THE HOTHOUSE

THE

HOTHOUSE

WOLFGANG KOEPPEN

Translated by Michael Hofmann

W. W. Norton & Company
New York   London

Copyright © 1953 Scherz & Goverts Verlag, Stuttgart

Alle Rechte bei und vorbehalten durch Suhrkamp Verlag Frankfurt am Main
English translation copyright © 2001 by W. W. Norton & Company, Inc.
Introduction copyright © by Michael Hofmann
Originally published in German as *Das Treibhaus* by Suhrkamp Verlag,
Frankfurt am Main
Interior photograph of Bonn courtesy Stadtarchiv Bonn
The publication of this work was made possible through a subsidy from
Inter Nationes, Bonn, Germany

The text of this book is composed in Fairfield Light
with the display set in Corvinus Skyline
Composition by Gina Webster
Manufacturing by The Haddon Craftsmen, Inc.
Book design by JAM Design
Production manager: Andrew Marasia

Library of Congress Cataloging-in-Publication Data

Koeppen, Wolfgang, 1906–
[Treibhaus. English]
The hothouse / Wolfgang Koeppen ; translated and with
an introduction by Michael Hofmann.
p. cm.
"The Hothouse is the second part of the author's trilogy . . . bookended by Tauben im
Gras . . . and Der Tod in Rom"—Jkt.
ISBN 0-393-04902-7
1. Hofmann, Michael, 1957 Aug. 25– II. Title

PT2621.O46 T713 2001
833'.912-dc21   00-069573

W. W. Norton & Company, Inc., 500 Fifth Avenue, New York, N.Y. 10110
www.wwnorton.com

W. W. Norton & Company Ltd., Castle House, 75/76 Wells Street, London W1T 3QT

1 2 3 4 5 6 7 8 9 0

Author's Note (1953)

The novel *The Hothouse* draws on current events, in particular recent political events, but only as a catalyst for the imagination of the author. Personalities, places, and events that occur in the story are nowhere identical with their equivalents in reality. References to living persons are neither made nor intended in what is a purely fictional narrative. The scope of the book lies beyond any connections with individuals, organizations, and events of the present time; which is to say, the novel has its own poetic truthfulness.

*God knows politics is a complicated business,
and the hearts and minds of men often
flutter helplessly around in it, like birds
in a net. But if we
are unable to feel indignant at a great injustice,
we will never be able to act righteously.*

—HAROLD NICOLSON

The process of history is combustion.

—NOVALIS

Introduction

WOLFGANG KOEPPEN (1906–1996) HAD A VERY LONG life and a very strange career. Following an obscure, provincial, peripatetic youth on the Baltic coast of Germany—nothing to record, no apprenticeships, no achievements, no landmarks, the only thing that characterized him a besetting love of books (asked what the crucial event in his life was, he replied: learning to read; asked another time how he would like to die, he said: in bed, with a book)—he had, by the late 1920s, made his way to Berlin (all roads then led, as they do again, to Berlin). There, Koeppen had his only period of regular employment, when he worked on the cultural pages of the *Berliner Börsen-Courier* for a couple of years, leaving in 1933, much as Keetenheuve does in *The Hothouse*, from dislike and apprehension of the Nazis. He left Germany, not for Canada and England, like Keetenheuve, but for Holland. He had, by this time, published a novel, *Eine unglückliche Liebe* (*An Unhappy Love Affair*, 1934) with the publisher Cassirer.

It was well reviewed, sold little, and the following year, there was another, *Die Mauer schwankt* (*The Tottering Wall*), again with Cassirer. Soon thereafter, the newspaper closed down: Cassirer, a Jew, fled, and Koeppen, in Holland with Jewish friends, who were themselves debating where to go and what to do with themselves, decided to return, in late 1938, to Germany, rather than wait to be apprehended. Koeppen lacked the fame, the contacts, on a banal level, the aptitude for languages, and perhaps ultimately, the brute necessity required to make a go of things in exile.

In 1939, extraordinarily, he was on a plane to Berlin. He said: "It is perhaps my only boast not to have served in Hitler's armies for a single hour." What Koeppen did was—Penelope-like—to work on unrealized film projects in the Berlin film industry. In 1944, fearing exposure from Nazi colleagues, he made use of the circumstance that his apartment building was destroyed in an Allied air raid, to go underground. He made his way to Munich, where he stuck for fifty years. Munich was the subject and the setting for the first of his second clutch of novels, the so-called "Trilogy" or "Postwar Trilogy." *Pigeons on the Grass*—which I describe elsewhere as "set in Munich in a single day, a modernist jigsaw in 110 pieces and showing 30 figures"—was published in 1951, closely followed by *The Hothouse* (1953) and *Death in Rome* (1954). Then and later (and, for that matter, earlier: Hermann Hesse had praised his second book for a Swedish newspaper), Koeppen was not short of influential supporters among fellow writers, critics, and publishers. Günter Grass referred to him in his Nobel Prize acceptance speech; Max Frisch and Hans Magnus Enzensberger have praised him in superlatives; Germany's most powerful literary critic, Marcel Reich-

Ranicki, has filled a short book with his encomia on Koeppen; Siegfried Unseld, the head of Suhrkamp, first acquired, then promoted and kept faith with and bankrolled his author for over thirty years. And yet, in spite of that, both within Germany and internationally, Koeppen has remained a marginal figure, one for the few, a writers' writer. Why is this?

In the first place, the idea of a literary career assumes a more or less even and continuous output, under more or less stable external conditions. And Koeppen's novels—he wrote no others in his remaining forty years, but more of that later—were written and published quickly, spasmodically, over very few years, but in two widely spaced periods. What good to him were his early books, published by a Jewish publisher in the Third Reich—both things that (it was part of his point) the good folks of the fifties were at pains to forget? Karl Korn, the outstanding critic who reviewed both *Pigeons on the Grass* and *The Hothouse* in the *Frankfurter Allgemeine Zeitung*, began by remarking unhappily that Koeppen's name was unknown to all but a couple of dozen people. Looked at in one way, he was a debutant; and in another, he was an experienced writer in mid-career, albeit ending a sixteen-year silence! No wonder people didn't know what to make of him!

And then there was the nature of the books themselves. Reich-Ranicki dubbed *The Hothouse* "a provocative elegy" and *Death in Rome* "an alarming provocation"—but that was years later. At the time, critics and readers merely felt themselves goaded beyond endurance. The reaction to Koeppen's poetically charged, scathing, rhythmic prose on the part of the morbidly sensitive, anxious, and protective media of the new Federal Republic can only be compared to that of some Soviet bloc country to certain works of samizdat literature—

with the difference that the work of the censor's blue pencil and the secret police was carried out by scribblers in the newspapers and an indifferent public. One review, in a leading German Sunday paper, was headed: "Not to be touched with a barge-pole," another ended: "The public will say 'Crucify him!' He won't care." Another, more "thinky" piece in a monthly magazine was actually followed, many years later, by a "recantation"—and how often does that happen in the literary world!? A bookshop in Bonn scheduled a reading from *The Hothouse* followed by a public discussion with politicians; this was canceled at short notice when the police said they would be unable to guarantee his safety! (They are very different writers, but in his ability to take on his own country, Koeppen reminds me of Tadeusz Konwicki, the great author of *The Polish Complex* and *A Minor Apocalypse*.)

The upshot of so much vilification and repression was to repress Koeppen as a novelist. He wrote no more novels. In another one of his characteristic little bursts of activity, he published a series of three travel books on Russia, America, and France, in 1958, 1959, and 1961. The tone taken toward him was transformed: there was, one observer reports, not a single adverse review to any of these! In 1962—as a reward for good behavior, the cynic might say—he was tossed the Büchner Prize. Thereafter, there were many sightings and promisings of further novels—not least after Koeppen moved to Suhrkamp—some of them even fully equipped with titles and settings and plots, but nothing ever appeared. The commodity that Koeppen traded in became silence. Journalists lined up to question Koeppen about his silence—as they did in the United States with the octogenarian Henry Roth, who had been silent for sixty years—and courteously, helplessly, evasively, he received them. A distressing book of these encounters was published (*Einer der schreibt* [*Someone Who Writes*], Suhrkamp, 1995), a cross between a bullfight and a game of grandmother's footsteps, painful to read:

INTERVIEWER: To put it another way, what do you do all day? Do you go for walks, do you watch TV?

KOEPPEN: I'm terribly busy.

INTERVIEWER: What are you busy with?

KOEPPEN: I don't know.

Sometimes Koeppen tried to deny that he was silent, claimed that he was writing all the time. But that was only half true, as he was writing only the kind of occasional things that writers don't see as writing—and that only with the greatest difficulty. The huge 700-page collection of his prose scraps that Suhrkamp published in 2000, *Auf dem Phantasieross* (*On the Wings of Imagination*), actually lays to rest the myth that he was all the time working on some secret project. Even so, to describe him as a victim of German circumstances is too easy.

Certainly, his decorated silence must have been easier to live with for the nation and its opinion of itself than any further novels of the ilk of *The Hothouse* or *Death in Rome*, but writing and not-writing are both mysteries. Just because there are three novels doesn't actually say anything about the feasibility of a fourth. Our technical, assembly-line model for the production of novels is entirely inappropriate to a writer of Koeppen's distinction. Besides, if one looks at his career, it is clear that not-writing—or not-publishing—preponderates.

Writing was the exception, not the rule. Reckon it up, and you find maybe one productive decade in six or seven as a writer. There were spates or spasms of it, that is clear from the dates, but there was also an admirable, even a lovely quality of truancy about it. *Death in Rome* he wrote while he had another project—an Eulenspiegel novel—on the go; he got a ticket to Rome to attend a meeting of the Gruppe 47, cut the meeting, discovered Rome, went home, and wrote a different novel. For *The Hothouse,* he spent a week in Bonn, then holed up in a bunker hotel in Stuttgart, his typewriter clattering up and down the concrete passages, and wrote his book in a few weeks. This quality of truancy, combined with violent necessity, has to be respected, and so, while—God knows!—I can understand the wish that there had been more books, I also understand that such a wish is unreasonable, and that it teeters along the boundary between gratitude and ingratitude.

The other writer about whom I have much the same feelings is Koeppen's coeval Malcolm Lowry (1909–1957), the author of *Under the Volcano.* There are some striking similarities between the two: earlier books in the thirties (*Ultramarine,* in 1937); one extraordinary, unrepeatable, Joycean masterpiece (taking, for the sake of argument, Koeppen's trilogy as a single work) that casts its shadow over the rest of their lives; difficulties with manuscripts (Lowry lost one in a taxi, and another when his house burnt down; Koeppen claimed to have left one behind in Holland); a deep interest in films (Lowry and his wife spent years over their script of Fitzgerald's *The Last Tycoon*) and music; the temptation to rewrite or double or shadow their masterpiece (Koeppen brought Keetenheuve back to life in some later fragments; Lowry wanted to write an *Under Under the*

Volcano); the way that both of them, in a phrase of Lowry's biographer Gordon Bowker, were "Coleridgean projector[s] of schemes." In 1955, Koeppen reviewed the German translation of *Under the Volcano* in terms that might have fitted, say, *The Hothouse*: "It is an intellectual book, you might almost say a book written for writers, full of civilization, quotations, allusions, doubt and asperity, the song of a cerebral despair, a protocol of failure, a plumbing of the depths of the soul, a laying bare of the emotions and the heart. . . . The novel is told at a breathless pace. But its panting breath has the moving, burning sniff of great poetry. It is an intoxicating book. The words flow over the reader like a cataract and make him delirious. But they are also elevating." *Unter dem Vulkan* was published in 1951. I wonder whether Koeppen might not have read it at about that time—and before he wrote *The Hothouse*. But even if he didn't, the Consul and the MP are surely kin; and the cantinas and barranca of Quauhnahuac are surely adjacent to "the Spanish colonial death veranda" in Guatemala.

I said Koeppen wrote no more novels in his remaining forty years. But in 1976, he published a short memoir, *Jugend* (*Youth*), and in 1992 a "novel" by the name of *Jakob Littners Aufzeichnungen aus einem Erdloch,* or *Jakob Littner's Notes from a Hole in the Ground,* which has become the subject of one more controversy at the end of this quiet controversialist's life. That book was one he ghostwrote, in 1948, in return for two CARE packets a month, at a publisher's suggestion drawing on the manuscript of the real Jakob Littner, a Jewish stamp dealer from Munich, who was shipped off by the Nazis to Poland, and then to Ukraine, where he survived the war under unspeakable circumstances. Littner emigrated to the

United States, and died in 1950. Recently, his original manuscript surfaced, and was published by Continuum in Kurt
Grübler's translation as *Journey through the Night*. This has
been used as a stick with which to beat Koeppen for his own
reissued work. This is, I think, unfair. Koeppen's version of
the story may not be—could not be—authentic, but sentence
for sentence and page for page, it is incontestably the better
book: it begins with the titles. Where I would take issue with
him is in allowing it to appear—however sheepishly and half-
heartedly and not altogether seriously—under his own name,
and as a novel. "I ate American rations and wrote the story
about the suffering of a German Jew. In doing so, it became
my story," he wrote. What speaks here is not arrogation, much
less theft, but a kind of wishfulness. My abiding memory of
the one occasion I met Koeppen was the fervor and regret
with which he spoke of the symbiosis of German and Jew.
Certainly, I don't question the blend of altruism and self-seek-
ing, of duty and imagination, of discipline and freedom that
Koeppen brought to the original enterprise, in 1948. To claim
that the story of a person or a group can only—or even best—
be told by that person or group strikes me as a misunder-
standing of what literature is. Whether there can be literature
about the Holocaust is a difficult problem, but Koeppen's
champion, the—Jewish—critic Marcel Reich-Ranicki, citing
Paul Celan, thinks there can, and I am inclined to agree.

THERE ARE not many novels—except for those by ex-politi-
cians, I suppose—that are situated in and around the corridors of power as *The Hothouse* is: Bulwer-Lytton and Anthony
Powell come to mind (neither of whom I've read), and so do

some of the South Americans such as Miguel Angel Asturias and Gabriel García Márquez (whom I have). In a longer time frame, one might think of Shakespeare's history plays—though, with the exception of *Henry VIII* (if that is Shakespeare), they tend not to be about recent history—or Aeschylus's play *The Persians*, which, with a brilliant switch of perspective, treats events (the Battle of Salamis) barely a decade old, and in which the author himself had been a participant. This will already show what a rarity *The Hothouse* is. It is further blessed—whether by luck or judgment—by having been written from a time that seems to lie at the source of many of the developments and institutions that have shaped the world we live in still, and by having as its theme an issue—the Western alliance or, more broadly, the matter of armaments or "deterrent terror"—that will continue to exercise us and our leaders for generations to come. And then, as if it were not enough to take us back to the early days of the Cold War, of NATO and the Montan-Union (or European Coal and Steel Union—the forerunner of the EC), both dating back to 1949; and to the founding of the Federal Republic of a divided Germany, ratified in the same year; it opens the brief chapter—now handily closed again, with the transfer of the seat of government back to Berlin—in which Bonn, a small, old university town on the Rhine was for half a century "the most arbitrarily designated capital city in Europe," in the words of one reviewer of *The Hothouse*. All these contribute massively to the unrepeatable and inescapable interest of the book: that it deals with artistry and detachment with things that, fifty years later, are still warm.

One of the many hostile critics of *The Hothouse* claimed that it was only the specific character of Bonn that made the book what it was, while complaining that it was somehow unfair or antidemocratic to write such a book. This is nonsense, as much as it would be if someone said *Under the Volcano* owed everything to Cuernavaca, or *Ulysses* to Dublin. The books are wonderful, even to people who have never been to the places. Koeppen—like Lowry, like Joyce—makes a Bonn that is part imaginary and wholly evocative, a derisive or cartoonish Monopoly board–like creation of "parliamentary ghetto," "pedagogic academy," press ship, station, church, park, wine bar, "American hive," and a few interiors, Knurrewahn's "avant-garde" office, Frost-Forestier's hi-tech multipurpose red grotto, and so on and so forth, with the turgid Rhine ominously at the back of everything. This all adds up to "Bonn"—and the place, and many of the characters thought they recognized themselves in Koeppen's descriptions. For instance, there was one Carlo Schmid (1896–1979), a leading socialist figure, an expert in international law, and—a translator of Baudelaire! But of course, Carlo Schmid isn't Keetenheuve, and no one would dream of reading *The Hothouse* as a roman à clef about the estimable Carlo Schmid, or as a naughty attack on Bonn, just as no one would read *Ulysses* because they wanted to find out about Dublin!

Koeppen said: "I wrote *The Hothouse* as a novel about failure," and I see no reason to quarrel with that. Many critics, even admirers of Koeppen, have made the mistake of seeing the failure in the novel itself. Reich-Ranicki quotes Thomas Mann's phrase "Helden der Schwäche," "heroes of weakness," but it doesn't help him to see the point and the necessity of Keetenheuve. To take on a strong, overbearing, even poisonous system, he would argue, requires a strong hero. It is a pity he has failed to understand that Koeppen's great idea was to inject, as it were, Hamlet into the world of one of Shakespeare's history plays. There is a glorious—and terribly sad—incommensurability in perhaps every one of the contacts in the book: how can Keetenheuve even talk to Korodin, say, or Frost-Forestier, or Mergentheim, or Elke, or Lena? But he, with his griefs and complications, is always more real than they are. The world needs more of him—the amateur in love, and writing, and politics—but it will only get—has only got—more of them: the career politician, the specialist, the Teflon man, before the threatened rise of a new and worse era of career miracle workers and cargo cults and apolitical money-men, Berlusconi, Tyminski, Forbes, Perot. *The Hothouse* is an elegy to the amateur and the dilettante: it already completely anticipates the plastic world of show, the world of newsreels, of sound bites, of calculation, of Piranesian or Pirandellian inconsequence, of near-virtuality, where, Koeppen wrote fifty years ago, "the century was reduced to imitating its own movie actors, even a miner looked like a film star playing a miner." Keetenheuve has an adolescent purity of heart, and that's what makes him such an inspired pendant to the corrupt drift and setting of this book, where there is Hiroshima and then business as normal, where there is Nuremberg and then business as normal; and such a perfect mouthpiece for a book that, as Koeppen says somewhere, is not a dialogue with the world, but "a monologue against the world."

None of the books I have translated have given me more pleasure than *The Hothouse* and *Death in Rome*. I find Koeppen's "hämmernder Sprechstil," as it was described by one critic, his "hammering parlando," completely congenial. I love the way he hides a phrase on a page, and a scene in a book; it takes many readings to become aware of the richness and the breadth of his vision, of his prismatic way with details and motifs. His rhetorical approach to a sentence, improvising and appositional, but wound tight in a mighty rhythm, is quite exhilarating. (You need to read them "aloud" to yourself.)

Koeppen describes *The Hothouse* as "a German fairy-tale, but, if anything, too mild." To that end, he has incorporated a lot of talismanic German material (German with a capital "D"). He takes "Wagalaweia" from the Rhine Maidens' song at the beginning of Wagner's *Rheingold*, and makes it into train noise; Alberich the dwarf, and Hagen, and the Norns (a sort of Nordic Fates) also come from Wagner. Novalis and Hölderlin and Heine all supply hugely famous tags. The historical Musaeus (1735–1787) was a collector of fairy tales (like the Grimms), a satirist, and a tutor to the court pages at Weimar. German politics, especially the short and often sadly compromised history of German socialism (the word is never mentioned in the book), is ransacked by Koeppen to similar effect. This system of allusions—to literature, to mythology, to politics—all serve to amplify the story, give it more, ironic, noise. As if it needed it: a man who emigrated in 1933, returned in 1945, was elected to Parliament in 1949, and drowned himself in the Rhine in 1953. As Karl Korn wrote in 1953: "*The Hothouse* is literature of a quality that is not often attained."

MICHAEL HOFMANN
September 2000

THE HOTHOUSE

1

He WAS TRAVELING UNDER PARLIAMENTARY IMMUNITY, seeing as they hadn't managed to catch him in flagrante. Although, of course, if it transpired that he was guilty, they would drop him just like that, hand him over with alacrity, the ones who called themselves the Noble House, and what a coup that would be for them, what satisfaction to have him depart under such an enormous and unforeseen cloud, off into the cells, safely to molder away behind the walls of some secure prison, and even in his own party, while they would witter agitatedly about the humiliation they would have been put through on his account (all of them, hypocrites to a man), secretly they would be rubbing their hands and be pleased that he had expelled himself, that he had had to go, because he had been a grain of salt, the germ of unrest in their bland and sluggish porridge of a party, a man of conscience and thereby an irritant.

He was sitting in the Nibelungen Express. There was a

whiff of fresh paint, of reconditioning and renovation; these days, you traveled in comfort on the Bundesbahn; while on the outside all the carriages were daubed blood red. Basel, Dortmund, dwarf Alberich, and the factory chimneys of the Ruhrgebiet; through-coaches to Vienna and Passau, Vehmic murderer Hagen had put his feet up; carriages to Rome and Munich, and there was a flash of ecclesiastical purple through a chink in the drawn curtains; carriages to Hoek van Holland and London, the exporters' twilight of the gods, their dread of peacetime.

Wagalaweia, went the wheels. He hadn't done it. He hadn't killed anyone. It probably wasn't in him to commit murder; but he might have done, and the mere imagining that he had done it, that he had picked up the ax and brought it down, that vision was so clear and irrefutable to him, that he drew strength from it. Fantasies of murder galvanized his mind and body, lending him wings, lighting him up, and for a brief moment he had the feeling that everything would turn out well now, he would make a better fist of everything, he would assert himself and get his way, he would break through to the world of action and make something of his life—but unfortunately his crime had been purely imaginary, he was still the old Keetenheuve, *sicklied o'er by the pallid cast of thought*.

He had buried his wife. And, not feeling at ease in bourgeois life, the act of interment alarmed him just as baptisms and weddings horrified him, and every other transaction between two individuals that became public and official. Her death grieved him, he felt deep sadness, choking loss when the coffin was lowered into the ground, he had lost the thing dearest to him in all the world, and, while the phrase had perhaps been devalued by appearing on millions of black-bordered death announcements sent by happy heirs, his dearest had been taken from him, his beloved was put in the ground, and the feeling *lost lost for ever I'll not see her again neither here nor in the hereafter I'll look for her and never find her* might have made him cry, but he felt unable to cry here, even though only Frau Wilms was watching him in the cemetery. Frau Wilms was his cleaning woman. She brought Keetenheuve a bunch of limp asters from her brother-in-law's allotment. For their wedding, Frau Wilms had brought a similar bunch of limp asters. On that occasion, she had said: "What a lovely-looking couple!" Now she didn't say anything. He wasn't a lovely-looking widower. Droll thoughts kept occurring to him. At school, instead of paying attention to the teacher, he had thought of ridiculous things, in the committee rooms and in the chamber, he saw his dignified colleagues as clowns in the ring, and even in situations when his life had been in danger, the grotesque side of it had not escaped him. "Widower" was a funny word, a grimly funny word, a somewhat dusty notion from a staider era. Keetenheuve remembered having known a widower when he was a boy, one Herr Possehl. Herr Possehl, widower, still lived in harmony with an ordered world; he was respected in the little town. He had assembled a widower's—one couldn't say weeds—garb, the stiff black hat, the morning coat, the striped banker's trousers, and later on an always slightly grubby white waistcoat, across which ran a gold watch chain that had a ram's tooth dangling from it, to symbolize that the animal in him had been set aside. And so, when Herr Possehl went to the baker Labahn to buy his bread, he was a living allegory of fidelity beyond the grave, a touching and estimable embodiment of loss. Keetenheuve was not estimable, and nor did he touch anyone. He owned neither a top hat nor any other kind of hat, and he had gone to the burial in his modish flapping trench coat. The word "widower," which Frau Wilms had not pronounced, but which had started up in him at the sight of her limp asters, pursued and embittered him. He was a knight of the sorrowful countenance, or a knight of the comical countenance. He walked out of the graveyard, and his thoughts raced toward his crime.

This time he did not remain coolly intellectual in his thinking, he acted on impulse, furiously, and Elke, who had always held it against him that he lived with his head between the pages of a book, Elke would have rejoiced now to witness the prompt and unswerving way he went about his business, while yet, like a film hero, remaining mindful of his safety. He saw himself striding through the street of secondhand stalls, saw himself purchasing his widower's raiment in various nooks and basements. He bought the striped trousers, the morning coat, the white waistcoat (grubby, just like Herr Possehl's), the stiff black hat, the gold watch chain, only the ram's tooth pendant proved impossible to find, and so he was unable to celebrate a triumph over the animal in him. In a large department store, an escalator carried him up to the floor where work clothes were sold, and there he bought a white overall of the sort that cattle drovers wear. The ax he stole from a timber yard. It was very simple; the carpenters were having their evening meal, and he saw an ax lying on a pile of shavings, bent down to pick it up, and slowly walked off with it.

A large and bustling hotel with several exits was the killer's chosen base. He took a room there, *Keetenheuve Member of the Bundestag/Possehl Widower from Kleinwesenfeld*. He got in disguise. In front of the mirror he slipped into his widower's outfit. Now he resembled Possehl. He was Possehl. Finally he had achieved respectability. In the evening he went out, with the drover's coat over his arm with the ax. In the gloomy street, a green scorpion glowed from the black glass of a pub window. That was the only light around, a marshy light in a grim story. The bakery and the little dairies and greengrocers all slumbered behind their rusty drawn shutters. There was a musty, moldy, sour smell, a smell of dirt, of rats, of potatoes germinating in basements and of rising bread dough. Phonograph music could be heard coming out of the "Scorpion." It was Rosemary Clooney singing "Botch-a-me." Keetenheuve moved into a gateway. He pulled on his drover's coat, he picked up his ax—he was a butcher waiting for the bull.

And there was the bull dyke, la Wanowski appeared, a coarse frizz of hair on her bull's skull, a woman who struck fear as a pub brawler, and had gained sway over the tribades; they felt a pang of sweetness when she appeared, they called her the mother of the nation. She wore a man's suit, a suit to fit a fat man, the seat bulged tautly around her buttocks, the square padded shoulders were a metaphor for penis envy, laughable and terrifying at the same time, and between the puffy lips under the burnt cork fluff, she was chewing on the sodden stump of a bitter cigar. No pity! No pity for the ogre! And no laughter to dispel the tension! Keetenheuve raised the ax, and smote. He smote the frizzy mat of hair that he supposed covered her all over, he split the skull of the bull. The bull sank to its knees. It rolled over. The drover's coat was stained by the blood of the bull.

He tossed the ax and coat into the river, did the widower Possehl, he leaned down over the railing of the bridge, ax and coat sank to the bottom, they were gone, the waters closed over them, *water from the Alps snow-melt glacier debris smooth flavorful trout.*

No one had seen him, no one could have seen him, because unfortunately he hadn't committed the act, once again he'd only dreamed it, it had been a daydream and a fantasy, and he had thought it instead of doing it, his old failing, it was always that way with him. He had failed. Failed at every one of life's crossroads. He had failed in 1933 and failed again in 1945. He had failed in politics. He had failed in his profession. He couldn't cope with existence, besides, who could, only idiots, it was like a curse, but this part of it concerned him alone, that he had failed in his marriage as well, and now that he was thinking sadly of Elke, with the widower's genuine and not at all ridiculous pain, Elke lying in the cemetery earth, already given over to the unknowable, to an appalling transformation if there was a void, and something just as appalling if it was more than that, it showed him he was capable of neither love nor hate, everything was just a lecherous fumbling, a groping of surfaces. He hadn't brained the Wanowski woman. She was alive. She was holding court in the "Scorpion." She was ruling, drinking, procuring for the dykes. She was listening to the Rosemary Clooney record, "botch-a-me, botch-a-me"—and then he felt his heart turn over, because he had murdered after all!

Wagalaweia, wailed the locomotive. Elke had come to him when she'd been hungry, and at a time when he'd had cans of food, a warm room, drinks, a small black cat, and, after a long fast, an appetite once again for human flesh, to use Novalis's phrase for love.

He had never ceased to feel German; but in the first summer after the war, it wasn't easy for someone who'd been out of the country for eleven years to orient himself. He was a busy man. After leaving him idle for a long time, Time reached for him, and took him in her toils once again, and he believed that, given time, something would become of him.

One evening found him looking out the window. He was tired. Darkness was falling early. There were ominous-looking clouds in the sky. The wind picked up puffs of dust. At that point he saw Elke. He saw her slipping into the ruins opposite. She slipped through a crack in the wall into the caverns of rubble and scree. She was like an animal taking refuge.

It started to rain. He went out onto the street. The rain and the storm shook him. Dust whirled into his mouth and eyes. He fetched Elke out of the rubble. She was soaked and filthy. Her soiled dress clung to her bare skin. She had no underclothes. She was naked against the dust, the rain and the bare stones. Elke had come out of the war, and she was sixteen years old. He didn't like her name. It made him suspicious. Elke to him was a name out of Nordic mythology, it reminded him of Wagner and his hysterical heroes, a wily, unscrupulous, and violent set of gods, and in fact Elke turned out to be the daughter of a Gauleiter and a governor of the lord.

The Gauleiter and his wife were both dead. They had swallowed the little death capsules they had been given for all eventualities, and Elke had heard news of their deaths when she was in the forest. She heard the news (and it was no more than news, because Time seemed to have chloroformed that particular day, and Elke felt all the knocks as though she'd been bedded in cotton wool and was being thrown around by rough hands while inside a box lined with cotton wool) from a sniffing and snorting radio transmitter, overexcited by cipher messages and appeals for support, among a group of

German soldiers who had surrendered and were waiting to be taken away to a prisoner-of-war camp.

Two Negroes were guarding them, and Elke could not forget them. The Negroes were lanky, loose-limbed types, who hunkered down in a strange and oddly vigilant kind of squat. It was a jungle posture. The rifles of civilization lay across their knees. Tucked in their ammunition belts, they had long, knotted leather whips. The whips looked altogether more imposing than the rifles.

From time to time, the Negroes stood up to relieve themselves. They relieved themselves with great seriousness and without taking their round white eyeballs (they looked somehow guileless) off the prisoners. The Negroes pissed in two great high streams into the grass under the trees. While they pissed, their whips dangled against their beautiful long thighs, and Elke thought of Owens, the Negro who had been victorious in the Olympic Games in Berlin. The German soldiers stank of rain, earth, sweat, and wounds, they stank of many miles of road, of sleeping in their clothes, of victories and defeats, of fear, exhaustion, weariness, and death, they stank of the word "injustice" and the word "futile."

And on forest paths behind the guarded enclosure, peeking shyly out of the bushes, still terrified of the soldiers, still suspicious of the Negroes, there emerged ghosts, famished bodies, broken skeletons, starved eyes, and anguished brows, they came crawling out of the caves where they had been hiding, they broke out of the death camps, they roamed as far as their bony, beaten feet could carry them, the cage was open, they were the persecuted, the harried, the prisoners of the government, who had given Elke her privileged upbringing, *games on Daddy's gubernatorial estate, butterflies flittering over the flowers on the terrace, a female prisoner sets the table for breakfast, prisoners rake the gravel, the stallion is led up for the morning gallop, Daddy's top boots cleaned to a mirroring shine, a prisoner brushed them, the saddle leather creaks, the beautifully turned out, well-fed stallion whinnies and paws the ground*—Elke couldn't remember how she had gone on from there; now with one refugee column, now another.

It was Keetenheuve's little kitty-cat that won Elke's trust. They were both young, the girl and the cat, and so they played together. Their favorite game was balling up Keetenheuve's loose manuscript pages and batting them to and fro. Each time Keetenheuve returned from one of his many avocations, which took up more and more of his time, and left him more and more disillusioned, Elke would call out: "Master's home!" Keetenheuve probably was master, to both of them. But soon the cat's companionship began to pall on Elke, she grew bad-tempered when Keetenheuve sat over his papers of an evening, still obsessed with the notion of helping, reconstructing, healing wounds, providing bread, and since their friendship had run aground, they decided to get married.

Marriage complicated everything. In all the questionnaires—a thing devised by the National Socialists, and now perfected by the occupying powers—Keetenheuve now appeared as the son-in-law of the dead Gauleiter. That alienated a lot of people, but he was unconcerned, he was opposed to clannishness in all its forms, and that included his wife's clan. What was worse was that marriage was deeply alien to his own nature. He was a bachelor, a loner, maybe a voluptuary, or then again maybe an anchorite, he wasn't sure, he swung between the two types of existence, but one thing was certain, that in getting married he had let himself in for an experience for which he had not been intended, and which was a further burden to him. He had, moreover (and happily), married a child, someone young enough to be his daughter, and, in the face of her youth, was forced to recognize that he was not grown-up himself. They were a match for love, but not for life. He could desire, but not educate. He had no great opinion of education, but he could see that Elke was unhappy in her excessive freedom. She didn't know what to do with freedom. She lost herself in it. Her life, apparently without duties, was like an immense body of water, that washed around Elke without hope of land, an ocean of emptiness, whose unending featurelessness was only ever animated by the riffling breeze of lust, the froth of excess, the wind of bygone days. Keetenheuve was a signpost that had been pitched beside the way of Elke's life, but only, it appeared, to lead her astray. Next, Keetenheuve made the acquaintance—it was a new experience for him, and, again, not one for which he had been intended—of a mortal fatigue and sadness after many conjunctions, the believer's sense of mortal sin. But first of all, he sated his appetite. Elke needed plenty of loving. She was a sensual creature, and, once awakened, her demand for tenderness was powerful. "Hold me tight!" she said. She directed his hand. "Feel me!" she said. Her thighs grew hot, her belly burned, she used uncouth expressions. "Take me!" she cried. "Take me!" And he was thrilled, he remembered his own hunger, the time he'd spent wandering the streets of the foreign cities into which the hatred of Elke's parents had exiled him, he thought of the thousandfold seductions of shop windows, the blandishments of the dummies, their crudely lascivious poses, the displays of lingerie, the poster models who tugged their stockings up to the tops of their thighs, the girls whose language he didn't speak and who passed him like ice and fire in one. Authentic passion had so far manifested itself to him only in dreams, in dreams he had felt eros, in dreams, and only in dreams, the myriad pleasures of the skin, the becoming one, the altered breathing, the rank heat. And the brief moments of pleasure he'd experienced in cheap hotels, on park benches, in doorways of old towns, what were they, in comparison with the exhaustive seduction of the string of seconds, the chain of minutes, the run of hours, the wheel of days, weeks, and years, the constant opportunity vouchsafed by the marriage vows, an eternity of seduction, which out of horror at so much time, spurred the imagination on to the unthinkable?

Elke stroked him. It was the time of power cuts. The nights were oppressive and dark. Keetenheuve had got himself a battery-powered lamp to work by. Elke brought it to bed, and its harsh light fell across their bodies, like the beam of a headlight catching a naked couple embracing on the roadway. Elke studied Keetenheuve long and attentively. She said: "You must have been good-looking when you were twenty." She said: "Have you had many girls?" He was thirty-nine. He hadn't had many girls. Elke said: "Tell me something." To her, his life was exciting and colorful, full of baffling leaps, like the life of an adventurer, almost. It was all strange to her. She didn't understand what star he was following. When he told her why he had rejected the politics of the National Socialists and gone abroad, she saw no reason for such behavior, and if there was a reason, it was something she couldn't herself see or feel; he was just a moralist. She said: "You're a schoolmaster." He laughed. But perhaps it was just his face that laughed. Maybe he had always been an old schoolmaster, an old

schoolmaster and before that an old schoolboy, a naughty boy
who wouldn't do his prep because he loved books too much.
Elke came to hate all Keetenheuve's books, she fulminated
against the innumerable documents, papers, notebooks, journals, digests, and drafts that lay about everywhere and took
Keetenheuve away from her bed into areas where she could
not follow him, kingdoms that were inaccessible to her.

Keetenheuve's pursuits, his involvement in the reconstruc-
tion, his eagerness to reinvent the nation as a liberal democracy, had brought it in their train that he was returned as a
member of the Bundestag. He was given a preferential place
on the list of candidates, and had won his seat without having had to exert himself on the hustings to any great extent.
The end of the war had made him somewhat optimistic, and
he thought it was right that he should now devote himself to
a cause, having been a marginal figure for so long. He wanted to realize his youthful dreams, at the time he had been a
believer in change, but he soon saw what a foolish belief that
was, people had naturally remained the same, it didn't even
occur to them to change, merely because the form of government had changed, because the uniforms thronging the
streets and making babies were now olive-green instead of
brown, black, and field gray, and once again everything came
to grief over petty matters of detail, the thick ooze on the
streambed that blocked the flow of fresh water, and left everything as it was before, in a hand-me-down type of life that,
everybody knew really, was a lie. At first, Keetenheuve
plunged himself enthusiastically into the work of the committees, he wanted to make up for all the lost years, and *he
would have blossomed if he'd gone with the Nazis, because that
was the break, the stupid miscalculation of his generation, and*

now all his eagerness was simply wasted and laughable, a graying youth, beaten from the start.

And what he lost in politics, what he had to give up on in his exhaustion, he lost also in love, for politics and love had both come to him too late in life, Elke loved him, but with his parliamentarian's free travel pass, he was chasing after phantoms, the phantom of liberty, of which people were afraid, and preferred to leave to the unfruitful investigations of professional philosophers, and the phantom of human rights, which raised its head only when people had suffered wrongs, the problems were infinitely difficult, and one might well despair at them. Keetenheuve could see himself back in opposition, but permanent opposition was no fun any more, because he asked himself: can I change anything, can I make things better, do I know the way?

He did not know it. Every decision was festooned with thousands of ifs and buts, like lianas, like jungle lianas. Practical politics was a jungle, you ran into big beasts. You might be brave and defend the dove against the lion, but while you were doing that, the snake snuck up on you from behind, and bit you. As it happened, the lions in this particular jungle were toothless, and the doves not as innocent as their cooing tried to make out, only the snakes' venom was good and strong, and they picked their moment to administer it. This was the terrain where he was fighting and losing his way. And in all that tangle, he forgot that a sun was shining on him, that a miracle had befallen him, that a woman loved him, that Elke, with her smooth young skin, loved him. Their embraces between trains were rushed, and he was back on his wanderings once more, a foolish knight, crusading against power that was so entwined with all the old power, that it could afford to laugh at the knight who sallied out to challenge her, and sometimes, in a spirit almost of kindness, to offer a target for his zeal, she tossed a windmill his way, good enough for that old-fashioned Don Quixote. At home, meanwhile, Elke fell into the lap of hell, the hell of solitude, the hell of boredom, the hell of apathy, the hell of daily trips to the movies—where, in the velvety darkness, the devil swaps a pseudo-life for your own life, the soul is dispelled by shades— the hell of emptiness, the hell of a tormenting eternity, the hell of a merely vegetative existence, which only plants could endure without losing heaven. "The sun? A deception," Elke told herself, "its light is black." *The only beautiful thing really was youth youth it'll not come back to us not once not twice it was scythed down in May and Keetenheuve a good fellow he was one of the harvesters she'd been without a schoolmaster now she had a schoolmaster in Bonn and he set her no tasks she wouldn't be able to perform any tasks how could she the governor's daughter prisoners raked the gravel,* and that was when she ran into Wanowski, Wanowski with her great padded shoulders, an invert from the National Socialist Women's Association, Wanowski with her enormous low imperious voice *she reminded her of home a strangely altered version of home but she was home she was Daddy's voice she was Mommy's voice she was the beer evenings of the old warriors that the Gauleiter liked to get himself up for and drop into as into a rejuvenating mud wallow and Wanowski said "Come, child" and Elke came,* she came into the tribade's embrace, where was warmth, where was oblivion, where was shelter from overmuch distance, shelter from the sun, shelter from eternity, where simple words were spoken, no blather of abstractions, not the ghastly, oppressive, voluble, swarming, frothing intellectualism of

Keetenheuve *who had stolen her when she was weak he a schoolmaster and a dragon and she the princess and now she took vengeance vengeance on Keetenheuve vengeance on the dragon vengeance on Daddy who had failed to triumph and took the cowardly way out and left her to the dragons vengeance on this damnable existence vengeance with female homosexuals they were the hellhounds of her vengeance,* and she avenged herself with others besides Wanowski, because Wanowski not only gave satisfaction herself, she was also a procuress and she recruited other disciples for the unholy Vestal rites, she had contempt for men, *milksops milksops the lot of them limp dicks* and so she could strut about with her padded shoulders, the cheeks of her stout ass in men's trousers, the cigar in her mouth a penile stump, she would have liked to deprive the unfairly kitted-out pathetic priapids of the woman altogether, monster of sexual envy, a fat and angry pub Penthesilea who had missed out on her Achilles. What Wanowski had to offer Elke was the irresistible offer of beer and company. Elke no longer felt abandoned when Keetenheuve was off in Bonn. She drank. She drank with bitter dykes who were waiting for her to get drunk. She drank bottle after bottle. She ordered beer over the phone, and it was delivered in iron rectangular crates. When Keetenheuve returned from his travels, the shameless so-and-so's squeaked out the door with sardonic grins like glutted rats. He lashed out at them; they skittered into their holes. The room stank of female sweat, fruitless arousal, senseless fatigue, and beer beer beer. Elke was stupid with beer, a drooling cretin. Dribble ran from her pretty, painted, lovable mouth. She drooled: "What are you doing here?" She drooled: "I hate you!" She drooled: "I love you." She drooled: "Come to bed." *The sun was black.* Could he fight? He could not fight. The women sat in their ratholes. They observed him. And in cahoots with them, also in their ratholes sat others—men—they too observing him. He leaned down over Elke's mouth, beer fumes, holy spirits, the bottle genies all rose toward him on her breath, it disgusted him, but he still felt impelled, and in the end it was he who had to yield to his own weakness. In the morning they made it up. Generally it was on a Sunday morning. The bells pealed for church. Keetenheuve was happy to hear them pealing, they didn't appeal to him, and maybe he even regretted that they didn't appeal to him, but any summons struck Elke as more in the nature of a demand, the bells represented the claim of some absolute, and she resisted them. She cried: "I hate that jangling. That jangling is so horrible." He had to calm her down. She cried. She fell into despondency. She started cursing God. Elke's God was a wrathful god, a monster and a sadist. "There is no God," said Keetenheuve, and he took away her last support, the belief in a bloody idol. They sang nursery songs in bed, and chanted counting rhymes. He loved her. He let her drop. He had been put in charge of a human being, and he let her drop. He set off in pursuit of his will-o'-the-wisps, wrestled in committee rooms for nebulous rights that were not secured, his efforts in the committee rooms were utterly ineffectual, he would not achieve anything for anyone, but he set off just the same, and he left Elke, the one person who had been entrusted to him, who was his sole responsibility, to fall into despair. The shameless so-and-so's killed her. Beer killed her. A few drugs also. But actually it was being abandoned that had asphyxiated her, a premonition of eternity and temporality, space, so confined and so boundless, space with its black light, space, the black baffling backdrop behind the stars.

*Keetenheuve schoolmaster, Keetenheuve rapist, Keetenheuve drag-
on from legend, Keetenheuve / Possehl widower, Keetenheuve
moralist and voluptuary, Keetenheuve member of parliament,
Keetenheuve chevalier of human rights, Keetenheuve killer*

*In a newspaper a wise countenance an old man a kindly face
under snow-white hair a figure in a gardener's well-worn outfit
Einstein pursued a fata morgana and found a fata morgana the
clear beautiful formula for the ultimate equation the connection
of results harmony of the spheres the unified field theory of the
natural laws of gravity and electricity traced back to their common source in the Fourth Equation*

Wagalaweia. They say the righteous sleep easy in their
beds. And could he sleep? With sleep came dreams that were
no dreams, that were ghosts and terrors. Lying crosswise,
east–west, his closed eyes facing west, what might
Keetenheuve have been able to see? The Saar, *la belle France,*
the Benelux states, the patchwork of Europe, the Montan-
Union.* Any arms dumps? Arms dumps. There was prowling
around the frontiers. Notes were exchanged. Treaties signed.
The game was on once more. The same old game? The same.
The Federal Republic was a player again. Writing letters to
the Americans in Washington and being irritated by the
Americans in Mannheim. The Chancellor found himself
seated at various round tables. As one among equals? One
among equals. What did he have behind him? Defense lines,
rivers. Hold the Rhine. Hold the Elbe. Hold the Oder. Attack
over the Vistula. What else? A war. Graves. Ahead of him? A
new war? Fresh graves? Retreat to the Pyrenees? The cards
were shuffled again. Who was it referred to the foreign min-

---

*The Europe Coal and Steel Community, avatar of the EU.

ister of one of the great powers as a jackanapes? An old
Wilhelmstrasse hand. He was feeling his way back to great-
power status himself, panting along the old running track,
along the Koblenzer Strasse, tongue out, and at the starting
line and the finishing line sat the obscenity and his wife. On
the Rhine, a line of coal barges labored upstream. They
looked like dead whales in the fog.

This was where the Nibelungs' treasure had lain, the gold
under the water, the hoard stashed in a cave. It was stolen,
plundered, embezzled, accursed. Ruse, furtiveness, deception, lie, murder, bravery, loyalty, betrayal, and fog, ever and
aye, amen. Wagalaweia, sang the daughters of the Rhine.
Digestion, decomposition, metabolism, and cellular renewal,
at the end of seven years you were someone else, only in the
area of memory there were certain encrustations—and to
them you owed obedience.

Wagalaweia. In Bayreuth the girls, glittering goddesses,
floated over the stage in swings. The dictator had been
aroused by the spectacle, he had felt a surge in his marrow,
his hand over his belt buckle, his kiss-curl flopping over his
eyes, his cap straightened, dark brooding gave rise to destruction. And then the high commissars were received with open
arms, come to my bosom! come to my bosom! Tears flowed,
tears of emotion, little salt streams of re-meeting and forgiv-
ing, the skin had turned gray, a little rouge bobbed along on
the tears, and Wotan's inheritance was safe again.

Flags are always available—rumpled prostitutes. Hoisting
the flag is duty. *Today I hoist one flag tomorrow the next I do
my duty.* The weathercocks clatter in the wind.* O Hölderlin,

*Direct translation from Hölderlin's great short poem "Hälfte des Lebens"
(Half of life): "im Winde / Klirren die Fahnen."

what's that rattling? The ringing phrase, the hollow bones of the dead. Society was once again disciplined, important tasks needed to be performed, fortunes to be saved, ranks to be closed, property to be preserved, contact to be maintained, because being there is all, in the creations of haute couture and the well-pressed dinner jacket, or, if nothing else is possible, with the stomp of boots. Tails flatter their wearer, but a uniform is snug and trim. It confers greatness, it gives security. Keetenheuve didn't give anything for uniforms. Did he not give anything for greatness, or security either?

He had been dreaming. Fallen into an unquiet sleep, he had dreamed he was on his way to a campaign rally. The little railway station was in a valley. No one had turned out to greet the incumbent. The tracks trailed off into infinity, without any other trains on them. The grass was withering beside the sleepers. Thistles sprouted from the ballast. The town was made up of four hills, which had on them the Catholic cathedral, the Protestant church, the war memorial of barren granite, and the trade union house swiftly and crudely knocked together from unseasoned timber. The four structures stood isolated like the Greek temples in the bleak landscape of Selinunt. They were the past, the dust of history, Clio's frozen slogan, no one gave a damn about them, but he had been instructed to go up one of the hills, to one of the sites and there to proclaim: "I believe! I believe!"

He was hot. Someone must have turned on the heat in the carriage, though it was a warm night. He switched on the light. He looked at his watch. It was five o'clock. The red second hand circled over the face with its luminous numbers like a high-pressure or explosion warning. Keetenheuve's time was ticking away. It ticked away luminously, that much could be

seen, and without meaning, which was less apparent. The
wheels of the train were conveying him to a meaningless and
unluminous destination. Had he used his time? Did he make
the most of each day? Was it worth the candle? And was the
question of the value of time not another expression of
human twistedness? "Only depravity has an end in mind,"
Rathenau had observed, and by that token Keetenheuve was
not depraved. Older now, he had the feeling of having barely
begun, and yet of already nearing the end of his life's road. So
much had happened that he had the impression he had just
been standing still and hadn't made any progress; the catas-
trophes he had witnessed, the momentous events, historical
decline, the dawning of new epochs whose parting gleam or
bloody rise (who could tell?) had tinted and tanned his own
features too, all that left him feeling, at forty-five, like a boy
who had just come out of a thriller and was now rubbing his
eyes, foolishly exhilarated, foolishly disappointed, and foolishly dissipated. He put out his hand to turn off the heat; but
the dial was on *cold*. Maybe the heat was controlled by some
further dial, maybe the conductor was responsible for adjust-
ing the temperature in each carriage; or maybe again the heat
wasn't on at all, and it was just the night that was oppressing
Keetenheuve. He lay back on the cushion and closed his eyes.
Nothing stirred in the corridor. The travelers lay in their pens,
consigned to forgetfulness.

And what if he wasn't reelected? He dreaded the grind of
campaigning. He was more and more wary of public meetings, the hideous breadth of the halls, the necessity of using
a microphone, the ghastliness of hearing his own distorted
voice droning out of the loudspeakers, filling the room with
its hollow and embarrassing echo, and coming back to him

out of a fug of sweat, beer, and smoke. He was not a con-
vincing speaker. The many-headed could sense his uncertain-
ty, and they did not forgive him for it. At Keetenheuve's
appearances, they missed the fanatic's performance, the genuine or play-acted fury, the calculating rant, the froth at the
mouth of the orator, the heartily familiar patriotic guff that
they couldn't get enough of. Could Keetenheuve be a propo-
nent of party optimism, could he lay out the cabbages in the
tidy seedbed of the party line so that they flourished in the
sunshine of the party agenda? Phrases leaped from the
mouths of his colleagues like croaking frogs; but frogs made
Keetenheuve's flesh creep.

He wanted to be reelected. Of course, didn't they all. But
Keetenheuve wanted to be reelected because he thought of
himself as one of the few who used their mandate against
established power. But what could he say? Should he paint a
ray of sunshine on the horizon, produce the old silver lining
that gets pulled out of the bag every time like tinsel at
Christmas (which was how the party wanted it), the hope that
things would get better, that fata morgana for simple minds
that goes up in smoke after every election, as if the votes had
been cast in Hephaistos's furnace? But could he afford not to
sell himself? Was he really choice goods, a star of the political knockabout? The voters did not know him. He did what
he could, but most of it was in the committees, not in the plenary sessions, and the work of the committees was done
behind closed doors, and not in full view of the nation.
Korodin from the other side, his opposite number on the
committee for petitions, dubbed Keetenheuve a human rights
romantic, always on the lookout for victims and the
oppressed, to relieve them of their chains, people who had

suffered injustice, Keetenheuve was always on the side of the poor and the hard done by, he supported the individual, and never the churches or cartels, nor even the parties, not even his own, and that cheesed off his party colleagues, and at times Keetenheuve felt better understood by Korodin, his enemy, than by the grouping with which he sat.

Keetenheuve lay stretched out under the sheet. Tucked in up to his chin, he looked like an ancient Egyptian mummy. There was stale museum air in the compartment. Was Keetenheuve a museum piece?

In his own estimation he was a lamb. But he wasn't going to make way for the wolves. Not this time. The trouble was that he was lazy; lazy even when he worked for sixteen hours a day, and not badly at that. He was lazy because he was uncertain, questioning, despairing, skeptical, and his own eager and honest advocacy of human rights was nothing but the last foppish remnant of the spirit of opposition and resistance to the state. His back had been broken, and the wolves would have little trouble taking everything away from him again. What else could Keetenheuve turn his hand to? He could cook. He could keep a room clean. He had housewifely virtues. Should he tend his conscience, write articles, address commentaries to the ether, become a public Cassandra? Who would print the articles, broadcast the commentaries, or give ear to Cassandra? Should he go on the barricades? If he thought about it, he would prefer to cook. Maybe he could prepare the evening meal for the monks in their cloister. Korodin would write him a recommendation. Korodin was a husband and father, he would have grandchildren in time, he had his faith, he had a sizable personal fortune and profitable directorships, he was a friend of the bishop's, and was on good terms with the monks.

There were some early risers in the capital. It was half past five. The alarm shrilled. Frost-Forestier was already awake. He had no dream, no embrace, from which to free himself, no nightmare had oppressed him, no early mass summoned him, no fear had caught him thrashing in its toils.

Frost-Forestier switched the light on, and disclosed an enormous room, a magnificent nineteenth-century salon, with stucco ceiling and carved pillars, and this served Frost-Forestier as bedroom, dining room, study, sitting room, kitchen, laboratory, and bath. Keetenheuve remembered the heavy curtains in front of the high windows, they were generalissimo red, and, permanently drawn, made a kind of fire wall against nature. All that was audible was a muffled twittering, the celebration song of the birds waking in the park outside, and what was performed in the salon was the beginning of a factory shift, the starting up of an assembly line, a succession of neat and sophisticated movements, precisely and logically calibrated, and the factory that was thus set in gear was Frost-Forestier. He chased after the electronic brains.

That was some twiddling and tuning! A large radiogram gave the news from Moscow. Its little brother glowed and bided its time. A coffee machine worked itself up into a froth. The boiler supplied the shower with ample hot water. Frost-Forestier stood under the stream. The plastic shower curtain was left open. Frost-Forestier liked to survey the battlefield while showering. First hot, then cold. He was a fit and well-proportioned man. He rubbed himself down with a rough khaki towel of American manufacture, a male nude in an empty barracks. His skin glowed. All quiet in Moscow. Appeals to the Soviet people. Frost-Forestier turned to the

muses, switched on music. Next to the shower cabinet was a
high bar. Frost-Forestier got in position; clean hands on clean
thighs. He leapt onto the bar, swung himself up and down.
Then back in starting position. His expression was serious.
His cock dangled, inert, well proportioned, between his mus-
cular thighs. The plug of an electric shaver was inserted into
a socket. There was a quiet purring sound as Frost-Forestier
shaved himself. There were disturbances to the reception.
Frost-Forestier switched off the big radio. The muses had
done their bit. He took a ball of cotton wool, and swabbed his
face with a pungent aftershave. The cotton wool ball vanished
under the patent lid of a hygienic pedal bin. A few pustules
stood out on his face. He pulled on a dressing gown, a hair
shirt, and tied it round his waist with a red tie. The time of
the little radio was at hand. It crackled and sang: "Dora needs
diapers." Frost-Forestier hearkened. The little radio repeated:
"Dora needs diapers." And that was all the little radio had to
say for itself.

The coffee machine trembled and steamed. A whistle hastened through its puckered mouth, the factory siren
announced the beginning of the day shift. Frost-Forestier
poured the coffee into a cup. The cup was of old Prussian
porcelain, an ornamental cup for amateur collectors.
Keetenheuve remembered the cup, its handle was broken.
Frost-Forestier scorched his fingers when he picked it up.
When Keetenheuve had been to see him, Frost-Forestier had
scorched his fingers too. Every morning he scorched them.
The cup had a colored picture of Frederick the Great on it.
The king looked out into the room from his cup with the
expression of a melancholy greyhound. Frost-Forestier took a
paper handkerchief, folded it around the porcelain and the

king, and began to sip his hot black morning beverage. All in all, less than fifteen minutes had elapsed since the alarm had gone off. Frost-Forestier opened the combination lock of his safe. Keetenheuve was amused by the safe. The safe was a gift to the insatiably curious. Documents, files, vitas, letters, drafts, films, and tapes waited here *how sweet the preserves in his old aunt's cupboard smelled to the boy,** and there were plenty of people who wouldn't have minded helping themselves. On the rough wooden table, a long piece of board on four trestles, there were tape machines. There were two cameras as well, one miniature, the other standard. Thieving equipment! One no longer stole the thing itself, that was left alone, one stole its shadow. And one could steal the voice of a man in the same way.

Keetenheuve always left so many things lying around. He was untidy. Frost-Forestier, a man in a political job, sat down at his desk. He began to think, he began to work. He had three hours ahead of him, the most important hours of the day, he concentrated, he got through a lot of work. He fitted a tape into the magnetophone, and switched it to play. He heard his own voice and another voice speaking. Rapt, absorbed, Frost-Forestier listened to the voices. Occasionally, they prompted him to write something down. Frost-Forestier had notebooks in red, green, and blue. He wrote down a name in one of them. Was it Keetenheuve's name? Frost-Forestier underlined the name. He underlined it in red.

General Yorck signed the agreement of Tauroggen. His king rehabilitated him. General Scharnhorst was recruiting. General Gneisenau was reforming. General Seeckt reminded

*Perhaps a memory of the opening scene of *Tom Sawyer*.

himself that the sun rose in the east. General Tukhachevski
wanted to roll up the carpet of the world. General de Gaulle
asked for tanks, no one paid him any attention and he was
right. General Speidel went to his allied colleagues. General
Paulus was still stuck in Russia. General Jodl was in his grave.
General Eisenhower was now President Eisenhower. Who
was the great informant to the Red Choir? Frost-Forestier
liked to remember his time in the Army High Command. He
was fond of military expressions. Once he said to
Keetenheuve: "I have a feeling in my water." What feeling did
he have in his water? That they would get together?

The morning barged through the blind. Keetenheuve
pushed back the sheet. He felt a draft—*Freud or Civilization
and Its Discontents. In the cafés in Berlin they talked about the
different psychoanalytical schools. Tulpe was a Communist.
Keetenheuve was a moderate. It was the time when moderates
and Communists still talked to each other. Fine. Futile. No
point. Struck with blindness? Struck with blindness.* It was
Erich who had first brought Keetenheuve along to a trade
union house. Erich had wanted to treat him, and
Keetenheuve was forced to accept his invitation, even though
he wasn't hungry. A small, worried-looking man with a mighty
mustache that was much too powerful for his shriveled face,
brought them charred potato pancakes and fizzy lemonade
that tasted like pudding out of packets. When Keetenheuve
had eaten the pancakes and drunk the lemonade, he felt rev-
olutionary. He was young. The town was small, dull, narrow-
minded, and the union house had a reputation for being the
citadel of dissent. But the popular rebellion the lads dreamed
of never came about, never never never, what there was and
what kept coming back, repeatingly, were the charred potato

pancakes of poverty and the pale pink drink of evolution, a lemonade brewed from synthetic syrups, effervescing when you unscrewed the top, and causing you to eructate after you'd drunk it. Erich had been killed. In the little town they had named a street after him; but the populace, dull, narrow-minded, and forgetful as ever, continued to refer to it as Short Street. Keetenheuve kept asking himself whether Erich had really died for his convictions, because it seemed likely that he would have lost them by then. But maybe at the moment of his death, Erich had returned to that hope, purely because the people of that small town were so god-awful in those days. It was lawlessness that caught up with Erich on the market-place, but what brought about his death was his own disgust.

Keetenheuve raised the lid of the washstand, water flowed into the basin, he could wash, could undertake—once more—the cleansing of Pontius Pilate, of course he was also innocent, he wasn't to blame for the course of the world, but precisely because he was innocent, he was confronted by the immemorial question, what is innocence, what is truth, o ancient governor of Augustus. He looked at himself in the mirror.

The eyes, without their spectacles, had a good-natured expression, and good-natured imbecile was what his col-league on the *Volksblatt* had called him, that last evening, the last time he saw the man. That was twenty years ago, on the day that the commissar had taken over the running of the newspaper. The Jewish editors were sacked on the spot, clever people, adroit leader writers, exquisite stylists, but they had misread the signs, done everything wrong, clueless calves in the abattoir compound; the others were given a few weeks to prove their worth. Keetenheuve declined the opportunity.

He took his back pay and went to Paris. He was free to go, no one stopped him. In Paris, though, people asked him in bewilderment: What are you doing here? Why have you come? Not until German troops were marching down the Champs-Elysées did Keetenheuve have an answer. But by then he was en route for Canada; together with German Jews, with German anti-fascists, German national socialists, young German airmen, German sailors, and German shop assistants he was way down in the belly of a ship bound for Canada from England. The captain of the vessel was a just man; he hated them all equally. And now it was Keetenheuve who was asking himself: What am I doing here, what's the point of this, is it just to avoid taking part, so that I can wash my hands in innocence, and is that enough?

Keetenheuve's head was in its usual place, no one had detached it from his trunk. Did that speak against Keetenheuve, or did it, as some thought, speak against the guild of the world's executioners? Keetenheuve had plenty of enemies, and there was no treason of which he was not accused. That's the way George Grosz would have painted me, he thought. His face already had the proud cast of the ruling class. He was a member of parliament and belonged to the loyal—oh, so loyal—opposition to the Chancellor.

Half-nude of a manager—that's what the mirror gave back. Mirror, mirror, on the wall, he was fleshy now, out of condition, the muscles slack, the skin matt white with a bluish tinge like watery skim milk in wartime, fat-free milk they called it now, a cute coinage of state euphemism, he belonged to the moderates, made his peace, accepted the situation, advocated cautious reforms in keeping with tradition, he was plagued by desire and circulatory disorders (*kiss me*) *you will go*. He was an imposing man. He displaced more air than he had ever expected to. What was the smell around him? Lavender water, a souvenir of the Empire, the long corridors of This-is-England *(kiss me) you will go*. Keetenheuve was no typical instance of the parliamentary elite. With those eyes, he couldn't be; they were too good-natured. Who wanted to be called good-natured and be thought of as something of an imbecile? And the mouth—the mouth was too thin, too pursed *schoolmaster schoolmaster* it wasn't garrulous, it was disquieting, and so Keetenheuve was never altogether demystified; "he was a handsome man / and what i want to know is / how do you like your blueeyed boy / Mister Death." Keetenheuve was a reader and devotee of contemporary poetry, and it sometimes amused him, while listening to his colleagues' speeches in parliament, to wonder who else in the room would have read Cummings. That set Keetenheuve apart from the party, kept him young, and caused him to lose out in the ruthlessness stakes. The little magazines, no sooner started up than wound down, the journals that devoted themselves to poetry, rubbed shoulders with the official files in Keetenheuve's briefcase, curious, yea verily, curious, to have the poems of the experimental poet E. E. Cummings scraping against the color-coded cardboard folders of a German parliamentarian marked *Confidential, Urgent, Secret (kiss me) you will go*

Keetenheuve went out into the corridor. Many ways led to the capital. There were many travelers toward power and livings.

They were all on their way, delegates, politicians, civil servants, journalists, party lobby fodder and party founders, interest groups by the dozen, unionists, publicity managers, jobbers, the corrupters and the corrupted, the fox, the wolf, and the sheep of the security services, the news hawkers and news fabricators, all the string pullers, the stage managers, the pact makers, the splinter groups, all those who wanted to strike it rich, the brilliant cineastes of *Heidelberg on the Rhine on the Heath in the tub for Germany at Dragon's Rock*, the spongers, swindlers, moaners, placemen, and Michael Kohlhaas was sitting in the train, and the alchemist Cagliostro, Hagen the Vehmic killer sniffed the dawn, Kriemhild wanted her pension, the lobby riffraff kept their eyes and ears peeled, generals still in their Lodenfrey suits came marching in to be reactivated, numerous rats, numerous panting dogs and plucked fowls, they had visited their wives, fucked their wives, murdered their wives, they had bought ice cream for their kids, they had watched the ball game, they had followed the priest in their chasubles, they had served as deacons, they had been chided by their bosses, received encouragement from their backroom staff, they had come up with an idea, drawn up an itinerary, they wanted to pull a fast one, they made plan B, they had drafted legislation, spoken in their constituencies, they wanted to get up the greasy pole, stay in power, keep their noses to the grindstone, their snouts in the trough, they made their way to the capital city, the tiny capital lowercase hamlet that they liked to poke fun at, and they failed to understand what the poet had meant when he said that the real capital of any kingdom was not in any case behind high walls and could not be stormed.

Make way for the people's representatives,* dime-store jibes, the joke already had a beard in the Kaiser's time *a lieutenant with ten men writing Germany awaken on the latrine*

*Freie Bahn dem Volksvertreter, an untranslatable and malicious pun—either "Make way for the people's representative" or "free rail travel for the people's representative."

wall, by now the beard was so long you couldn't even see where the joke had been. What did the people want, and what did it mean anyway, the people? Who was it on the train, on the street, at the station? Was it the woman in Remagen pushing the beds over to the window, beds for birth, copulation, or death, then the building was hit by shrapnel, was it the maid with the milk pail staggering to the cowshed, up so early tired so early, or was he, Keetenheuve, the people? He distrusted the simplifying collective. What did it mean, the people, was it a herd to be fleeced or shod or led, was it composed of groups, to be brought into action by the planners according to their terms and their needs, sent into battle, driven to their graves, the German boy in action, the German girl in action, or was the people millions of individuals, each one different, each one thinking for himself, separately, away from any center, toward God, or toward a void or madness, impossible to lead, to direct, to bring into action or to shear? Keetenheuve hoped it was the latter. He belonged to a party that believed in majority rule. So what did the people mean? The people worked, the people funded the state, the people wanted to live off the state, the people complained, the people muddled along.

It wasn't given to talking about its representatives much. The people was not as mannerly as the people in school textbooks. It didn't share the author's notion of civics. The people was resentful. It resented the title of its deputies, their seats, their immunity from prosecution, their diet, their free travel passes. The dignity of parliament? Laughter in the bars, laughter in the streets. The loudspeakers had humiliated the parliament in people's front rooms for too long, the representation of the people had been a male voice choir for too long, a simple chorus to beef up the dictator's solo. Democracy was held in low repute. It failed to galvanize. And the repute of the dictatorship? The people said nothing. Was it silent because it was still afraid? Or was it silent out of unabating adoration? The jury acquitted the men of the dictatorship on all charges. And Keetenheuve? He was engaged on the work of rebuilding, and he was traveling on the Nibelungen Express.

Not all the parliamentarians traveled on the sleepers of the Bundesbahn. Others came to the capital by car, claimed the mileage allowance and the depreciation, and did very well out of it; they were the sharper cookies. On the Rhine highway, the black Mercedes roared downstream beside the water. Downstream washed the ooze, the driftwood, the germs, the excrement, and the industrial discharges. The men sat next to their drivers, or they sat behind their drivers, and they nodded off. Their families had taken it out of them. Sweat poured down their bodies, under their coats and jackets and shirts. The sweat of exhaustion, the sweat of memory, night sweat, death sweat, sweat of rebirth, sweat of being driven somewhere or other, sweat of naked panic fear. The chauffeur knew the road and hated the scenery. The chauffeur's name might be Lorkowski and he might have come from East Prussia. He came from the pine forests; there were dead bodies in the pine forests. He remembered the lakes; there were dead bodies in the lakes. The member of parliament had a soft spot for displaced persons. I thought it was supposed to be pretty here, thought Lorkowski, I shit on the Rhine. *He shat on the Rhine, Lorkowski, parliamentary driver from East Prussia, Lorkowski, hearse driver from the POW camps, Lorkowski, ambulance driver from Stalingrad, Lorkowski,*

National Socialist Motorized Column driver from the old Kraft durch Freude *days, shit the lot of it, corpses, parliamentarians, and cripples all one and the same load, load of shit, he shat everywhere not just on the Rhine.*

"There's an eyeful."

The lobbyist left the lavatory, adjusted his cock, *nihil humanum*, etc. He rejoined the other lobbyists in their compartment at the front of the carriage, a man among men.

"Bit on the pale side."

"Who cares."

"Rumble, fumble, tumble."

"Spent too long underneath."

Wagalaweia.

The girl came in a floating gown, an angel of the line, a night angel in a floating night gown, lace brushed the dust, snot, and dirt of the varnished corridor, nipples, full buds rubbing against the lace, the feet tittupping in dainty slippers, laced with satin ribbons, *Salome's feet like white doves*, the toenails lacquered red, the girl was still half asleep, moody, sulky, lots of girls wore sulky expressions on their pretty china dolls' faces, it was the fashion for girls to be sulky, in her throat she felt her smoker's tickle, the men watched as the girl, tittupping, lacquered, long-legged, pretty and sulky, went to the little girls' room. Perfume tickled their noses and mingled behind the door with the lobbyist's steady consumption of bocks the previous night—he wasn't one on whom hops and malt were wasted.

"Nice case you've got there. Real diplomat's accessory. Like it's just come from the Foreign Ministry of the Reich. Black red and gold stripe and all."

"Black red and mustard, we used to call it."

Wagalaweia.

The Rhine was now wending its way between flat beds, a winding silver ribbon. Distant hills arced up out of the early morning haze. Keetenheuve breathed in the mild air and straightaway felt sad. Chambers of commerce and tour operators described the area as the Rhine Riviera. A hothouse climate flourished in the basin between the hills; the air stagnated over the river and its banks. Villas stood beside the water, roses were bred, prosperity strode through the parkland wielding hedge clippers, gravel crunched crisply under the pensioner's lightweight footwear, Keetenheuve would never join their ranks, never own a home here, never trim or breed roses, the *nobiles, Rosa indica,* which put him in mind of *Erysipelas traumaticum,* faith healers were at work here, Germany was one large public hothouse, Keetenheuve took in rare flora, greedy, curious plants, giant phalluses like chimney stacks full of billowing smoke, blue-green, red-yellow, toxic, but it was a fertility without youth and sap, it was all putrid, all ancient, the growths swelled, but it was all *Elephantiasis arabum.* Engaged, it said over the door handle, and on the other side the girl was peeing—prettily, sulkily—over the tracks.

Jonathan Swift, the dean of St. Patrick's in Dublin had taken a seat between Stella and Vanessa, and was offended by their corporality. In old Berlin, Keetenheuve had known one Dr. Forelle. Forelle had had a general practice in a tenement block in Wedding. He was squeamish about bodies, for decades he had been working on a psychoanalytical study of Swift, and at night he would line his front door bell with cotton wool, in case he was called out to a birth. Now he lay in the ruins of his tenement together with all the other detested

bodies. The lobbyists, with empty bladder, with voided bur-
bling intestines, gabbled and slanged, they knew what they
were after.

"I'd go see Hanke if I were you. Hanke's been in the
Defense Ministry for as long as I can remember. Tell him I
sent you."

"But I can't just treat him to a frankfurter."

"Take him to the Royal. Three hundred. But it's first rate.
Worth every penny. Never fails."

"Or else just go and tell him we can't provide the mer-
chandise after all."

"I think the minister ought to take care of the bond. What's
he a minister for?"

"Plischer was at Technical College with me."

"Then Plischer's my man."

"Soft knees."

Wagalaweia.

The girl, pretty and sulky, tittupped back to bed. The girl,
pretty and sulky, was headed for Düsseldorf, she could go
back to bed for a little, and the men's lusts slipped in beside her,
pretty and sulky under her blankets. Lust chauffed. The girl
worked in fashion, beauty queen in some competition or other.
The girl was poor, and lived, not badly, off the rich. Von Timborn
opened the door of his compartment, von Timborn neatly
shaved, von Timborn comme il faut, von Timborn already pre-
senting his credentials to the Court of St. James.

"Good morning, Herr Keetenheuve."

Where did he know him from? Some foreign press ban-
quet. People toasting each other and listening out for scraps.
Keetenheuve didn't remember the occasion. He didn't know
who was greeting him. He nodded a greeting. But Herr von

Timborn had a remarkable memory for names and faces, and
he trained it for professional reasons. He set down his suitcase on the grille of the heater in the passage. He observed
Keetenheuve. Timborn had the habit of thrusting out his
lower lip, a rabbit snuffling in clover. Maybe the Lord had
provided for His servant in the night. The rabbit didn't hear
the grass growing, but he did hear the whisperings in the corridors and anterooms. Keetenheuve had a dodgy scent, he
was hard to discipline, he was uncomfortable, he gave
offense, he was an enfant terrible in his particular party, that
might yet harm a body, for Timborn that would have meant
the end of all his hopes, but then again, these outsiders, you
could never be sure, their mistakes might be the making of
them yet. There were good jobs and pressure jobs, government jobs and dead-end jobs a long way from Madrid, and
Timborn once more was led by the nose, trotting along the
strait path, not of virtue exactly, but of promotion, step by
step, up or down, that couldn't be ascertained just yet, but all
the same, one was back at the center, eight years previously
one had been in Nuremberg, eight years before that one had
also been in Nuremberg, on the podium then, the Nuremberg
Laws were promulgated, the first of them, the system of
mutual reinsurance seemed to be working, he was on the
comeback trail, and everything was up for grabs once more.
And now if Herr Keetenheuve gambled on the election result
and maybe was rewarded with a ministerial portfolio? Then
Keetenheuve would kick up. Idiotic of him—even Gandhi
didn't milk his own goats any more. Keetenheuve and
Gandhi, he could see them walking hand in hand on the
banks of the Ganges. Gandhi would have been irresistible to
Keetenheuve. Timborn retracted his lip and gazed dreamily

across the Rhine. He could picture Keetenheuve seated under palm trees—not a pretty sight. Timborn himself would look far better in a safari suit. The gateway to India was open. Alexander killed his best friend with a spear.

The train stopped in Godesberg. Herr von Timborn doffed his hat, the correct, the becoming, the Antony Eden felt. Godesberg was where the top people lived, the Foreign Ministry wallahs. Herr von Timborn strode briskly away over the platform. The engine driver swore. What a line! Get up steam and break. It was supposed to be an express. They'd used to rattle through Godesberg and Bonn. Now they stopped. The lobbyists blocked the doorway. They had sharp elbows, and they were the first into the capital. Schoolchildren came running up the stairs of the underpass. It smelled provincial, the staleness of tight little streets, cluttered rooms, fusty wallpaper. The platform was roofed in and gray—

and there at the gate, in the drab hall, he set foot in the capital, hunt him, catch him, O God Apollo O, and they grabbed hold of him again, fell upon him, overwhelmed him, dizziness and shortage of breath, a cardiac cramp shook him, an iron band laid itself around his chest, was tightened, soldered, riveted fast, every step helped to solder and rivet it, the movements of his stiff legs, his numb feet, were like hammer blows knocking in rivets in a wreck on the devil's wharf, and so he took one step after another (where was there a bench where he might sit, a wall he might lean against?) walked, even though he thought walking was beyond him, wanted to put out his hand for support, even though he didn't dare put out his hand for support, emptiness, emptiness stretched mightily in his skull, pressed, climbed like the pressure of a balloon rising into remote atmospheric dis-

tance, but like a balloon that was filled with the merest nothing, a void, an un-substance, non-substance, something baffling that had the urge to expand, that wanted to break through his bones and skin, and he could hear, it wasn't yet happening but he could hear it, the silk ripping like a glacial wind, and that was the extreme instant, an invisible juncture not even definable in mathematics, where everything stopped, there was no beyond, and this was the interpretation of it, see, see!, you will see!, ask, ask!, you will hear, and he lowered his glance, coward, coward, coward, his mouth remained closed, poor, poor, poor, and he clutched at himself, and the balloon was a disappointing dirty shell, he felt terribly exposed, and then he began to fall. He showed his travel permit, and his sense was that the station official saw him naked, the way prison guards and corporals see the men in their charge before they are put into uniform.

Sweat beaded his brow. He walked over to the newsstand. The sun was just paying a call, peering through a window and casting its spectrum over the latest news, over the Gutenberg picture of the world, an ironic flicker of iridescence. Keetenheuve bought the morning papers *No Discussions with the Russians*. Well, evidently not. Who wanted to discuss or not discuss what? And who came running at the sound of a whistle? Who was a dog? A constitutional dispute—was there some disagreement? Could someone not read? The Basic Law had been drawn up. Were people saying they shouldn't have bothered? What was going on in Mehlem? The High Commissar had been up the Zugspitze. He had enjoyed the wonderful view. The Chancellor was a little off color, but continued to perform well. Seven a.m.—he would be at his desk already. It wasn't just Frost-Forestier who worked in Bonn. Keetenheuve still hadn't got over his panic. The main section of the station restaurant was closed. Keetenheuve went into the little buffet room, schoolchildren were sitting around a table, charmlessly clad girls, boys already with the faces of civil servants, smoking furtively, they too were industrious, like the Chancellor, had open books spread out in front of them, were studying, striving (like the Chancellor?), grim-faced young people, because that was supposed to be sensible and help them to get ahead, they steeled their hearts, they were mindful of the timetable and not of the stars. The waitress gave it as her opinion that she should have been born with wings, Keetenheuve could see her float off, a halibut with pinions, the establishment wasn't large enough to accommodate all the custom issuing from the big trains, the lobbyists were cross, they wanted their eggs, Keetenheuve ordered a lager. He loathed beer, but on this occasion the bitter fizz seemed to calm his heart. Keetenheuve opened the newspaper at the local page. What was happening in Bonn? He was like the spa guest, who, having been banished to a bleak watering hole for too long, ends up listening to all the village scuttlebutt. Sophie Mergentheim had agreed to a soaking for the benefit of the refugees. There, she never failed. At a reception for God knows whom, she had charitably knelt under a watering can. Sophie, Sophie, the ambitious goose, didn't save the Capitol. You paid your money and you got to give her a drenching. Pretty tulip. The newspaper carried the photograph of a wet Sophie Mergentheim in a wet evening gown, wet to her panties, wet to her powdered scented skin. Colleague Mergentheim was positioned by the microphone, gazing pluckily into the flashlight through his thick black horn rims. Let's see your owl! *All quiet in Insterburg. Dog barks.* Mergentheim specialized in Jewish jokes; on the old

Volksblatt, he had been in charge of the funnies. *What, who barked in Insterburg? Yesterday? Today? Who barked? Jews? Silence. Dog joke.* In the cinema—Willy Birgel riding for Germany. *The loathsome beer foam on his lips. Elke, a name from Nordic mythology. The norns Urd, Werdandi, and Skuld under the tree Yggdrasil. Polished boots. Death in capsule form. Beer over a grave.*

2

KORODIN GOT OFF THE TRAM AT THE MAIN STATION. A traffic policeman was playacting at being a traffic policeman in the Potsdamer Platz in Berlin. He waved the traffic on down the Bonner Strasse. It swarmed and buzzed and squeaked and honked. Cars, bicycles, pedestrians, and wheezy asthmatic trams squeezed out of narrow side streets onto the main station square. This was where coaches had once trundled, drawn by four horses, steered by royal coachmen, Prince Wilhelm had been a student at the university—and was thereby a few meters closer to his ultimate exile in Holland— he wore a tailcoat, the order of the Saxo-Borussian fraternity and their white cap. The traffic got snarled up, impeded and constricted by construction sites, cable laying, canalization pipes, concrete mixers, asphalt boilers. The snarl-up, the labyrinth, the knotty tangle, emblematic of losing one's way, of wandering and erring, the insoluble, inextricable knot, the ancients already had known the curse, had experienced the deception, found themselves ensnared, had lived it and thought about it and described it. Always the next generation would be wiser, would arrange things better for itself. (And this for five thousand years now.) Not everyone had a sword. Anyway, what was a sword good for? You could wave it around, kill people with it, die by it. And the point? None. You needed to show up in Gordium at the right moment. Opportunity makes the hero. By the time Alexander breezed in from Macedonia, the knot was tired of resisting. Besides, the event was without consequence. India did not fall; at the most, some fringe territories were occupied for a few years, and between the locals and the occupying forces there was barter.

What was the scene at the real Potsdamer Platz? A wire enclosure, a new international frontier, the end of the world, the Iron Curtain that God had caused to fall, God alone knew why. Korodin hastened to the stop for the trolleybus, the proud, modern conveyance commensurate to the needs of the capital city, the carrier for the masses traveling between the widely separated government quarters. Korodin did not, strictly speaking, have to join the line of those waiting at the stop. Two automobiles were garaged at his house. It was an act of modesty and self-denial for Korodin to ride to politics on public transport, while his chauffeur, alert, rested, and comfortable, drove Korodin's kids to school. Korodin was greeted. He acknowledged the greetings. He was a man of the people. But greetings from anonymous citizens not only incurred his gratitude; they also made him uncomfortable. The first bus came. They piled onto it, and Korodin stood back, modestly and self-denyingly he stood back, but he also felt squeamish (a sinful feeling) at the thought of these hurrying people struggling for their daily bread. Then the conveyance set off for parliament, the various ministries, the proliferation of offices, they were packed together like sardines, the gaggles of secretaries, the armies of pencil pushers, the companies of middle-ranking officials, all one trawl, emigrated from Berlin, emigrated from Frankfurt, emigrated from the caves of the Wolfsschanze,* relocated along with their jobs, bundled up together with their files, by the dozen they had been shoehorned into apartments in the new prefab blocks, where the walls barely separated their bedheads from the bedheads of others, perpetually under observation, never alone, always snooped on, always snooping, who's the visitor in the corner apartment, what are they saying, are they talking about me, they sniffed, who's been eating onions, who's having a late bath, it's Fräulein Irmgard, she's the one who uses chlorophyl soap, she needs it, who's been combing his hair over the sink, who's been using my towel, they were irritable, rancorous, embittered, indebted, separated from their families, seeking consolation, but not seeking it too often, anyway they were too tired in the evenings, they slaved away, typing up the new laws, doing overtime, sacrificing themselves for their boss, whom they hated, and on whom they snooped, against whom they intrigued, to whom they addressed anonymous letters, whose coffee they heated up, in whose window they put flowers—and they wrote proud letters home, sending bleached box brownie snapshots showing themselves in ministry gardens, or little Leica pictures that the boss had taken of them in the office: they were working for the admin-

*Literally "Wolf's Lair," the East Prussian headquarters of Hitler, who liked to style himself "Wolf" or even "Wolfi."

istration, they were governing Germany. It struck Korodin
that he hadn't prayed yet that day, and he decided to step out
of the stream, and finish his journey on foot.

Keetenheuve hadn't been in to his apartment in the parliamentary ghetto in Bonn that morning, for him it was just a
joyless pied-à-terre, a doll's chamber of constriction *tomorrow,
children, we'll be joyful, tomorrow we will celebrate*, why
should he go there; everything he needed was in his briefcase,
and even that sometimes seemed to him like useless ballast
on the journey. Keetenheuve had declined to take the bus. In
the square in front of the cathedral, Keetenheuve encountered the modest Korodin. Korodin had prayed to Cassius and
Florentius, the patron saints of the place, and he had con-
fessed to the sin of pride *I thank thee God that I am not as
these men are,* and he had absolved himself for now and for
today of his guilt. Being seen coming out of the cathedral by
Keetenheuve made Korodin feel uncomfortable again. Were
the saints perhaps dissatisfied with the delegate's prayers and
were they now punishing Korodin by putting Keetenheuve in
his way? Or perhaps the encounter had been arranged by a
kindly Providence, and was a sign that Korodin was in good
odor once again.

It was accounted unusual if members of hostile parties—
while they might work together, and even on occasion vote
together in committee—went for walks à deux. For each it
was suspicious to be seen with the other, while for the party
bosses the sight ranked with that of one of their flock openly
consorting with rent boys, a display of straightforward perversion. Gossip inevitably put the worst construction on every
casual conversation, which might revolve around the oppressive climate or a still more oppressive heart condition, gossip

suspected conspiracy, collusion, betrayal, heresy, and the overthrow of the Chancellor. The town, moreover, was crawling with journalists, and the photograph of the individuals in question might appear in Monday's *Spiegel,* where it would give rise to furious indignation. All this Korodin was mindful of, but Keetenheuve (he felt like saying "God damn him") was not unsympathetic to him, with the result that he hated him sometimes with a personal animus, and not just with the chilly routine rejection of party rivalry, because he had ("Damn him") the striking and unignorable feeling that here was a soul to be rescued, that Keetenheuve might yet be brought back to the straight and narrow, might even, ultimately, be converted. Korodin, with his two large and expensive automobiles generally consigned to their garage, had an honest infatuation with the new generation of worker priests in the industrial Ruhrgebiet. They were grumpy men in clumping shoes, who, Korodin liked to think, had read their Bernanos and their Bloy, whereas in fact it was only he himself who—and this was to his credit—had been perturbed by these authors, and so the grumpy men from time to time would receive a check from Korodin, though apart from that, he seemed to them rather a cold fish. To Korodin, however, these checks represented a kind of primitive Christianity of pure opposition to the existing order, against one's own class and against expensive automobiles, and already he was experiencing difficulties on account of his "radicalism," and receiving mild rebukes, and his friend the bishop, who, like Korodin, had read Bernanos, but had not been disturbed, but merely appalled, the bishop would have preferred to see the check on some other offertory tray elsewhere.

Korodin, who always knew everything, always had a list of

birthdays committed to memory, if only so as not to alienate
anyone in his wife's extensive landed family, Korodin wanted
to express his condolences to Keetenheuve, and maybe he
hoped that a moment of shattering grief might make him
more amenable to conversion, that the loss of transitory
earthly happiness might turn his mind to the joys of eternity,
but then, standing in front of Keetenheuve, Korodin thought
commiseration was not called for, would even be unpleasantly and tactlessly intrusive, because to such a man as
Keetenheuve, everything that would be taken for granted in
Korodin's circles, such as, for instance, expressions of sympathy, was dubious, one could not say for sure whether
Keetenheuve was even grieving, there was nothing visible, no
black armband, no mourning riband on the lapel, and no tears
in the widower's eyes, but that again made the man attractive,
perhaps he wasn't one to make a public display of his grief,
and so Korodin, lowering his gaze, and fixing the cobbles in
front of the cathedral, said: "We are standing on the site of a
huge cemetery from Roman-Frankish times." And there it
was—the sentence, already spoken, no longer merely a casual or thoughtless conversation opener, a chance association
that had come up, the sentence was more crassly stupid than
any condolence, and Keetenheuve might take it as an allusion
to his grief, but at the same time as a banal and cynical ignor-
ing of it. And so, in his confusion, Korodin went from the
cemetery straight onto the question he might otherwise have
spent a long time circling round, without perhaps even putting in the end, because it was an invitation to him to commit
betrayal, albeit betrayal of a wicked party.

He asked: "Might you not change your position?"

Keetenheuve understood Korodin. Keetenheuve understood too that Korodin had wanted to express his sympathies, and he was grateful to him that he had not done so. Of course, he might change his position. He might easily change his position. Anyone might change his position, but the fact was that, with Elke, Keetenheuve had lost the only person with intimate knowledge of his position, the only spectator at his turbulence, and that meant that he could not now change his position. He could not change it himself, from within, because he *was* that position, it was an ancient disgust in himself, and he could change it least of all now when he thought of Elke's short life ruined by war and criminality, and Korodin had already given him the answer with his Roman-Frankish cemetery.

Keetenheuve said: "I don't want any more cemeteries."

He could just as well have said he didn't want any more cemeteries in Europe or in northern Europe; but that would have had a little too much pathos. But of course you could use the cemetery as an argument against the cemetery. Both of them knew that. Korodin didn't want any more cemeteries either. He wasn't a militarist. He was an officer in the reserve. But he was willing to risk the sort of cemetery that Keetenheuve was thinking of in order to forestall the digging of another, much larger and otherwise unavoidable cemetery later (in which he himself, and his automobiles and his wife and children, would all be buried). But what could or could not be forestalled? History was a clumsy child or an ancient guide with a blind man in tow, it alone knew the way, and it was in a hurry to get there. They were strolling toward the Hofgarten now, and stopped in front of a playground. Two little girls were playing on the seesaw. One of them was fat; the other little girl was slender, with long, shapely legs. The fat one had to push to get off the ground.

Korodin saw the possibility of a metaphor. "Think of the children!" he said. Even to his own ears, it sounded sanctimonious. He was annoyed with himself. Keetenheuve wouldn't be converted like that.

Keetenheuve thought of the children. He would have liked to go over to the seesaw to play with the pretty girl. He was an aesthete too, and the aesthete is unfair. He was unfair to the fat girl. Nature was unfair. Everything was unfair and unfathomable. Now he longed for bourgeois domesticity, for a wife to be a mother to his children. An attractive wife, of course, and a charming child. *He lifted a little girl on to a swing, he stood in the garden, the beautiful wife and beautiful mother called him in to lunch, Keetenheuve head of a household, Keetenheuve kind to children, Keetenheuve trimmer of hedges.* There were unused feelings of tenderness curdling within him.

He said: "I am thinking of the children!"

And he saw a scene that often came to him, that he always remembered as a moment of eerie prophetic vision. When Keetenheuve had voluntarily left the Fatherland, driven by nothing beyond his own profound disagreement with what was happening and what would shortly happen, on his way to Paris, Keetenheuve had spent a night in Frankfurt, and in the morning, outside the theater in Frankfurt, breakfasting on a café terrace on Himalayan blossom tea and crisp croissants, he had watched a procession of the Hitler Youth, and there before his eyes the large and colorful square had widened, and all of them, with their flags and pennants, and fifes and drums and daggers, they had marched into a wide and deep grave. They were the fourteen-year-olds following their Führer, and by 1939 they were twenty-year-olds, which made

them storm troopers, airmen, and sailors—the very generation that died. Korodin gazed up at the sky. Black clouds were
gathering. A child had been struck by lightning just where
they were standing, and Korodin was afraid once more of the
wrath of heaven. He flagged down a passing taxi. He hated
Keetenheuve. A man without responsibility, a vagabond,
childless, doomed. Korodin felt like leaving Keetenheuve
behind. Hope he gets struck by lightning! And maybe Korodin
was endangering himself and the taxi if he gave the pariah a
lift. But in the end Korodin's good breeding prevailed over
fear and dislike, and with a chilly smile he allowed
Keetenheuve to climb into the car.

They sat together in silence. It spattered and flashed, and
sheets of rain swathed the tops of the trees like fog, but the
thunder boomed feebly, as though the storm were already
tired or still far off. There was a powerful smell of damp, of
earth and blossom, the air grew warmer, he sweated, his shirt
clung to him, and once again Keetenheuve had the impression of being in a gigantic hothouse. They drove past the back
of the presidential mansion, and the front of the Chancellor's
villa, the wrought iron gates stood open. Sentries guarded the
open drive, they could see flower beds, sweeping lawns, ornamental beds, flowers glowed, a dachshund and a German
shepherd walked together, an odd couple, as though deep in
conversation, slowly along the gravel paths. A botanical landscape, botanical gardens, princesses had lived here and sugar
manufacturers, con men had dined with them and still not
managed to melt their fortunes. A few bombs had fallen too.
Blackened stumps of masonry reached out of the dense
greenery. The federal flag was waving. A man walked slowly to
work, a ridiculous pop-up lady's umbrella dangling unused

from his wrist, in spite of the rain. A former, a future, a once-and-future ambassador? Extras on the political stage wandered down the alleys, and with them wandered their biography, their printed vita, a versatile whore on many sidewalks. There were the extras. But where was the director grazing? Where was the protagonist cropping his grass? But of course there had never been any directors or protagonists. The taxi merely passed a lot of so-called resisters, who had prevented worse things from happening. It was raining; otherwise, they should have been sunning themselves in their fame.

They stopped outside the Bundeshaus. Korodin paid the taxi. He refused to allow Keetenheuve to pay any share of the short ride, though he asked the driver for a receipt, Korodin wasn't about to make the state a present. Hurriedly, fearfully—it was flashing again—he said goodbye to Keetenheuve with his frosty smile. He hurried off, as though the Law had summoned him and none other. Keetenheuve felt like going into the press barracks, but Mergentheim wouldn't be up yet, he had the exorbitant Sophie at home, and he wasn't a morning type anyway. Keetenheuve was loath to go up to his office. Then he saw that visitors had been bussed in to view the federal capital, to view the federal parliament, to lunch in the restaurant of the Bundeshaus, and were gathered together for a guided tour, and just as an old Berliner had once had the idea of taking part in Käse's tour, Keetenheuve joined the group as it set off. How strange! The official in his dark uniform, who was charged with conducting the sightseers, looked just like the Chancellor. He had a somewhat pinched face, dry, cunning, creased with humor, he looked like a wily fox, and he spoke with the same touch of dialect as the celebrated statesman. (In the time of the monarchy, loyal servants went around with the same style of beard as their respective emperor or king.) They walked up the steps to the plenary room, and their guide, whose resemblance to the Chancellor seemed to have gone unnoticed to the others, because no one paid him any particular attention, the guide was telling them that the building they were in had started life as a pedagogic academy, and unfortunately he forgot to play the German cultured card and pull his Goethe on them, and refer to the pedagogical province that might be ruled from here. Did the Chancellor know that his parliament was short of philosophers to go out and work the land for him?

For the first time Keetenheuve found himself standing up in the gallery of the plenary room, and saw the uncushioned seats that were reserved for the public and the press. Down below, all the seating was plush green, so even the Communists might enjoy the green comfort of the upholstered benches. The room was empty. A large empty classroom with row upon row of tidy desks. The teacher's desk at the front, fittingly elevated. The perchance Chancellor brought up the significant facts. He said the room had over a thousand meters of neon tubing. Delegates who were hard of hearing might have recourse to headphones, said the Chancellor-cum-guide. One joker among the group wondered if you could switch over to a music station. The Chancellor look-alike looked askance at the ribald suggestion. He pointed out the voting doors of the chamber, and alluded to the tradition of the division.* Keetenheuve at this juncture might have offered an anecdote for the amusement of the group, a charming little anecdote from the life of a politician.

*The German is *Hammelsprung*, literally "the jump of sheep."

Keetenheuve, the sheep in question, had once jumped the wrong way. Which is to say he didn't know whether he had jumped the wrong way or not, all at once he had felt uncertain, and he had skipped through the door with the ayes, while his grouping had decided in favor of the noes. The coalition had applauded him. They were mistaken. Korodin had seen his conversion campaign beginning to bear fruit. He was mistaken. In the party assembly room, they told off Keetenheuve in no uncertain terms. They too were mistaken. Keetenheuve had found the matter at issue rather trivial, and he had acted on the spur of the moment, he wanted to be a yea-sayer rather than a nay-sayer, and so he had fallen in with some minor government proposal. Why shouldn't the government sometimes be in the right? It seemed to him idiotic to seek to deny that, and to conduct a politics of stubbornness, or of political principle, which came to the same thing. Keetenheuve saw schoolboys seated there, farmers' sons, blockheads, quarrelsome and submissive, quarrelsome and turbulent, quarrelsome and slow-witted, with a couple of eager beavers in their midst. "Talking-shop" said one of the visitors. Keetenheuve looked at him. The visitor was of the beery nationalist sort, who loved to have a dictator grinding him down, so long as he himself got a pair of boots to trample on those below him. Keetenheuve looked at him. "In the chops," he thought. "Well, don't you agree?" said the man, with a challenging look at Keetenheuve. Keetenheuve might have replied: It's always seemed to me the least worst option, even this parliament here is the lesser evil. What he said was: "You damned well keep your mouth shut in here!" The man went purple, then he felt unsure of himself, and he cravenly knuckled under. He edged away from Keetenheuve. If he had recognized the delegate Keetenheuve, he could have thought to himself: I'll remember you, you're on my list, you wait till Judgment Day, I'll get you in the swamps or in the heath. But no one knew Keetenheuve, and the Chancellor perchance led his little troop out into the open.

The journalists were based in a couple of barracks. The barracks were long and low, and faced the Bundeshaus; from the outside they looked like military constructions, meant to last for the duration of a war (and wars go on for a long time), to accommodate military staffs and run a new exercise yard. But through the center of each building ran a central aisle that was like the corridor of a ship, perhaps not exactly a luxury liner, but at least a tourist vessel, with the cabins cheek by jowl on either side, and the clatter of typewriters and the ticking of telexes, the incessant shrilling of telephones giving the impression that beyond the various correspondents' quarters was the open sea with mewing gulls and steamer sirens, and so the press barracks became a pair of barges that were carried on the waves of the times, and rocked and shaken. "Press releases" arrived at intervals, like the tides. They were dropped on a pine table in the entrance, pale blurred snippets of information on cheap paper, left there by the indifferent messengers from the various arms of government, all concerned to talk up the activity of their ministries, to inform the public, to spread federal propaganda, to conceal or deny or throw smoke screens around events, to allay concerns, to deny truths or lies, and occasionally to toot into the horn of righteous indignation. The Foreign Ministry informs, the Federal Treasury, the Central Statistical Office, the Ministry of Post and Railways, the Occupying Forces Liaison Committee, the Ministry for the Interior responsible for

Police or Justice, they all were informing of this or that, were loquacious or tight-lipped, as the case might be, showed their teeth, or an expression of concern, and a few even had a smile for the public, the encouraging come-hitherish smile of an available beauty. The press spokesman for the government let it be known that the opposition claims that the government had applied to the French secret service for help in the forthcoming elections were completely and utterly without foundation. This was something they were in earnest about, they threatened to take the matter to a prosecuting attorney because election funds, party coffers were always strictly off-limits, always a touchy subject; they needed money just as every citizen did, and from where else would it be forthcoming but from wealthy friends. Korodin had wealthy friends, but as is the way of rich people they were tightwads (Korodin could understand that) and they wanted something in return for their money.

The press ship was bobbing along that morning in a slight breeze. Keetenheuve could sense there wasn't anything particular going on. The planks were not atremble, no doors were thrown open and slammed shut; but then there are storms that break suddenly and unpredictably, unannounced by any weatherman. Keetenheuve knocked on Mergentheim's door. Mergentheim was the capital correspondent for a newspaper that rightly accounted itself one of the Republic's "most highly respected" newspapers (but what of the others? were they not respected or not respectable? poor little wallflowers at the national folk dance!), and on important days he spoke suave and trenchant commentaries on the wireless that were by no means uncritical, and had even provoked angry protests from the morbidly sensitive and gypsyishly jealous coalition parties.

Keetenheuve and Mergentheim—were they friends or enemies? They wouldn't have been too sure themselves: hardly
friends, and neither would have spoken of the other with
schoolboy fervor: my friend Mergentheim, my pal
Keetenheuve. But on occasion they found themselves drawn
together, because they had set out and been colleagues together at a time when everything might have turned out different-
ly, and if history had taken a different course (inconceivable
that it could), without the Austrian lunatic, without the mon-
strous upsurge, without crime, hubris, war, death, and
destruction, then perhaps Keetenheuve and Mergentheim
might have spent years of their lives in the same gloomy
courtyard room of the old *Volksblatt* (Keetenheuve would have
liked that, Mergentheim not at all) and really would have had
the feeling, they were still young, of joint effort, shared opin-
ions, and a common friendship. But in '33 there came a parting of the ways. Keetenheuve, dubbed a good-natured fool,
wandered off into exile, while Mergentheim successfully took
the probationary path that was to see him become senior editor, or *Hauptschriftleiter,** as it was then known, of the somewhat changed newspaper. Later, admittedly, in spite of an
obedient change of course that cost it readers, the *Volksblatt*
ceased to publish, or it was swallowed up by the *Arbeitsfront,*†
one couldn't say for certain, and it continued to exist in the
form of a subtitle with a party member at the helm, and
Mergentheim got himself made a Rome correspondent. In

---

*The aversion of Goebbels and Hitler to borrowings from the French or Latin,
like the more normal *Chefredakteur*, led to such ugly and zany Teutonisms as
this "main-writing-leader."
†The Nazis compulsorily reorganized every enterprise in Germany under this
"work front."

the nick of time! The war began, and life in Rome was pleasant enough. Later again, in Mussolini's Northern Italian republic, things got tricky for Mergentheim once more, he might easily have copped a bullet from the SS or the partisans, or fallen into the hands of the Allies, but once again, Mergentheim managed to get out in time, and so had made himself a sought-after and well-supported figure in the rebuilding with a relatively unbesmirched past record. It made Keetenheuve happy each time he saw Mergentheim in his office, because as long as Mergentheim was at his desk, as long as he hadn't taken off again to become Washington correspondent or whatever else, it signaled to Keetenheuve that the state was on a reasonably even keel, and its enemies distant.

For his part, Mergentheim had completely wiped Keetenheuve from his memory, and when he spotted him as a member of parliament in Bonn, a poacher in his own preserve, he was frankly astounded. "I thought you were dead," he stammered the first time Keetenheuve paid him a visit, and he thought the game was up and he would be made to account for himself. Though account for what? Was any of what had happened his fault? He was a man who liked to clarify things for the people, not uncritically so long as it didn't cost him his life or his job, and his chosen profession after all was newspaperman and not martyr. But Mergentheim quickly recovered himself. He saw that Keetenheuve had come to him in friendship, with his head full of sentimental memories, and not in any accusing spirit. The only thing that Mergentheim was left at a loss to explain to himself was how Keetenheuve too had managed to catch the wave and, even more than that, how he had managed to ride it and take Fortune (as Mergentheim would see it) by the throat. But when he noticed during their first conversation that Keetenheuve had not come home armed, as Mergentheim had expected him to be, with a British or a Panamanian passport, and that he had come to see his old chum on foot, then Mergentheim changed from being apprehensive to being benevolent, and he took Keetenheuve and put him in his chrome company car, and drove him home to Sophie.

Sophie, fragrant, alluring, wearing a housedress designed by some Düsseldorf Dior, and apparently alerted by telephone of the visitor's coming (how had Mergentheim managed to pull that off?), greeted Keetenheuve with a purring "Yes, we've met," and with a flutter of the eyelids that suggested to him that he had slept with her. It was unlikely. But then it turned out that Sophie had once worked as an office junior in the circulation department of the *Volksblatt,* and even if Keetenheuve couldn't place her in his memory, that was where Mergentheim must have discovered her, unless it was she who had made a play for him, and the rise to *Frau Hauptschriftleiter* must have made her socially ambitious; she was the Muse who advised, supported, and encouraged Mergentheim on the path of success, career, and timely trimming.

No, Keetenheuve hadn't slept with her, though perhaps he might have done so. Sophie gave herself to important and influential men without arousal on her part, she felt aroused only when she talked about these copulations afterwards, she scorned boys and men who were merely good-looking, and, while Keetenheuve was perhaps not his party's concertmaster, he was at least among its first violins, and therefore worthy of being slept with. But it had never come to a kiss or sexual embrace between them; Keetenheuve's response had been lukewarm, and, since he made a point of not participating in the social life of the upper echelons of the new Republic, he wasn't a tempting quarry for Sophie either, but just a fool. The epithet "good-natured" was left off this time, and Mergentheim too didn't add it to his description of his old friend. Seeing as Keetenheuve had made it to MP, it stood to reason that he would be a fool, but it seemed unwise to gamble on his good nature.

What plunged the loose friendship between them into something approaching enmity was Mergentheim's discovery in the Bundestag's register that Keetenheuve was married. Sophie's curiosity was piqued. Who was this wife whom Keetenheuve didn't produce? Was she so beautiful or so ugly that he kept her concealed? Was she a wealthy heiress, and was he afraid she might be stolen from him? It would probably be something like that, and Sophie in her imagination was already pairing off Elke with young first secretaries, not in order to hurt Keetenheuve, but merely to restore the natural order of things, because clearly a Keetenheuve didn't merit a young and beautiful heiress. Eventually, the two women met and took an instant dislike to each other. Elke was naughty and mouthy, she didn't want to go to the ball (which delighted Keetenheuve, who didn't want to go either, couldn't go, as he didn't have a black tie), but in the end Sophie got her way, and Elke drove to the ball with Mergentheim, after whispering in Keetenheuve's ear that Sophie was wearing a corset (which embarrassed Keetenheuve). The evening had been ghastly. Both women, feeling an inexplicable aversion to one another, thought: Nazi bitch (that's how mistaken women can be), and Elke didn't cosy up to the embassy first secretaries, she cosied up to the embassy gin, which was imported duty-free and was excellent, and when alcohol had fogged her brain, she announced to the astonished gathering, whom she called a bunch of ghosts, that her Keetenheuve would bring down the government. She dubbed Keetenheuve the man of the revolution, who felt contempt for the restoration that was now strengthening its grip on the country; so highly did Elke think of her husband, and how badly she must have felt let down by him. Once the astonishment at her display had died down, and Elke was driven home by an attaché—though, instead of canoodling with him, she swore at him—the silly incident had the unexpected effect of raising the profile of the MP, because Elke hadn't betrayed (if she had even known) what sort of putsch Keetenheuve was gearing up for, for what side, with whose help, with what weapons, and to what end he wanted to remove the government, and so, after that evening, many people viewed Keetenheuve distrustfully and anxiously as a politician to be reckoned with, and perhaps kept in with.

Mergentheim sat behind his desk like a fluffy melancholy bird, his face getting ever broader, his eyes more and more veiled, his glasses thicker, their horn rims heavier and blacker, and so the impression grew of confronting an owl, a bird that frequented ruins and boskage, who wore his handmade suits, and might be satisfied and merry and amused, but wheezed a little with so much fluffy activity, was a little exhausted by his dynamic consort's night flights, and the assumption that the wisdom associated with that bird was melancholy was perhaps a mistake based on the visitor's ignorance. Mergentheim sent his secretary away to get something. He offered Keetenheuve a cigar. He knew that Keetenheuve didn't smoke, but Mergentheim pretended to have forgotten.

Keetenheuve should remember not to get above himself.
Mergentheim took a black cylinder of tobacco out of a crinkly
tin wrapper and lit it. He eyed Keetenheuve through the blue
haze. Mergentheim knew that Elke had died, under mysterious
circumstances, it was rumored, gossip traveled quickly, but, like
Korodin, Mergentheim was unable to offer a word of sympathy
to Keetenheuve, he too felt that to bring up family tragedy and
personal loss with Keetenheuve was inappropriate, tactless, and
intrusive; Mergentheim wouldn't have been able to explain why
this was so—Keetenheuve was just like that. This time,
Mergentheim was correct in his intuition. Keetenheuve was not
a family man, he was sensual and capable of love, but he had so
little of coupledom in his makeup that he wasn't even husband
material. Keetenheuve was a man without contact, with occasional yearning for contact, and that led him to his party, to difficulties and confusion. It was marriage, and not love, that to
Keetenheuve was a contrary form of existence, and maybe he
was a stray monk, a caged tramp, or even a martyr who'd missed
his cross. Poor guy, thought Mergentheim. Elke's death must
have affected Keetenheuve badly, and the way Mergentheim
saw it (and he wasn't completely wrong), Keetenheuve had
come back from exile feeling thoroughly deracinated, and Elke
had represented his desperate attempt to put down fresh roots
here, and to win love and to have love. The attempt had failed.
What would the man do now? An unexpected run of fortune (as
Mergentheim persisted in seeing it) had borne Keetenheuve
aloft, into the arena of big-time political decision making, and
through a variety of circumstances, which Keetenheuve had not
particularly intended or worked to bring about, he had ended up
occupying a pivotal position, which wouldn't allow him to put
into effect whatever he wanted to put into effect (whatever that

might be), but in which he could certainly make a major nuisance of himself. That was dangerous! Perhaps Keetenheuve himself didn't even know how dangerous his position was. Maybe he hadn't changed at all, an idiot, a well-intentioned fool. That would make him unusual, at least among the new intake of parliamentarians, and Mergentheim viewed him with new benevolence.

"You need to watch yourself," said Mergentheim.

"What for?" Keetenheuve wasn't really interested. Why should he watch himself? What was Mergentheim getting at now? What was he doing here, Keetenheuve, what was his purpose? The room in the old *Volksblatt* had been more gemütlich. It was in ruins now. *Forget it!* What was Keetenheuve doing in this barrack, where the walls were throbbing with industriousness and hysterical busyness? Keetenheuve had gradually stopped caring whether it was rain or shine. He had his trench coat.

"The knives are out for you," said Mergentheim.

He was right! The knives were out for him. He sensed it himself. He had fallen victim to the pleasures of the table. Maybe it was to make up for so much thin gruel. It couldn't be made up for. But he had become heavy. Layers of sluggish fat slept under his skin. Mergentheim, admittedly, was much fatter. But on Mergentheim it looked good; on himself, it didn't. Well then, he had better fight.

He asked: "What information do you have?"

"None," said Mergentheim. "I'm just thinking aloud." The owl put on an intelligent expression. It shrouded itself in smoke. The thick spectacle lenses misted in front of the veiled eyes. Owls looked like that in old pictures of witches. Actually, they looked stupid.

"Don't be oracular. What's going on?" He couldn't really care less. He was just drifting along today. *Rotten*

Mergentheim laughed. "If you want to hang a dog . . ." *A dog barked in Insterburg*

"I don't have a hook," said Keetenheuve, "not one they can use!"

"Now, Major . . ."

"Don't be stupid. That's such an idiotic old story."

"Truth is often just a question of packaging," said Mergentheim.

So that was it! That's how they proposed to gag him. It was that old canard that they were going to wheel out against him. Shortly after his return, the rumor had spread around Keetenheuve that in England during the war, he had worn the uniform of a major in the British army; and of course people came forward, prepared (people are prepared to do anything) to claim they'd seen him in that uniform. It was absolute rubbish, so easy to disprove that Keetenheuve didn't even feel like defending himself. For anyone who knew him, it was a ridiculous vision, Keetenheuve mincing around as a British major, with his swagger stick tucked under his arm. It was particularly absurd, because in fact it was Keetenheuve's proud Achilles' heel (and he was quite unyielding about this) that he had never worn a uniform of any description, even though (purely hypothetically—it had never quite come to that), if he'd had to choose, he would have preferred a British uniform to a German one—for ethical reasons (i.e., Hitler) to which Keetenheuve gave far more weight than the patriotic ones, which to him were merely atavistic. A dead man is no good to his Fatherland, and people die for ideas they are at best incapable of grasping, and whose implications they fail to see. The flogged warriors on the battlefields, the tortured nations, were the victims of quarrelsome, selfish, self-righteous, and completely hopeless thinkers, unable to get clarity in their poor warped brains, and incapable, furthermore, of understanding, or of getting along with one another. Maybe armies were irrational notions of God, unleashed against one another. Better to abstain! Better still to try and call a halt to the whole thing!

Keetenheuve gestured dismissively. "That's crap, why are you telling me that?"

"I'm not so sure," said Mergentheim, "call it crap if you like, sure, you were never in His Majesty's Armed Forces, I don't believe for a moment you were, but it's a good story, and it's a good picture of you for the masses to keep in their heads. Keetenheuve, member of parliament and major in the British army. Surely some mistake? Something not quite right there. We know it's a lie, a completely baseless story. But one day a newspaper decides to print it, for the hell of it. If you're lucky, it's forgotten again. But then someone else runs it. You know Hitler knew a thing or two about black propaganda, and what is it he says in his book? You repeat the lie over and over again. A man's name is Bernhard. You call him Isaac. You do it again. You keep on doing it. Never fails."

"We're not at that stage yet."

"You're right. Not yet. But maybe someone, maybe friend Frost-Forestier, has turned up some old photograph of you. You won't remember. But say the photograph shows you behind a BBC microphone, the letters are clearly visible, and if they're not, there are ways of making them visible, and then everyone can see them, and everyone can understand them. Do you know what's coming? Then someone, say Frost-

Forestier, gets his hands on a bit of old tape, maybe from the
Ministry of Defense, or old Gestapo archives, and it's of you,
and you're addressing your electorate, who are huddled in
their basements, while you . . ."

*This is England. This is England. The long corridors of
Broadcasting House. The blacked-out windows. The lightbulbs
daubed blue. The smell of carbolic soap and moldy tea. He didn't
go down to the bomb shelter during air raids. The blackened windows shook. The blue daubed lightbulbs trembled and swayed.
My heart! My heart! He came from the forests . . .*

He came from the forests of Canada. As an interned enemy
alien, he had worked as a lumberjack. Physically, it had been
a wonderful time: plain food, cold ozone-rich air, physical
labor, sleeping under canvas . . .

*But no sleep for Keetenheuve! What am I doing here? Why
am I here? Just so as not to participate? Not to be there? Stay out
of the picture? To nurture my carefully tended innocence, mis-
leading, bogus? Is that enough? In winter snow fell on the tents,
fell silently through the great forest, poured a quiet anonymous
grave of gentle foreign snow, because had he not brought it upon
himself, wasn't it his fault, had he not always tried to stay out of
it, oh-so-sensitive and babied, in his ivory tower, distinguished,
starving, without shelter, miserable, sent from country to country, but always out of it, always enduring, never fighting, was he
not at the root of all the atrocities that were breaking out all over
the world like bleeding and purulent sores . . .*

After a few months in the Canadian logging camp, they
separated the inmates into black sheep and white, and
Keetenheuve, put up and vouched for by a Quaker, returned
to London.

He spoke in England. He fought behind the microphone,

and he fought not least for Germany, he thought, for peace and the fall of the tyrant; it was a good fight, and not one to be ashamed of. An end to madness, was the slogan, and an early end would have been useful to the world, and extremely useful for Germany. Keetenheuve felt he stood shoulder to shoulder with anyone rebellious, including those in the military, the men of the 20 July.* He said as much to Mergentheim.

But he gave back: "I'm not a missionary. I'm a journalist. Take a look at the members' register of the High House! Resistance is something your colleagues have already scrubbed from their vitas. This is the latest edition here. You seem to be stuck with the last one. And that's been pulped! Don't you get it! Why don't you make peace! There are plenty of people who say they can do business with your boss, but they can't talk to you. Knurrewahn was a noncommissioned officer. You confuse him. They call you his evil spirit. You make him wobble." Keetenheuve said: "That would be worth doing. That would mean I was getting somewhere. If Knurrewahn hesitates, he'll begin to think. And thinking will make him hesitate still more about his politics." Mergentheim interrupted him impatiently. "You're mad," he cried. "You're past help. But I've got one more thing to say to you: you'll lose. You'll lose more than you can imagine. This time you won't be able to emigrate. Where would you go? Your former friends think like us about most things, and every continent, I tell you, every continent is sealed by mistrust. Maybe you're just a gnat. But the elephants and tigers are afraid of you. And you'd better watch out for them."

*An attempt to assassinate Hitler in 1944, led by aristocratic military men, such as Stauffenberg and Beck. Four people were killed, but Hitler escaped with only minor injuries. The site of the attempt was the Wolfsschanze.

The ship's corridor between the press offices didn't sway any more than it usually did under his departing steps. He didn't have any feeling of going down or personal risk. Mergentheim's warning didn't particularly bother Keetenheuve. It only made him sadder, and he was sad already; but it isn't shocking to hear a confirmation of what one has already known and been afraid of for a long time, in this case the national restoration, the restorative nationalism, that everything was pointing toward. The borders weren't falling. They were going up again.

And then a man was back in the cage he'd been born into, the cage called Fatherland, which dangled along with a bunch of other cages called Fatherland, all on a rod, which a great collector of cages and peoples was carrying deeper into history. Of course Keetenheuve loved his country, loved it as much as anyone who noisily said so, perhaps even more because he'd been away from it for a long time, had missed it, and had idealized it from a distance. *Keetenheuve Romantic.* But he didn't want to sit in a cage, access to which was controlled by the police, who only let you out with a passport that you had to get off the head of the cage, and then it went on from there, you stood in the inhospitable space between cages, and you rubbed up against all the bars, and to get into one of the other cages you needed something called a visa, a residence permit from the head of that cage. He didn't like giving permission. In all the cages, they were worried about declining population numbers, but the only additions that were welcome came from the wombs of the female denizens of the cage, and that was a terrible image of the lack of freedom all over the world. Another factor was that you were swung on the pole that the great cage bearer had over his shoulder. Who

could say where he was going? And did you have any say in
the matter? You and your cage might wind up on the pole of
the other cage bearer, who was just as unpredictable as the
first (and who knows what daemon, what idée fixe was actu-
ating him) in heading for the unknown—an anabasis that
would be taught to the children in time. On his way out of the
press building, of the news ship, beside the pine table with
the communiqués, Keetenheuve ran into Philip Dana, a God
of true rumors, high above ebb and flow of official proclama-
tions, sifting the meager fare. Dana took Keetenheuve by the
hand and led him off to his room.

The Nestor of the foreign correspondents was an old man,
and handsome. He was the handsomest of all the handsome
and busy old men in politics. With his shining snowy mane and
his fresh complexion, he looked as though he'd just come in
from the gale that he had caused to blow around his ears. It
was hard to tell whether Dana was a personality of his own,
or whether he only seemed to be important because he had
spoken to celebrities and notorieties, who perhaps had only
been able to give the world and themselves the illusion of
importance, because Philip Dana had interviewed them on
the telephone. At bottom, he despised the statesmen he interviewed; he had seen too many of that ilk rise, glitter, fall, and
sometimes dangle from a gallows, which secretly was a more
pleasing sight to Dana than seeing them robust and self-
justifying in their presidential armchairs, or lying in state with
their contented smile of natural death in their fat faces, while
their people were cursing them. Dana had been present at
every war and every conference that followed the fighting and
paved way for a fresh wave of hostilities for forty years now;
he had been fed diplomatic lies by the shovelful, he had seen

blind men as leaders and had vainly tried to warn the deaf of approaching catastrophe, he had met rabid dogs who wrapped themselves in the flag, and Lenin, Chiang Kai-shek, Kaiser Wilhelm, Mussolini, Hitler, and Stalin had all stood before him in white angels' robes, with a dove on their shoulder, and the palm branch in their hand, and blessed was peace on earth. Dana had drunk with Roosevelt and dined with Negus, he had known cannibals and true saints, he had witnessed all the insurrections, the revolutions, the civil wars of our era, and invariably he had seen the defeat of ordinary people. The vanquished were no better than the victors; they only seemed briefly more attractive because they were the vanquished. The world whose pulse Dana had taken was now waiting for his memoirs, but it was his present to the world that he wasn't writing them—it would have been one long horror story. And so, mild and it would appear wise, he sat in Bonn, in a rocking chair (he had set it in his office for comfort and for the symbolism of it), and as he rocked he observed the to-and-fro of world politics in a diminished, but still neuralgic, way. Bonn was Dana's last detail; perhaps his grave. It was less taxing than Korea would have been, but here too he could hear the seed of incomprehension sprouting, and watch the grass of discord and inevitability grow. Keetenheuve knew Dana from the old *Volksblatt* days. Keetenheuve had written a piece for the *Volksblatt* on the great transport strike in Berlin, in which the Nazis and the Communists had briefly formed a bizarre, expedient, and highly volatile unity front, and Dana had picked this up for his international news-gathering service, and found readers for Keetenheuve all over the world. Later, Keetenheuve ran into Dana in London. Dana was writing a book on Hitler, which he conceived and sold as a best-seller; he turned his revulsion to good account. Keetenheuve's own antipathy to the Browns had merely served to impoverish and unhouse him, and he half envied Dana's diligence, with the caveat that Dana's book on the seducer was nothing but a best-seller, a smooth and canny piece of work.

God was in a good mood. He passed Keetenheuve a sheet from a news agency with which he stood in regular contact. Keetenheuve straightway spotted the item that Dana had wanted him to see, it was a bulletin from the Conseil Supérieur des Forces Armées, an interview with French and British generals, who were in the process of setting up a European army, and who saw the evolution of the peace, cemented by treaties, portending a perpetuation of the division of Germany; in their eyes, this division was the one positive outcome of the past war. In the context of the Federal Republic this was dynamite. Its kilotonnage would be highly significant if it were detonated at the right moment in parliament. There was no doubt about that. Only, Keetenheuve was no thrower of bombs. With that news, though, he could strengthen and support Knurrewahn, who dreamed of becoming the man of reunification (a common enough dream). But had the newspapers not picked up on the report yet, and run with it, so that the government would be tipped off, and have their denials already in place? Dana indicated no. The press in the Republic would give the interview little space, if any. The delight of the generals was too touchy a matter, a real body blow for the government, and so, at best, it would be tucked away somewhere where it would be overlooked. Keetenheuve had his dynamite. But he didn't care for explosives. All politics were squalid, it was like gang warfare, the means were dirty and divisive; even someone who was on the side of good, might easily become another Mephistopheles, who invariably does ill; for what was good and what ill, in this field that stretched, like a vast empire, far into the future? Keetenheuve looked sadly out the open window at the rain now spurting again like steam. Through the window came the botanical smell of warm dampish soil and plant mulch, and pale lightnings twitched over the hothouse. Even the storms seemed to be manmade here, an artificial entertainment in the restoration businesses of Fatherland & Sons, Inc., and Dana, the mild and experienced old man, had dropped off in spite of the rumble of thunder. He lay back in his sensitive rocking chair, a balanced observer, a sleeper, and a dreamer. He was dreaming of the Goddess of Peace, but unfortunately the goddess came to him in his dream in the guise of Irene, an Annamite prostitute, whom Dana had consorted with a quarter of a century ago, in a brothel in Saigon. Soft had been her arms, frisky as small rushing streams, and her skin had smelled of flowers. Dana had fallen asleep peacefully in the arms of the peaceful Irene, only later to have to take bitter medicine. That's the way it was with the Goddess of Peace. It's a game. *We're playing cops and robbers cops and robbers again and again*

3

KEETENHEUVE HAD GONE TO HIS OFFICE IN THE NEW section of the Bundeshaus, the annex built onto the Pedagogic Academy. The corridors and the MPs' offices were floored with a waxy, dust-free linoleum. In their gleaming salubriousness, they were reminiscent of the antiseptic wards of a clinic, and maybe the politics that were practiced here on the sick electorate were sterile as well. In his office, Keetenheuve might be a few steps closer to heaven, but he was no nearer to clarity; new clouds and new thunderstorms kept rolling up, and the horizon was draped in brooding black or sulfurous mists. To help his concentration, Keetenheuve had switched on the neon lighting and sat in a kind of twilight where its brilliance encountered the uncertain light of day. His desk was full of mail, full of petitions, full of cries for help; it was full of abuse and insoluble difficulties. Under the neon, Elke was eyeing him. It was just a little picture of her that he had here, a snapshot of her with untidy hair in a street of rubble (but dear to him, because that was how he had found her), but now it seemed to him as if she was as big as a flickering shadow on the cinema screen, and her hair was now brushed, and she was regarding him with friendly mockery, as if to say: "Well, you can have your politics now and your deals, because you're rid of me!" It pained Keetenheuve to hear her talking like that, particularly as it was her voice from the grave that was talking to him, and that could no longer be revised. He picked up Elke's picture and put it away. He filed Elke away, laid her *ad acta*. But what did that mean, *ad acta*, to be filed? The files were unimportant, and what was important, whether it appeared in the files or not, was current and pending, was there all by itself, and would remain until sleep, until dream, until death. Keetenheuve put off the moment of dealing with his correspondence, the pleas and the abuse, the letters from professional beggars, moaners, business people, and madmen, the cries of despair—he would have liked to sweep the lot of them off his desk. He picked up a sheet of official stationery, and wrote out "*Le beau navire*," "The beautiful ship," because Elke had reminded him of that wonderful poem in praise of women, that was how he wanted her to live on in his memory, and he tried to translate Baudelaire's deathless lines from memory, "*je veux te raconter, o molle enchanteresse*," I want to say to you, let me tell you, let me confess to you . . . , he liked that, he wanted to confess to Elke that he loved her, that he missed her, he was looking for the right word, the *mot juste*, he thought, he scribbled, he crossed out, he emended, he sank back in feelings of aesthetic melancholy. Was he lying? No, he felt it; his love was great, and his sorrow profound, but along with them was an undertow of vanity and self-pity and the suspicion that, in poetry and in love, he was a dilettante. He bewailed Elke, but he also dreaded the desolation he had called for all his life, and which now gripped him. He translated from *The Flowers of Evil*, "*o molle enchanteresse*," my sweet, my soft, my warm rapture, *o my soft, my smooth, my enraptured word;* —he didn't have anyone to write to. There were a hundred letters on his desk, wails, bewildered stammerings, and cursings, but no one was expecting a letter from him, except by way of reply. Keetenheuve had written Elke letters from Bonn, and if they were written with one eye on posterity as well, still Elke had been much more than a postal address; she was the medium that permitted him to speak and put him in touch with the world. Pale as one of the damned, Keetenheuve sat in the Bundeshaus, pale lightnings twitched outside his window, clouds freighted with electricity, charged with the emissions from the chimneys of the Ruhr, steaming broody mists, gassy, toxic, and sulfurous, eerie untamed nature moved stormily past the roof and walls of the hothouse, whistling its contempt and its scorn for the sensitive plant within, the grieving man, the Baudelaire translator and MP in his neon cell the other side of the window. And so the time passed until Knurrewahn sent for him.

They lived symbiotically, in the way that different creatures lived together for mutual advantage; but they weren't sure they weren't damaging themselves as well. Knurrewahn might have contended that Keetenheuve was bad for his soul. Only, Knurrewahn, an autodidact from the period before the First World War, when he had stuffed himself with a progressive-minded and optimistic literature that even then was no longer new (the riddles of the world had all been solved, and once he'd got rid of his ill-advised god, man needed only to put his house in order), denied the existence of the soul. And so the discomfort he experienced through Keetenheuve was comparable to the irritation that a conscientious noncommissioned officer might feel with a one-year volunteer who doesn't understand the point of training and, worse, can't make himself take it seriously. Unfortunately, though, the army needed its one-year volunteers, and the party needed Keetenheuve, who (Knurrewahn guessed) wasn't an officer at all, wasn't even officer material, but was a straightforward confidence trickster, a vagabond, who for some reason, perhaps bound up with his arrogant manner, was taken for an officer. On this last point, Knurrewahn erred; Keetenheuve was not arrogant, he was merely unconventional, and that struck Knurrewahn as the height of arrogance, and so in the end it was he who took Keetenheuve for an officer, whereas Keetenheuve himself would have been quite happy to admit he was something else, a drifter, for example. He respected Knurrewahn, whom he called a boss from the old school, which was said slightly mockingly, but not unpleasantly, whereas when it was reported back to Knurrewahn's ears, it sounded irritating and conceited. He truly was a man from the old school, though, a craftsman from a family of craftsmen, who had aspired first to knowledge, and then to justice, and once knowledge and justice had turned out to be uncertain of definition and always on a sliding scale, to power and control. Knurrewahn didn't want to make the world do his bidding either, but he did think he could be a force for good in it. And as such, he needed companions and helpers, and he had come across Keetenheuve, who didn't strengthen him, but only confused him. Keetenheuve wasn't the type to make a fourth at cards, and he wasn't a beer drinker, and that excluded him from the

circle of fellows that gathered around Knurrewahn of an
evening, raising their tankards and slapping down their cards,
fellows who decided the fate of the party, but who didn't
make up a government in waiting and who couldn't even
organize the proverbial piss-up in a brewery.

Knurrewahn had been through a lot; but it hadn't made
him wise. He had had a kind heart; now it had steeled itself.
He had come home from the First World War with a bullet
lodged in him, and to the surprise of the doctors he had survived; it was at a time that the medical profession still hadn't
known that a man could live with a bullet in his heart, and
Knurrewahn had gone from one hospital to the next as a living corpse, until he became cleverer than his doctors, accepted a job in the party, and by diligence and occasionally with
the help of his remarkable wound, which made its appearance on election posters, was promoted to member of the
Reichstag. In 1933, some veterans appealing to veteran values threw the veteran Knurrewahn, who carried the veteran
experience around with him in the form of a piece of lead in
his heart, into a camp. His son, who, it had been hoped,
would continue the academic ascent of the family, was
instead, following an older family tradition, apprenticed to a
carpenter, and, embittered about the loss of status, and angry
with his father's political misjudgments, and in the deluded
belief that he had to prove himself (all over the country there
were appalling examples of people proving themselves), he
volunteered for the Condor Legion in Spain, where he met
his death as a *monteur*. Keetenheuve too had entertained the
idea of Spain, and he too, to prove himself, only on the other
side (he hadn't done it, and he sometimes reproached himself
for having failed here as well), and it wouldn't have taken

much for Keetenheuve in an ack-ack emplacement outside
Madrid to bring down Knurrewahn's son out of the southern
sky. The lines of battle snaked right through the middle of
countries, and most of those who were flying or shooting no
longer remembered what had caused them to fetch up on one
side of the front or the other. Knurrewahn never got it. He
was a patriot, and his opposition to the government's nationalist politics was, so to speak, a patriotic opposition.
Knurrewahn wanted to be the liberator and the unifier of the
divided Fatherland, he could already see himself as the
Bismarck statue in Knurrewahn Park, and he forgot all about
his old dream of the International. In his youth, this
International with its red flags had stood for human rights. In
1914, it had died. The new era marched behind different
flags, and whatever was still around and called itself
International now were little groupings with numbers after
their proud names, factions and sects, which didn't exempli-
fy peace at all, but all too evidently discord, from the way they
were forever at one another's throats. Maybe Knurrewahn was
right to fear an old mistake. In his opinion, the party's position had been insufficiently patriotic in the first German
Republic; it hadn't found any support from the already splin-
tered International, and within the nation it had lost the
masses, who had been drawn away from it by the siren words
of primitive nationalistic egoism. This time, Knurrewahn
meant to make sure the patriotic wind would not be taken
from his sails. He was in favor of having an army, the burnt
child doesn't always fear the flame, but he was in favor of a
troop of patriots (the French Revolution blinded him with
folly, and perhaps Napoleon was *redivivus*), he was in favor of
generals, so long as they were socialist and democratic gener-

als. Fool, thought Keetenheuve, the generals weren't as stupid as they looked, they would lead Knurrewahn up the garden path, they would promise him the earth, they would lay down and open their legs for him, they wanted to bulk up their staffs, they kept half an eye on their shopping lists, they wanted their toys and their sandboxes to play with. What happened now, nobody knew. Tailors like to sew. National regeneration was one of those dicey things. Maybe that wind had lost some of its puff. A patriotic government, cleverer and wilier now, might sail under an international breeze, and a nationalist Knurrewahn might find himself becalmed, instead of making the running as an internationalist, a race with new ideals for sails, making for new shores. Unfortunately, he couldn't see them. He could see neither the new ideals nor the new shores. He failed to enthuse, because he lacked enthusiasm himself. He was like the populist figures out of cheap nationalist and socialist pamphlets, he wanted to be a Bismarck cleansed of hysteria and unscrupulousness, an Arndt, a Stein, a Hardenberg, and a bit of a Bebel, all rolled into one. Lassalle* was a portrait of the MP as a young man. That young man hadn't made it; the doctors had been right after all, and he hadn't managed to survive the bullet in his heart. The Knurrewahn of today looked good in the homburg he didn't wear. He was a stubborn, ornery so-and-so, not just at cards, he was as stubborn and ornery in his way as Prussia's old soldier king, or as Hindenburg, and so in politics everything had its wires crossed, the winds paid no attention to the

---

*Quite a lineup. Bismarck is Bismarck. The next three were part of a broadly liberal German opposition to Napoleon. August Bebel (1840–1913) co-founded the Social Democratic Party (SPD) with Karl Liebknecht. Ferdinand Lassalle (1825–1864) was a writer and politician.

courses the parties were trying to keep, and only weather charts, which no one understood, perplexing lines traced between points that had the same temperature (though they might be far apart in other ways) showed the fronts and warned of the impending storm. In a situation like that, Knurrewahn could no longer orient himself, and he clung to Keetenheuve (his well-intentioned Mephistopheles) that he might take the helm and, in the dark and starless sky, steer the little ship by the seat of his pants.

It was progressive chez Knurrewahn, in a style that he held to be radical and that corresponded roughly to the aesthetic of a bourgeois art monthly. The furniture was practical, the chairs comfortable; furniture, chairs, lamps, and curtains were all the sort of thing that might have appeared in the window display of an interior designer of moderately progressive outlook, labeled "The Modern Chief Executive's Office," and the bunch of red flowers bought and tended by his secretary stood in exactly the right place, under the watery Weser landscape on the wall. It tickled Keetenheuve to imagine Knurrewahn reading cowboy stories in his chair, but the head of the party had no time for private reading. He listened to Keetenheuve's report, and at the mention of the generals of the Conseil Supérieur des Forces Armées, glamour and treachery entered the room, the perfidy and arrogance of the wicked world, he could see the foreign military men striding across the German weft of his carpets in their riding boots and silver spurs, the French like odalisques in their baggy red pants, and the Brits ready to beat a tattoo on his desk with their little sticks. Knurrewahn was dismayed. He waxed indignant, whereas Keetenheuve could understand the generals talking about the perpetuation of the division of Germany as a scant gain from the last war from the point of view of their specialization. An expert opinion was always going to be narrow, and in this case it was the opinion of generals, so it was bound to be of limited intelligence as well. Knurrewahn didn't share this view; generals impressed him, whereas Keetenheuve tended to bracket them with firemen. The bullet burned in Knurrewahn's heart, the lead that was flesh of his flesh burned, and it was the pain of youth that animated and rejuvenated him. He felt hatred. It was a hatred, furthermore, that the leader of the socialist peace party could afford to feel, a double hatred, doubly legitimated and doubly founded, it was a hatred of the class enemy and the nation's enemy, which presented itself to him and his rage in the same group of persons. Fundamentally, it was the name of their confraternity that sounded arrogant to his ears, it was the expression Conseil Supérieur des Forces Armées that riled Knurrewahn, and that Keetenheuve had held out to him in elegant and calculated provocation, like the torero his cape.

Keetenheuve loved it when Knurrewahn lost his rag. What a magnificent man he still was, with his massive skull, and his Iron Cross shyly in its little box in his desk drawer, and the medal for his wound, both of them wrapped, as it might be, in the release form from the concentration camp and the farewell note from his son before he went off to find his death, fighting for the Condor Legion. But now Keetenheuve had to concentrate, lest Knurrewahn slip away. The party leader wanted to advertise the generals' interview, and let people know what the heads of the European army thought of Germany. He wanted the words *Permanent division* posted on the walls, and then to turn to the people: "See, we are betrayed and sold down the river, this is where the govern-

ment's policy has landed us!" But such an action would be to
defuse the bomb for parliament; the Chancellor would organize the denials and the statements of support from the
European powers before the matter was even discussed in the
plenary, and in the end only the fly-poster would be called
mean and treacherous. There might be public agitation, but
that would have little effect; the government wouldn't be put
off by public opinion. Knurrewahn believed that the generals,
who had expressed themselves so satisfied about the partition
of Germany, couldn't simply be denied, but Keetenheuve
knew that the politicians in England and France would call
their generals to order. They would give them a rebuke
because (and on this point it was Keetenheuve who was
biased) foreign generals accepted rebukes from their political
masters, whereas German generals automatically represented
actual power in the state, and they would restore what
seemed to them the natural order of things, namely the pri-
macy of the military over the political. The German general
was to Keetenheuve a malignancy on the German people, and
even his respect for the generals who were murdered by
Hitler wasn't enough to affect his judgment on this point. He
detested the old barracks types, who, with expressions of
fatherly decency, addressed adult citizens as "my lads" or "my
boys," and promptly packed his boys off to their deaths.
Keetenheuve had seen the people sickening and dying from
this outbreak of generals; and who, if not the generals, was
responsible for growing the Braunau bacillus! Force had
always led only to misery and defeat, and Keetenheuve wanted to give nonviolence a chance of procuring moral victory, if
not happiness. Was that the much touted Final Victory? It
meant that Keetenheuve could be only a temporary ally for

Knurrewahn, who dreamed sincerely of a German national army, and a German people's general, a fit and unpretentious man in gray mountaineer's garb, who shared meals with his troops, and, a good and solicitous father, would share them just as readily with his prisoners. Keetenheuve wanted an end to prisoners, and for that he needed Knurrewahn to oppose the Chancellor's plans for rearmament, but the day would certainly come when he would have to turn his opposition to his friend's much more dangerous idea of a people's army. Keetenheuve espoused a pure pacifism, a putting down of weapons, once and for all! He knew what responsibility he was taking upon himself, it was oppressive and it gave him sleepless nights, but even though there was no one of like mind in the Republic, and he was friendless and misunderstood in West and East alike, the lesson he persisted in drawing from history was that the abjuring of force and self-defense had never brought such evil in its train as their use. And when there were no more armies, then the frontiers would fall; the idea of sovereign nation states that was such an anachronism in the age of jet travel (you broke the sound barrier, but stuck to air corridors that had been dug by maniacs) would be renounced, and man would be free and free to move, and free, in fact, as a bird. Knurrewahn gave in. He thought he probably gave in too much and too often, but he gave in again, throttled back his fury, and they agreed that Keetenheuve would use the generals' little moment of crowing as a surprise weapon during the debate on the security contracts.

He went back to his room. He sat down in the neon again. He left the tubes on, even though the sky was now clear and bright, and the sun, momentarily, bathed everything in a bril-

liant light. The Rhine sparkled. An excursion steamer plowed
past in the white spray of its wheels, and the passengers could
be seen pointing at the Bundeshaus. Keeteneuve was dazzled.
The translation of the *"beau navire"* had been left unfinished
among unopened correspondence, and more had arrived now,
more cries for help, more screeds, more complaints, more
castigations of the Honorable Member, they came flowing in
like the water of the river outside, faithfully scooped up onto
the table by postmen and clerical staff, without abatement.
Keetenheuve was the addressee of a nation of letter writers;
it drained him, and only the intuition of the moment saved
him from the flood that otherwise would have broken over his
head. He devised a speech to hold in front of the assembly.
He would shine! A dilettante in matters of love, a dilettante
in poetry, and a dilettante in politics—and he would shine.
Who else could save them, if not a dilettante? The experts,
sexperts, texperts, were still following their old paths into old
deserts. They had never led anywhere else, and it took a dilettante to stumble upon the Promised Land, the kingdom
flowing with milk and honey. Keetenheuve poured himself a
brandy. The thought of honey flowing somewhere was disagreeable to him. And the description of the Promised Land
should not be taken literally either, that was why children
didn't find it, why they grew tired, grew up, and set up as tax
lawyers, which says everything that needs to be known about
the condition of the world. Our forefathers had been expelled
from Paradise. That was a fact. Now, was there a way back?
There wasn't even the most tenuous path to be seen, but then
again the path might be invisible, or maybe there were millions upon millions of invisible steps that lay in front of everyone, just waiting to be trodden. Keetenheuve had to follow his

conscience; but a conscience was no more visible and palpable than the right way, and you only heard it bleating very occasionally, and that was something you might equally attribute to circulation disorders. His heart was irregular, and his writing slithered on the smooth official notepaper. Frost-Forestier rang to ask if Keetenheuve would like to have lunch with him. He would send his car around to pick him up. Was that the declaration of war? Keetenheuve thought it was. He accepted the invitation. It was time. They wanted to get rid of him. They wanted to set the pistol to his chest and blackmail him. Mergentheim had known it already. Very well, he would fight. He left the correspondence, he left the files, he left the Baudelaire translation, he left his notes for the debate, and the page from the news agency that Dana had given him, he left everything lying in the neon, which he forgot to switch off, because the sun was still shining, and its light broke in thousand prisms in the mirror of the river and in the droplets on the green leaves on the tops of the trees. It shone, dazzled, glittered, sparkled, flashed.

Government cars look like official black coffins, there is something unimaginative and dependable about them, they are of squat construction, cost a lot of money, but still have a reputation for being solid and economical, but also prestigious, and ministers, councillors, and officials feel themselves equally drawn to solidity, economy, and prestige. Frost-Forestier's office was out of town, and Keetenheuve was driven solidly, economically, and prestigiously through little villages on the Rhine that had collapsed without being historic, that were narrow without being romantic. The villages looked wrecked, and Keetenheuve had a sense of frowning people behind the crumbling walls; maybe their incomes were too low; maybe they felt oppressed by their taxes; or maybe the only reason they were frowning and letting their houses crumble was that so many black cars drove past them with important people inside them. And in among the old tumbledown villages, dotted about on cabbage patches, on fallow land and poor grazing, were the ministries, the offices, the administrative centers, they squatted in old Hitler buildings, they lugged their files behind façades of Speer sandstone, heated up their little soups in former barracks. The ones who had slept there were dead, the ones who had been brutalized were in jail, they had forgotten it all, it was in the past, and if they were alive and at liberty, then they struggled to get a pension, or they chased after a job—what else was there for them to do? It was the government quarter of a government in exile that Keetenheuve was driven through in his government car, sentries stood guard behind senseless fences that had been drawn right across fields, it was an administration that depended on the kindness and hospitality of its people, and Keetenheuve thought: My not being part of the government is a joke; it's the perfect government for me—exiled from the nation, exiled from the natural order, exiled from the human order (although he did still dream that all men were brothers). There were also men in uniform trekking along the road to see Frost-Forestier. They lived somewhere locally; but they walked individually, albeit with the stride of civil servants, and not marching all in a heap like soldiers. Were they civilian policemen, were they border guards? Keetenheuve couldn't tell; he was determined that even if he knew the rank, he would reply: "Senior Forester."

Frost-Forestier was installed in an erstwhile barracks and was in charge of an army; but it was an army of secretaries whom he kept on their toes. They worked in Stakhanovite shifts here, and Keetenheuve felt dizzy when he saw a secretary talking on two telephones at once. What fun children might have here, what unlikely parties could be put in touch with one another! If the nation was writing to Keetenheuve, then the whole world was on the phone to Frost-Forestier. Was that Paris on the line, or Rome, or Cairo, or Washington? Was the call from Tauroggen already in? What did the shady man in Basel want on the phone? Had he snared himself? Or were there negotiation partners waiting at the Hotel Stern in Bonn, singing their songs from the earpieces of the telephone into the whorled ears of the ladies? There was a trilling and a buzzing and a ringing, an incessant tolling of miserere, a continuous confessional murmur, with the girls' periodic breathy refrain: "no, Herr Frost-Forestier regrets, Herr Frost-Forestier is unable, can I take a message to Herr Frost-Forestier"— Herr Frost-Forestier did not have any official title.

The much demanded one did not keep his guest waiting. He came right away, welcomed his Daniel in the lions' den, and asked him out to the canteen. Keetenheuve groaned. The enemy was advancing his heavy weapons. The canteen was a fearsome great barn of a place, reeking of rancid fat, stinking of burnt flour. There was German Beefsteak Esterhazy on a Bed of Mashed Potatoes, Meat Balls with Green Beans on a Bed of Mashed Potatoes, Spare Ribs with Sauerkraut on a Bed of Mashed Potatoes, and right at the bottom of the menu it said: "Schnuller's soups* for connoisseurs turn every meal into a feast." It was a tactical decision on the part of Frost-Forestier (an inexpensive tactic, at that) to take the MP,

*Typical of Koeppen's way with names, a *Schnuller* is a "dummy" or "comforter."

whose gourmet tendencies were widely known, to the canteen. He wanted to remind Keetenheuve of the mean fare to which it was possible to be reduced. To left and right of them, secretaries and petty officials sat at oilcloth-covered tables, tucking into the German Beefsteak Esterhazy. What had Esterhazy ever done to cooks, to make them name all scorched onion dishes after him? Keetenheuve made a mental note to look into the matter. Frost-Forestier paid for their lunch with a couple of tin coupons. They ordered matjes herrings with green beans, boiled potatoes, and bacon gravy. The matjes was a longtime inmate of salt barrels. The bacon gravy was black and full of slimy clumps of flour. The potatoes were black as well. Frost-Forestier ate with relish. He devoured his herring, sopped up the black gravy with the black potatoes, and left none of the stringy string beans. Keetenheuve was astonished. Perhaps he was utterly mistaken about everything, and Frost-Forestier wasn't eating with relish, and wasn't human; perhaps he was a high-performance motor, a cleverly designed digestion engine that needed to be refueled periodically and enjoyed it about as much as a car in a filling station. While he stuffed himself, he told stories about the class struggle and the office pecking order, pointing recklessly at individuals who sat nearby. The steel expert was not on speaking terms with the cast-iron man, except during office hours, and the girl who did English-language stenography ate her spare ribs with sauerkraut and mashed potatoes at a different table from the poor creature who merely did German shorthand. Even here, though, beauty was at a premium, and Frost-Forestier reported on Trojan Wars that had broken out between rival offices when the head of personnel had a pretty girl on his books, and there was Helen, envied, reviled, eating her meat balls and mashed potatoes with the head of the working group on agricultural land degradation. *And there was a cute hermaphrodite to be seen as well.*

What now? Something reminded him of a singer, a whisperer. *A cute hermaphrodite. Where was that? By the sea, on the beach? Forgotten. Sagesse, a poem of Verlaine's. Wisdom, beautiful and melancholy. I kiss your hand, Madame. A singer. Womanish. Flotsam. I kiss your hand. Whisperer. What was his name again? Paul. I kiss your hand, Monsieur Paul. Monsieur Frost. Frost-Forestier, the matjes motor, the bacon gravy high-performance engine. The electron computer. Reel-to-reel man. Steel gymnast. Virile. Placid phallus. What does he want? The fish is dished up. Alas, poor herring. The widower. Pickled in brine. Frost-Forestier bachelor. Passionless. Incorruptible. Frost-Forestier the incorruptible. Robespierre. No great revolution. No chance. Feels it in his water. What? A tickle? A tinkle? Lives dangerously. Pisses with privates. All privates together. Writing on the wall. Informs shady characters.* Kohlenklau* *walls have ears. Dark jungle of the airwaves. Pisses waves in the ether. Pissoirs. Swastikas on the walls. Lobby groups. Know their man. Beer. Piss.* He said: "Can you get a drink here?" *No. You can't. Not for you. Coffee and lemonade. Coffee accelerated the heart rate. Not on. Beat fast enough as it was. The pulse in his throat. The pallid lemonade of evolution, fizzing and repeating. What then?* Frost-Forestier ordered a coffee. *What then?* What did he want?

Frost-Forestier asked him a question. He looked at him. "Do you know Central America?" he asked. He added: "Interesting place, by all accounts." *No my snake not that pep-*

---

*Literally, "coal grab," a ubiquitous Nazi propaganda creature, exhorting the populace to economize on scarce fuel.

per tree, you'd have known all about it if I had been there, it would have been in your files. No good to you. I'm no good to you. It'll have to be the old British major. Sir Felix Keetenheuve, Commander, Member of Parliament, Royal Officers' Club, dropped bombs on Berlin.

"No. I've never been to Central America. I once had a Honduran passport, if that's what you're getting at. I bought it. That's what people did. I could travel anywhere on it, except Honduras." *Why am I telling him? Buttering his bread for him. Who cares. Keetenheuve falsifier of documents. I showed my face in Scheveningen. You know, the sea, the beach, the sunsets? I sat outside the Café Sport, and the singer came and sat at my table. He sat at my table because he was alone, and because I was alone I let him sit there. The young girls walked past, Proust's "jeunes filles en fleurs" from the beach at Balbeck. Albertine, Albert. The young men walked past. Young men and women promenaded down the seaside boulevard, they swam through the evening light, their bodies glowed, the orb of the sinking sun sparkled through their sheer clothes. The girls lifted their breasts. Who were they? Salesgirls, schoolgirls, seamstresses. The apprentice hairdresser from the Haager Plein. She was just a sales assistant in a shoeshop—that too was something the singer in his heyday had whispered on disk, softly and campily. He was murdered. We watched the girls and boys walk by, and the singer said: You're as hot as monkey shit.* What was going on now? He'd better pull himself together, he hadn't been paying attention. Frost-Forestier wasn't talking about Central America any more, he was talking about Keetenheuve's party, which hadn't had its share of diplomatic jobs recently, well, it was only natural that the government would think of its friends first, though it was hardly an equitable way of proceeding, then again Keetenheuve's outfit was short on suitable candidates, and when one appeared, well, Frost-Forestier was taking preliminary soundings, he was showing his hand, of course everything at this stage was unofficial, the Chancellor hadn't been consulted, but he was certain to give his approval—Frost-Forestier was offering Keetenheuve the ambassadorship in Guatemala. "Interesting place," he said again. "Right up your alley! Interesting people. Left-wing government. Not a Communist dictatorship, mind you. A republic, respect for human rights. An experiment. You'd be our man on the spot, keep a weather eye on developments for us, represent our interests."

Keetenheuve Ambassador Keetenheuve Excellency. He was stunned. But the remoteness of it tempted him, and perhaps that was the solution. The solution to all his problems! It was running away. It was running away again. It was his last escape. They weren't stupid. But maybe it would be freedom; and he knew it was retirement. *Keetenheuve pensioner on the state.* He saw himself in Guatemala City, on the pillared veranda of a colonial villa, watching the dusty street glowing in the sun, the dust-coated palms, the dry and dust-laden cactuses. Where the street widened out into a square, the dust in the park toned down the obscene colors of coffee blossom, and the memorial to the Unknown Guatemalan seemed to melt in the sun. Huge silent automobiles, clattering fire-red motorcycles leapt out of the sun haze, drove past, and disappeared like visions in the heat. It stank of petrol and putrescence, and from time to time there was the ping of a ricocheting bullet. It might be his salvation, it might be the chance to grow old. He would spend years on the pillared veranda, and years surveying the hot dusty road. At intervals, he would send dispatches home, which no one would read. He would drink endless quantities of bitter gassy soda water, and in the evening he would try and lose the taste by adding rum to it. He would complete his translation of *"Le beau navire,"* on stormy nights he would talk to Elke, maybe even reply to the letters he had got as an MP, which wouldn't do any good to anyone, and one day he would die—and the flags would fly at half-mast in the Guatemalan Foreign Ministry and on the colonial verandas of the other embassies. *Excellency Keetenheuve the German Ambassador passed away* Frost-Forestier wanted an answer. His secretaries, his telephones, his tape recorders, were all calling him. Keetenheuve was silent. Was the bait not juicy enough? Did the mouse smell a rat? Frost-Forestier threw in the fact that, as an ambassador, Keetenheuve would be working for the diplomatic service. What prospects! And if Keetenheuve's party happened to win the elections, Keetenheuve would be foreign minister. "And the next time the government changes, you'll be our man in Moscow!" Frost-Forestier evidently didn't believe the opposition party had a chance in the elections.

Keetenheuve said: "I'd be persona non grata."

Frost-Forestier smiled a thin-lipped smile. "It could be that time's on your side." Did he feel that in his water too? Would they still make music?

He went back to his barracks, back to the twittering mouths of his secretaries, to the humming wires, to the enigma of wireless communication. Keetenheuve, meanwhile, asked to be driven to Godesberg, the town that, as legend had it, had fifty retired mayors living in it, all of them aspiring to follow a great example, all of them having grasped, like Morgenstern's polyp, the reason for their existence, namely to steer the ship of state, and all of them practicing hard at the family dinner table. The mortarboard that came with the honorary doctorate was invisibly inclining over the sponge cake. If he accepted Guatemala, Keetenheuve would probably be given a black official car to take with him, maybe even one of the new models, where prestige had finally got the better of economy. Keetenheuve was heading for Godesberg because after the salty herring and the—albeit unofficial—conferral of the ambassadorship, he wanted to eat a diplomatic lunch, and where better than on the celebrated *Rheinterrasse,** where the great diplomatic calamity had occurred? He was all alone in the hall, all alone on the carpet, the carpet was new; maybe the Führer had breakfasted on the old Persian rug because Chamberlain and the gentlemen from the Foreign Office were late, and his neurotic character couldn't bear to be stood up. Now industrialists came here to relax. The Führer had been a bad investment, or had he not? A dilettante shouldn't be the judge of that. Maybe the savior of the people had been worth it. How many million dead? The chimneys are smoking. Coal is being cut. The foundries have fire in them. The steel glows white. Keetenheuve looked every inch the manager too. He had his briefcase with him; the MP's imposing briefcase. Poems of Cummings, Verlaine, Baudelaire, Rimbaud, Apollinaire—he knew them all by heart. *Keetenheuve industrialist, Excellency Keetenheuve, Sir Keetenheuve Knight of the Realm, Keetenheuve traitor, well-intentioned Keetenheuve.* He went out onto the terrace. He sat down beside the Rhine. Four waiters observed him. Haze. Storm haze. Hothouse atmosphere. Sun glare. The windows

---

*Site of one of the abortive meetings between Hitler and Chamberlain.

of the hothouse could do with a clean; the air-conditioning wasn't functioning. He sat in a vacuum, around him haze, above him sky. A pressurized chamber for the heart. Four waiters softly approached; heralds of death, formal, in tails, an initial approach, an opening bid? "Cognac, please." Cognac to stimulate him. "One cognac Monnet!" What's bobbing along on the Rhine? Steel, coal? The flags of the nations over the black barges. Low in the water, these new tales of the riverbank, fantasy accounts, the myths of write-offs while the substance remained untouched, one-to-one exchange rates, ore and coal, shipped from mine to mine to yours, from the Ruhr to Lorraine, from Lorraine back to the Ruhr, your Europe, gentlemen, *visit the art treasures in the Villa Hügel*, and the panties of the bargeman's wife, panties from Woolworth's in Rotterdam, panties from Woolworth's in Düsseldorf, panties from Woolworth's in Basel, panties from Woolworth's in Strasbourg, panties on the line, across the deck, fluttering in the west wind, the mightiest flag in the world, rosy pink over the sub rosa coals. A little spitz, furious and white, a little spitz, very full of itself, switches from bow to stern. On the opposite bank, the retirement villages of the rose growers stifle a yawn: siesta time.

He ordered a salmon, a salmon from the Rhine, and straightaway he regretted it, he imagined the waiters a-leaping, the formally tail-coated welcoming committee of death, overly excited like silly children, overly grave like silly old men, they staggered down to the riverbank, stumbled over sticks and stones, dangled nets in the water, pointed up at Keetenheuve on the terrace, nodded at him, were assured of his agreement, caught the fish, pulled him up, the beautiful, the golden-scaled salmon in shining armor, like a haul of gold and silver he bellied the net, torn from his powerful element by ghosts, from his kindly world of storied, babbling water— oh, to drown in light and air, and the diamond flash of the knife blade in the sun! The salmon was sacrificed to Keetenheuve. *Keetenheuve the god to whom innocent fishes were sacrificed.* Once again, he hadn't wanted it. Temptation! Temptation! What did the anchorite do? He slew grasshoppers. The fish was dead. The wine was moderate. Excellency Keetenheuve ate his diplomat's lunch with moderate appetite.

He conducted diplomatic talks. Who were his guests? Herr Hitler, Führer, Monsieur Stendhal, Consul. Who officiated? Mine host, Mr. Chamberlain.

Hitler: Soft air; historic Rhine scenery; a stimulating terrace. Only nineteen years ago—

Stendhal: My respect and my admiration! Oh, to be young, when you set off from this very terrace for Wiessee to murder your friends! How the fates of youths do commove me! How the novels written under your aegis arouse me! I would have followed your army's progress, as I did Napoleon's. I would have seen Milan again, and Warsaw and the Beresina. With man and horse and chariot, the Lord has you in his lariat. You quoted the poem following your victory over Poland. You spoke in the Reichstag. You rewarded your generals with marshal's staffs and estates in West Prussia. You had a couple of them hanged. Others helpfully shot themselves. To one of them you sent poison. And all your shining youths, your heroes of the air, your heroes of the sea, your heroes in tanks, and your boys in Berlin, Monsieur Hitler! What are your men of literature doing, Monsieur Keetenheuve? You are translating Baudelaire? How fine, how brave! But what of Narvik, Cyrenaica, the Atlantic, the Volga, the places of execution, the prisoner-of-war camps in the Caucasus and the prisoner-of-war camps in Iowa. Who writes of them? What is interesting is truth, nothing but truth—

Keetenheuve: There is no such thing as truth here. Just tangles of lies.

Stendhal: You are an impotent gnostic, Monsieur Keetenheuve.

The tangles of lies form themselves into a chorus line in the air over the Rhine, and flash their dirty undies.

Hitler: In my table talks for the Germanic Historic Institute of United Illustrated Magazines, I've been fighting for years to get German culture cleansed firstly from Jewish, secondly from Christian, thirdly from moralistic sentimental, and fourthly from international cosmopolitan bloodthirsty pacifist influences, and I'm happy to be able to tell you today that I've won all down the line.

Six globes come rolling down the Rhine. They bear flags and weapons. Loudspeakers shrill: Raise high the flags! Chamberlain's hands tremble. He tips melted butter onto the tablecloth, and says: Peace in our time.

The corpse of Czechoslovakia rises out of the water, stinking. Destiny is trapped in the belly of the corpse and wanders witlessly back and forth. Three loudspeakers fight it out. One of them yells: According to plan! The second roars: Plan deficit! The third sings the chorus from the *Threepenny Opera*: Yeah, make a plan. Loudspeakers one and two furiously attack loudspeaker three and beat it to a pulp.

Senator McCarthy sends a couple of lie detectors over to investigate.

The first lie detector turns to Hitler: Mr. Hitler, are you now, or have you ever been a member of the Communist Party?

Hitler: As an obscure lieutenant, I decided to go into politics so that the beast of Bolshevism will never, believe me, rear its ugly head again . . .

The indicator on the lie detector wags enthusiastically.

Hitler glares at it, breaks off his reply, and screams: Show me your Aryan passport!

The first lie detector is utterly bewildered. It blows a fuse and withdraws in confusion. The second lie detector turns to Keetenheuve: And did you at any stage belong to the Communist Party?

Keetenheuve: No. Never.

Second Lie Detector: Did you or did you not on 9 August 1928 take out *Das Kapital* by Karl Marx from the National Library in Berlin, and did you or did you not tell your then girlfriend Sonia Busen not to remove her shirt, since it was more important to study *Das Kapital*?

Keetenheuve is frightened and embarrassed. The pointer on the lie detector swings hard left. Rhine maidens rise up out of the Rhine. They wear sexy, sky-blue air hostesses' uniforms, and sing: Wagalaweia, you won't get to America, Wagalaweia, you stay where you are.

Keetenheuve is distraught.

Stendhal attempts to comfort Keetenheuve: Guatemala is no more boring than Civitavecchia, where I was consul. Don't go on vacation, you'll only have a stroke.

Keetenheuve looks reproachfully at Chamberlain and says: But Beck and Halder wanted a coup! Please remember, Beck and Halder wanted to get him!

Hitler smacks his thigh with amusement, and laughs with somnambulistic confidence.

Chamberlain looks heartbrokenly at the remains of the fish

as he takes it away. He whispers: A general who is planning a coup may not be a suitable partner for the United Kingdom; the general with a successful coup behind him is a welcome guest at the Court of St. James.

He had better go. It was time. The four waiters were standing around him. Before long they would be serving generals again. It was probably inevitable. The villages on the opposite bank were waking from their siestas. Coffee tables were being prepared. There too, the generals would have a place. The villages wanted their generals back. They felt like rose petals on a black mere. What might not climb up out of the depths? Toads, algae, embryos. Maybe a toad would leap onto a rose petal, hop up to the table, and say: "I'm in charge here." Then it was a good thing to have generals with sabers around. The waiters bowed. He always tipped too much, and it was a good thing that he tipped too much, because Death's welcoming committee let him go this once.

Frost-Forestier's black official car had been waiting for Keetenheuve. Frost-Forestier had wanted Keetenheuve to get used to the amenities that life and the Federal Republic reserved for high officials and government representatives. When he climbed into the car, Keetenheuve saw the French High Commission building, and the tricolor waving on its roof. *"Le jour de gloire est arrivé!"* Well, was it at hand, the day of glory? Or was it always at hand? Every day for a hundred and fifty years, one day of glory after another? It wasn't even all that long ago, but it seemed such a long time. It wasn't that long ago that the tricolor was waving in America, they put up a statue to liberty, *"qu'un sang impur abreuve nos sillons."* For a century and a half, the nations had been screaming for impure blood and irrigating their furrows with it. They couldn't get enough of that impure blood to cover all the demand for it: German blood, Russian blood, English blood, French, Italian, Spanish, and American blood, blood from the Balkans and blood from Asia, Negro blood, Jew blood, Fascist blood, Communist blood, a horrific lake of blood, the flow kept coming, so many philanthropists had helped dig channels for the blood, so many well-intentioned people, the Encyclopedists, the Romantics, the Hegelians, the Marxists, and the Nationalists of various stripe. Keetenheuve saw red trees with red leaves, he saw red heavens and red earth, and the philosophers' god saw, and he saw that it was not good. Then he whistled up his physicists, who thought in waves and quarks, and they managed to split the atom, and they murdered in Hiroshima.

He passed children in his car. French children, German children, American children. The children went around or played by nationality. The different groups did not speak to each other. Keetenheuve drove through the American village. There was an American village on the Rhine. A little American church had been built in the style of those the American settlers of the pioneer era had built on the edge of the prairie, once they had killed or driven away the Indians. In the church they prayed to a god who loved successful people. The American God would not have loved Keetenheuve. Keetenheuve was not successful, he had never conquered a prairie.

They came to Mehlem, they reached the American High Commission, and Keetenheuve got out of the car. The American High Commission was a pile construction in the forest, a modern design with concrete, steel, and glass, but it was as exotic here as a Romantic castle from a German fairy

tale, a skyscraper brought over from Broadway and set on concrete stilts, as though it was afraid the Rhine would rise up
out of its banks to swallow it up, and the herds of automobiles
that were parked underneath the building, in between the
concrete stilts, were like little lifeboats that were kept ready
for an emergency. Even though it was daytime, thousands of
neon tubes were lit throughout the large building, and they
heightened the magical, the unreal aspect of the pile struc-
ture standing in the middle of the forest. The High
Commission was like a mighty magician's palace, and it was
also like a huge beehive, where the neon-dripping windows
were like honeycombs. Keetenheuve could hear it buzzing.
The bees were busy. Keetenheuve walked boldly into the
magic kingdom, plunged into the conjurer's domain. He
showed his papers to a guard, and the guard let him in.
Elevators rose and fell like the circulation of a living creature.
Bustling men and women with little files had themselves
pumped up and down, they were the bacteria specific to this
body, they kept it alive, they strengthened or weakened it. (It
would take a microscope to tell whether they were construc-
tive or destructive particles.) Keetenheuve boarded one of the
elevators and went up. He got out halfway, and walked down
a long, neon-lit corridor. The corridor was ghostly, unreal and
pleasant, cool air from an air-conditioner flowed over him in
a friendly stream. He knocked on a door and entered a
double-lit neon chamber. It was like an artificially lit aquarium in sunshine, and Keetenheuve recalled that he too liked to
work in a similarly double-lit aquarium. What specialized
breeds they were, in their aquariums and hothouses! He
encountered two German secretaries. He asked about an
American, and one of the secretaries replied that the American

was somewhere in the building, but she didn't know where. Nor was there any point in looking for the American, chipped in the other secretary; they would never find him, and anyway the matter that Keetenheuve had come about hadn't been decided yet, it was currently being considered by other Americans, higher up than the boss of this little aquarium. Keetenheuve thanked them for the information. He stepped out into the singular illumination, the pure neon, of the corridor again, and the futility of what he was doing was revealed to him. The only dark stain on all this meaningless and beautiful clarity was the people somewhere, who were waiting for their case to be decided. Keetenheuve reached the elevator. He rode on up. He reached a rooftop canteen that afforded wide views of the Rhine, and at the same time he set foot in a basement dive in the lower depths of Paris. The ladies and gentlemen who had bustled in the corridors and elevators liked to linger here over coffee, cigarettes, and problems— they scratched at the surface of existence. Did they exist? They seemed to think they did, because they drank coffee, they smoked, and hypothetically or factually they rubbed against one another. They thought about their existence, and about their existence relative to all the other existences, they contemplated the existence of the building, the existence of the High Commission, the existence of the Rhine, the existence of this Germany, the existence of the other states bordering on the Rhine, and the existence of Europe, and in all these existences there was the worm of doubt and unreality and disgust. *And Thor threatened them with his giant hammer!* "America is perhaps the last experiment and the last great hope of mankind to achieve its purpose," Keetenheuve had heard a speaker say in the Keyserling Society, and he thought about that now. He would have liked to visit America. He would have liked to see the new Rome for himself. What was it like, America? Big? Free? Not the way one imagined it to be from the banks of the Rhine, for certain. This building wasn't America. It was an extraterritorial office, an outpost, perhaps a certain kind of experiment in a certain kind of vacuum. "America is not about being, but all about becoming," the speaker had said. Keetenheuve was all in favor of becoming; up until now, he had seen only destruction. The girls in the rooftop café wore sheer nylons that held their thighs in a warm, slippery embrace, a second skin of pure sex, that disappeared alluringly under their skirts. The men wore ankle socks, and when they crossed their legs, you could see the hairy calf. They worked together, the bustling ladies and gentlemen, did they sleep together as well? While Thor thundered up above, Keetenheuve envisioned grimly promiscuous bacchanals in the room, all of them busy as they had been before with their files in the elevators and corridors, now given over to a pansexual orgy, from which Keetenheuve was excluded, as he had been excluded by their busyness previously, and for a moment he envied them, but he knew it wasn't love and passion that actuated them, but the hopeless scratching of an ever-recurrent itch. He drank his coffee standing up, and he watched the pretty stockinged girls, and the young men in their little ankle socks, standing around like dissatisfied angels, and then he saw that their attractive faces were marked, marked by emptiness, marked by mere being. *It wasn't enough*

4

THE DIPLOMAT HAD LUNCHED, THE DREAMER HAD GONE awol, with the result that now Keetenheuve was late, and the members of the committee shot reproachful glances at him. His party colleagues Heineweg and Bierbohm looked at the late arrival with a mien of stern disapproval. With their expressions, they seemed to be accusing Keetenheuve, who had yet to miss an hour of these sessions, and who had been industrious and productive in the committees, of having done irreparable damage to the party and its standing.

Korodin also looked at Keetenheuve, but in his expression there was less blame than expectancy. Once more Korodin wondered whether Keetenheuve might have undergone a transformation, whether he was perhaps delayed because he had been to a church, praying to God for enlightenment, and had now come to them to say: I have found God, I am reborn. Korodin would have accepted a conversation with the Lord as a reason for being delayed, and he would have forgiven Keetenheuve. But Keetenheuve didn't mention anything about having found enlightenment, he muttered a casual and inaudible apology and sat down. He sat down (only they didn't notice) feeling ashamed of himself, ashamed like a bad pupil, unable to think of any defense for his laziness. He had let himself drift today. Like an old boat that had broken away from its mooring, he had slipped away on the variable current of the day. He thought. He had better look after himself. What was the mooring that he had lost? He had lost Elke, the Gauleiter's daughter, the war orphan, and he didn't think of her now as a woman, he saw her as a child that had been entrusted to him, and that he had failed to protect. The child or the duty of care he felt for her, they had been his mooring, a fixed point in the flowing stream, the anchor to his vessel in the, it now appeared, sterile lake of his life, and the anchor had sunk down, the chain had snapped, the anchor would remain for ever in the scary, unknown, dismal depths. Poor little anchor! He hadn't kept it clean. He had allowed it to rust. What had become of Elke at his side? An alcoholic. Where had she fallen in her drunken stupor? Into the arms of lesbians, the arms of those thoroughly damned by love.* He had failed to look after Elke. He couldn't understand it. He had attended committee meetings, he had written hundreds of thousands of letters, he had spoken in parliament, he had revised legislation, he didn't understand it, he could have stayed at Elke's side, stayed on the side of youth, and perhaps, if he hadn't done everything wrong, it might have been on the side of life as well. One human being was enough to give

*Not the opinion of Keetenheuve, much less of Koeppen, but taken from Baudelaire's *Les Fleurs du Mal*, where it was the title of one of the poems to which the French censor took exception in 1857.

meaning to life. Work wasn't enough. Politics weren't enough. Those things didn't protect him from the colossal futility of existence. It was a mild futility. It didn't hurt. It didn't stretch out long ghost arms to catch at the MP. It didn't throttle him. It was just there. And it remained. Futility had shown itself to him, it had introduced itself to him, and now his eyes were open, now he could see it everywhere, and it would never disappear, it would never become invisible to him. What was it? What did it look like? It was the void, it had no appearance. It looked like everything else. It looked like the committee, like the parliament, like the town, like the Rhine, like the country, it was all futile, it was all the void in a terrifyingly infinite vista, which was indestructible, because even the end, even entropy could do nothing to the void. The void was in fact eternity. And Keetenheuve just then felt his own existence very clearly, he was there, he was something, he knew it, he was surrounded and riddled by the void, but he was something by and of itself, an I, all alone against the void, and that represented a tiny hope, a slender chance for David against Goliath—only David wasn't sad. Keetenheuve was full of sadness. Korodin would have told him that despair—wanhope—was a mortal sin. But how would it have helped Keetenheuve to know that? Besides, he did know it. He was no more ignorant than Korodin. —Keetenheuve couldn't follow the language of the committee any more. What were they speaking in? Chinese? It was committee German. It was a language he knew! He had to force himself to understand it again. He began to sweat. He sweated with the effort of following the discussion; but the others were sweating as well. They wiped away their sweat with handkerchiefs; they wiped their faces, they wiped their bald heads, they wiped their

necks, they stuffed their handkerchiefs inside the damp col-
lars of their shirts. In the room it smelled of sweat and lavender, and Keetenheuve smelled the way they did: there was
always something rotting, and people always used scent to try
to mask the smell.

Now he saw the members of the committee as gamblers
seated around a roulette wheel. Oh, how vain their hopes, the
ball leapt, luck deserted them! Heineweg and Bierbohm
looked like small-time players, who played for low stakes,
each of them with his system, hoping to extort a day's money
from Lady Luck. But the game was about people, about large
sums of money, and about the future. This was an important
committee, it had important questions to debate, it had to
provide people with housing. And how complicated that was!
Every proposal had to be steered through dangerous rapids, if
it was even committed to paper, the little paper boats were
terribly vulnerable, got caught up on one of a thousand rocks,
bogged down, and went under. Ministries and other committees got involved, questions of war compensation, of government bonds, of taxation, were touched upon, the effect on
interest rates had to be considered, the accommodation of
displaced persons, reparations for bomb victims, property
rights, care for the mutilated, the laws of the regions and city
planning should be respected, and how could the poor people
be given anything if nobody was offering to contribute, how
could one expropriate when the Basic Law was explicitly in
favor of private ownership, and if one took the decision to
expropriate anyway, cautiously, in a few special cases, then
that opened the door to further injustice; if someone was
clumsy enough to get tangled up with the paragraphs, that
laid them open to punishment. Keetenheuve heard figures

being quoted. It was like the sound of running water to him, impressive but so what. Six hundreds and fifty millions of public money. So and so much from central funds. Separate budget for pilot schemes; only fifteen millions. But then there was still the money that would accrue from debentures. Korodin read the figures out, from time to time he shot Keetenheuve a look, as though he expected him to object or perhaps agree. Keetenheuve didn't open his mouth. All at once, he had as little to say to Korodin's figures as someone at a magic show has to say to the baffling but ultimately inane goings-on on the stage; he knows that there's a trick somewhere, and he's being duped. Keetenheuve had been given his seat on this committee by the nation, to make sure that no one was deceived. But for him, this whole discussion was nothing but baffling numbers games! No one would see the millions that Korodin listed. No one had ever seen them. Even Korodin, the conjurer, hadn't seen them. They were on paper, they were handed on on paper, and they would be allocated—on paper. They were fed through an infinity of calculating machines. They were pumped through the calculating machines of the ministries, of the accounting departments, the main offices and the subsidiaries, they appeared in the statements of government bank accounts, diminished, melted away, but they remained paper, a number on a piece of paper, until they finally materialized somewhere, and became forty marks in someone's pay packet, and a stolen fifty-pfennig piece in a little boy's hand for an Indian comic book. No one truly understood it. Even Stierides, the plutocrats' banker, didn't understand the juju of the numbers; but he mastered a kind of yoga by which his accounts grew. Keetenheuve wanted to speak. Couldn't something be done? Couldn't twice the sum be fed through the calculating machines, as much again as had been suggested, and then wouldn't eighty marks arrive in the pay packets, instead of forty? But Keetenheuve didn't dare talk in those terms. Once again, Korodin was looking at him expectantly, encouragingly even, but Keetenheuve couldn't meet his eye. He was afraid of his party colleagues, he was afraid of Heineweg and Bierbohm, their astonishment, their dismay. Keetenheuve saw trams running across the committee table, and the trams were ringing their bells: We're doubling, we're doubling our prices; and he saw the bakers demonstrating: Twice the price for loaves; and he saw the greengrocers altering their price signs for potatoes and turnips. Doubling the paper sums was useless. The wage packet would remain half empty. It was a law of economics, or a law of relativity. Keetenheuve would have dearly liked to put more in the wage packets; but he couldn't see how it might be done either, and his head was spinning. All day, he had felt dizzy.

They were talking about apartments for mine workers now, a new settlement on the slag heaps, and an expert had worked out how many square meters per person, and a second expert had thought about how crudely and inexpensively the walls might be fashioned. Korodin had shares in the pits. The workers hacked out the coal, and by some mysterious mechanism, their efforts swelled Korodin's bank account. The workers rode the elevator down to the coal face, and Korodin read his new balance. The workers went home exhausted. They trudged through the suburb, walked past the slag heaps, which were still growing like the mountains in the early days of the earth, black table mountains, changing the face of the earth, and on whose dusty peaks dirty children were playing cops and robbers or cowboys and Indians. So Keetenheuve imagined the miner arriving at the new home in the settlement that they were discussing in the committee, that they crunched numbers for, that they passed into law, and for which they approved the means, the substantial insubstantial (paper) sums. The miner entered the minimum number of square meters that the experts had agreed. He shared them with his wife and his children and some relations that fate, tragedy, or unemployment had suddenly thrown upon his household, and with the lodgers whose rent he needed to pay the installments on the hideous, impractical, far too big and showy furniture, for the "Erika" style bedroom, and the "Adolf" style lounge, those torture chambers and housewives' dreams in the windows of the never-never shops. The miner was home. There was buzz and there was talk, and screams and creaks and squawks from mouths and loudspeakers, and yells and barks, oaths and smacks and shouts coming through the expert's cheapo walls in the form of *Iphigenia in Tauris* and the lottery results, and the miner remembers the pit, he thinks his way back down the long shaft, and thinks: Out there, when the pneumatic drills are droning, when the rocks are crunching and splitting, it's quiet in the middle of the din. And many went gladly to fight because they hated the daily grind, because they couldn't stand their tight lives any more, because, with all its terrors, war represented escape and freedom, the possibility of travel, the possibility of withdrawal, the possibility of living in Rothschild's villa. Tedium filled them, a creeping tedium that sometimes manifested itself in violence, in suicide, in apparently motiveless family drama, but there was so much tedium in the noise of the settlements, displeasure in the proximity of other beings, disgust at the miasma of kitchen and bathroom, at the stink of often worn clothes and clothes soaking in the tub, the miner felt sickened by his wife's sweat (he loved her), and by the excreta of his children (he loved them), and by the incessant blabber from their lips that swirled around him like a tornado.

Heineweg and Bierbohm were content. They supported the proposals of the experts; they approved the minimum expenditure, the minimum number of square meters, the minimum dwelling. The dwellings would be built. Heineweg and Bierbohm advocated the joys of allotments. They saw little gabled houses being created, and they imagined them as cosy; they saw satisfied laborers class-consciously planting seeds in their own little plots, and through the open window the wireless was broadcasting an uplifting speech of Knurrewahn's. *We may face the future and face the world with confidence.* And Korodin was content. He supported the proposals of the experts; he approved the minimum expenditure, the minimum number of square meters, the minimum dwellings. The dwellings would be built. Korodin too advocated the joys of allotments for the workers, he too found favor in gabled huts in the green; only he saw the doors and windows decorated with birch on Corpus Christi, and the radio was broadcasting the bishop's sermon, and the contented workers were kneeling in the front garden, devoutly on their own sod, in front of the Holy of Holies that was carried past in the procession. *The Lord is my shepherd, I'll not want.* They wanted mollification. Heineweg, Bierbohm, and Korodin were rival brothers. They didn't know they were brothers in spirit. They thought they were enemies. But they were brothers. They all got tiddly on the same watery lemonade.

What was Keetenheuve after? Any roof was better than

none. He ought to know that. He had known bunks in barracks and Nissen huts, put-you-ups in bomb shelters, rubble
billets, emergency lodgings, he knew the slums of London
and the basement holes in Rotterdam's Chinatown, and he
knew that the minimum apartments that the committee was
putting its weight behind were a step up. But he didn't like
mollification. He couldn't see any allotment heaven. He
thought he could see through the designs: he sensed poison
and bacteria. How were these settlements any different from
the National Socialist settlements for large families, or the
SA and SS settlements, only cheaper and narrower and grim-
mer and shabbier? And if you looked at the blueprints, it was
the Nazi idiom they were still building in, and if you looked
at the names of the architects, it was the Nazi architects who
were still working, and Heineweg and Bierbohm approved of
the brown style and okayed the architects. The program of the
National Socialist Union for Large Families was Heineweg
and Bierbohm's program, it was their approach to the mollification of the population, it was their idea of social progress.
So what was Keetenheuve after? Did he want the Revolution?
Such a big and beautiful word, toppled in the dust! No,
Keetenheuve didn't want the Revolution, he couldn't want it
any more—it no longer existed. The Revolution was dead. It
was withered and dead. The Revolution was an offshoot of
Romanticism, a crisis of puberty. It had had its time. Its pos-
sibilities had not been investigated. And now it was a corpse,
a dry leaf in the herbarium of ideas, a dead notion, an anti-
quated word to look up in the encyclopedia, that didn't come
up in daily speech. Only a gushing youth would still enthuse
about Revolution for a while longer, and after that it would be
nothing but a pash or dream, an odorless bloom—the pressed

blue flower of Romanticism.* The time for the tender faith in liberty, equality, fraternity, it was over *the morning of America the poems of Whitman strength and genius it was all onanism and the epigone lay down contentedly in the broad marital bed of law and order the night stand with the calendar that marked the fruitful and unfruitful days of his wife's cycle next to the pessary and the encyclical from Rome.* Korodin had prevailed over the Revolution, and he guessed he had lost something in the process. Heineweg and Bierbohm had prevailed over the Revolution, and they felt they had betrayed something of themselves in the process. Between them, they had succeeded in emasculating religion and the Revolution. Any idea of society had gone to the Devil, and he was holding it in his claws. There might still be the occasional coup d'état, they came in hot or cold versions, like punch, but the drink was always mixed from cheap ingredients and it left the people who tried it with sore heads. Keetenheuve was not in favor of mollification. He was in favor of looking the Gorgon in the eye. He didn't want to lower his gaze in front of horror. But he wanted an agreeable life, and he wanted to trick the devil of his due. He was in favor of happiness in despair. He was in favor of a happiness built from convenience and solitude, a happiness within reach of everyman, a lonely, convenient and despairing happiness in the technological world that had been created. There was no need to feel cold as well as miserable; or hungry as well as suicidal; one shouldn't have to wade through dirt while one's thoughts were on the void. And it was in such a spirit that Keetenheuve wanted new homes built for the working class, Corbusier machines-for-living, contempo-

---

*Die blaue Blume is the title of Novalis's novel and is used, in a wider way, for the object of any unattainable quest.

rary castles, an entire city in a single high-rise, with artificial roof gardens, artificial climate control, he saw the possibility of insulating man from excesses of heat and cold, of freeing him from dust and dirt, from housework, from domestic squabbles and noise. Keetenheuve wanted to have ten thousand under a single roof to isolate them from one another, in the way that metropolises take a man out of his neighborhood and make him alone, a lone beast of prey, a lone hunter, a lone victim, and every room in Keetenheuve's gigalith would be soundproofed against every other, and everyone should be able to set the temperature to his own liking, and he should be alone with his books, alone with his thoughts, alone with his work, alone with his idleness, alone with his love, alone with his despair, alone with his human reek.

Keetenheuve wanted to get up. He wanted to address them. He wanted to persuade them, and perhaps he only wanted to provoke them, because he no longer believed he was capable of persuading them. He wished for new architects, young and enthusiastic master builders, to draw up new plans, a mighty construction, to transform the ugly landscape of the slag heaps, the vomit of the pits, the waste products of industry, the rubble and landfills into a single beaming sparkling edifice, which would get rid of all the pettiness of the suburban settlements, their pokiness, their poverty, their pathetic mania for ownership, which was encouraged as a way of overcoming social envy, the woman's enslavement to housework, the man's enslavement to the family. He wanted to tell them about his tower, and the thousand ingenious and comfortably equipped apartments of explicit solitude and proudly borne despair that it would contain. Keetenheuve wanted to erect the profane monastery, with hermits' cells for the masses. He saw the people, and he saw them clinging to things in which they had long ceased to believe. One of their illusions was family happiness. But even Korodin dreaded the drive back (not to mention Heineweg and Bierbohm, who had three-room apartments stuffed full of family and junk), home to his stately inherited home, home to the soirées, the feebleminded and enervating orgies of falsehood that his wife, bitten by some imp, put on to bore him, home to the self-absorption of his half-grown children, who tormented and appalled him, pampered savages, confronting him with their cold pitiless faces, features behind which lurked greed, dirt, and loathing, and where even his celebrated paintings, his exorbitantly insured Dutch, disappointed him, their landscapes with placid bullocks on juicy pastures, their polished gleaming interiors, their winter scenes with ice-skating, fog and frozen mill wheels, the sight of them made him freeze too, and so he chose to occupy himself with politics (in the sensible belief that he needed to do something, seeing as his work had been taken from him, the mines and factories were ruled by managers now who knew how to deal with the work force, and how to get the best out of the brutes, Korodin didn't know) or to sit around anxiously in churches, calling on the bishop, he spent time with the likes of Keetenheuve, and he enjoyed walking in cemeteries at night. They wouldn't understand Keetenheuve. They would think his tower was a tower of Babel. He didn't speak. Korodin looked up at him encouragingly one last time, disappointed by his silence, and Heineweg and Bierbohm looked at him again, they too were disappointed and reproachful, and they wondered what had happened to him, a wreck, a man with heart trouble, what a shocking transformation, it was as though the work in parliament had robbed him of his strength, and they remembered the younger Keetenheuve, who, like them, had eagerly and keenly done the needful, who had helped them feed and clothe the victims of the horrible war, and find them somewhere to live, and give them new hope—well, that was once, and so they decided to have the calculations gone over again, to send the plans back to the experts for one last look, and Heineweg said to conclude, with a mild glance at Keetenheuve: "I think we've made a bit of headway today."

Keetenheuve walked through the passageways of the parliament building, up some steps to his office, from time to time he encountered filing clerks who looked like ghosts. The typists had already gone home. Only a few eager beavers were still creeping around the building. Keetenheuve thought: the labyrinth is empty, Minos's bull is trotting among the adoring population, while Theseus wanders through the maze for ever. His desk looked just the way he had left it. The piece of paper from the agency that Dana had passed on to him was lying openly on top of the delegate's correspondence, on top of the delegate's scribbled rendition of Baudelaire's *"Beau navire."* Guatemala or no—that was the question. The interview quotes from the generals on the Conseil Supérieur des Forces Armées stood between him and Guatemala. If Keetenheuve took up Dana's suggestion and brought up the interview in the plenary session tomorrow, then he wouldn't be able to retire any more, because they would shoot him down in flames here instead, and not throw him the sop of Guatemala. It took cunning to hold out that particular morsel to him. Not that it was an especially appetizing bit! Guatemala—who bade each other good night there?

Foxes?*—You got them on the Rhine. Guatemala meant peace, Guatemala meant oblivion, Guatemala meant death. And whoever's idea it was knew that, he knew that was what would tempt him, peace and oblivion and death. Otherwise they could have kept The Hague open for him, Brussels, Copenhagen, maybe Athens, he was probably worth that much; but Guatemala, that meant the veranda in the baking sun, the square with the dusty palms, that was the slow and inevitable moldering away. They had his measure! Knurrewahn, if it had been him in power, would have offered him Paris, to get rid of him. Knurrewahn had no idea. Paris meant continuing to blunder around and remaining a player; Guatemala was dissolution, a cynical surrender to death. It was like pulling your pants down for Mr. Death—a comparison that Frost-Forestier would have appreciated. A rainbow had appeared over the Rhine. Its arc ran from Godesberg, from Mehlem, from the American hive, across to Beuel, where it disappeared next to the bridge, behind a wall on which was written *Rheinlust*. The rainbow was like a heavenly ladder going up and down, spanning the river, and it was easy to imagine that angels were crossing it, and that God was at hand. Did the rainbow signify conciliation, did it signify peace, was it a token of friendliness? The President in his presidential palace must be able to see it, the friendly arch of peace from Godesberg to Beuel, maybe the President was standing out on his flowered terrace, gazing across the river, staring into the evening air, which was still now as an old painting, and maybe the President felt sad and didn't know

---

*"*Wo sich die Füchse gute Nacht sagen*" (Where the foxes wish each other a good night), a fragrant German expression for "the boonies."

why,* or the President felt disappointed and didn't know why
either. And Keetenheuve, standing by the window, the window of his office in the parliament building, invented a character whom he called Musaeus, who was the butler of the
President. It was perfectly possible that the President didn't
have a butler, but Keetenheuve endowed him with one by the
name of Musaeus, and Musaeus resembled the President. He
was the same age as the President, he looked like the
President, and he thought he was the President. His work left
him with enough time to imagine it. Musaeus was a trained
barber, and had "gone to Court," he talked about it sometimes, that was something he didn't forget, in his early years
he had "gone to Court" in a tailcoat, to shave the young
Prince, and while he lathered him up, he had spoken to him
boldly about the plight of the common people, and after the
Prince abdicated in 1918, Musaeus hadn't wanted to shave
anyone else, and he became an usher in the Office of the
Minister President, and then he entered the service of
Hindenburg, and then he showed some character and refused
to serve the guy from Braunau. He got through the dictatorship and the war years, and then the new state remembered
him, and appointed him butler to the President. Well and
good; but he was confused, was Musaeus. He read too much
Goethe, which he borrowed from the President's library in the
sumptuous Sophien Edition, and in the evening, when the
rainbow spanned the banks of the Rhine, Musaeus stood by
the rose-covered balustrade, thought he was the President,
looked far into the countryside, and rejoiced that everything

*"Ich weiß nicht, was soll es bedeuten," the first line of Heine's Lorelei poem,
shamelessly re-ascribed by the Nazis as an "anonymous folk song," in view of
Heine's Jewishness!

in the Pedagogic Academy at his feet was coming up roses.
But somewhere in his heart he felt a twinge, he felt as though
he'd forgotten something that had once been his in the days
when he'd "gone to Court," the voice of the people, the whisper of the people, the unmeaningful monotonous murmur
that he had sloshed around the jaws of the young Prince along
with the shaving foam, now he could no longer hear it, and it
bothered him that it wasn't there. Musaeus wanted to be
good, he wanted to be a good father to the country, maybe
back then he had even wanted to train the Prince to become
a good father to his country, but the Prince hadn't been in
power for very long, and now it was Musaeus' turn, and unfortunately he had forgotten his educational principles for young
princes. Musaeus wasn't able to govern properly, they were
dragging him into horse trading, he thought crossly, and the
leading statesman, Musaeus thought that evening, he was
feeding Musaeus too well, and making him fat and deaf and
sluggish, till he finally couldn't hear the whisper of the people
or, worse, what he was hearing was a confected murmur,
recorded in a record factory, who could tell, Musaeus couldn't
feel the difference any more, previously he had, and then he
decided to go on a diet, cut down on food, cut down on drink.
For three days he didn't eat, good old Musaeus, for three days
he didn't drink, but then—the job was too cushy, and the
kitchen and cellar were too good, Musaeus ate a little chop
and he drank a little claret, and so he appeased and mollified
his twinge of anxiety. Keetenheuve turned down Guatemala.
He turned down the Spanish colonial death veranda. There
were terraces on the Rhine as well. He was determined not to
let them get rid of him. He would remain. He would remain
at his desk, he would remain in parliament; he wouldn't scale

the barricades, but he would scale the rostrum. He would speak with holy rage against the policies of the government. The end justified the means. The end was peace. The end was a friendlier planet. Wasn't that an end worth pursuing? Perhaps he would get there. He stopped planning his speech. He would speak without a script, with passion and zeal. Keetenheuve *retired ambassador orator tribune of the people* was one of the last to leave the Bundeshaus that day. A guard had to unlock the door to let him out. For a while Keetenheuve walked with light feet into the evening. What had he left behind him? The unfinished translation of a poem, a deskful of unanswered letters, the beginnings of a speech, *and with him went the new era*

Before long, he noticed he was sweating. The evening was still sticky, even with the rainbow up there. There was a stench of sewage. Fragrance of roses wafted from the gardens. A lawn mower clattered over the carpet of grass. Trim dogs sauntered down the avenue. The great diplomatic averter of the worst, his little twerpish ladies' umbrella dangling coquettishly from his limp wrist, was taking his evening turn, excogitating a new chapter in his lucrative memoirs, while other extras on the political stage and honest balladeers strolled proprietorially about. Keetenheuve greeted the averter, whom he didn't know, and the great memoirist acknowledged him, flattered. "Rumbled! Rumbled!" Keetenheuve felt like calling after him, and tapping him on the shoulder. Bismarck already had known the type: "Every politician is burdened with a mortgage to vanity." They were vain, they were all of them vain, ministers, officials, diplomats, MPs, and even the porter who unlocked the door of the parliament building was vain because he unlocked the door of the parliament building, because he belonged to the government, and because he occasionally got his name in the paper, when a journalist wanted to prove he had really been inside the ministry and had seen the porter. They all thought of themselves as historic personages, as public figures, just because they had an office, because their mug shots appeared in the papers, because papers need fresh faces, because their names went out on air, because radio stations also needed their daily bundle of hay, and then the wives saw their great husbands or their little lovers waving enraptured from the cinema screen, and standing with an appealing little grin they had copied off the Americans, who didn't scruple to cosy up to photographers like models. And while the world might not think all that much of its official historic figures, it did keep brandishing them about, to prove that the stock of vacuity and horror was not exhausted, and that history was still being made. Why was there history? And if it was a necessary thing, a necessary evil, why so much clucking over no eggs? The minister is visiting Paris. Okay. What to do? He's being received by his opposite number. Well, isn't that nice. The ministers will breakfast together. How lovely. Lovely. Hope they had good weather. The ministers will retire for bilateral talks. Excellent! Then what? They say goodbye. Yes, and then? One minister will accompany the other to the airport or the railway station. Yes, but then what happens? Nothing. The minister will fly home, and his opposite number promises to visit him soon. And the whole thing, station, airport, breakfast, handshake makes banner headlines in newspapers, is shown in cinema news-reels, and broadcast into sitting rooms all over—what's it all been in aid of? No one could say. Go to Paris quietly, why can't you!! Have yourselves a good time. It would be so much

better for all concerned. Can't we forget all about them for a
year? So we don't recognize their faces, don't remember their
names. Maybe legends will form around them. *Keetenheuve
hero of legend.* It was his world, and he was thinking it to bits,
because how was he going to become a minister if he didn't
use all the tools of propaganda to try to persuade the world
that it needed ministers? *Keetenheuve minister burdened with
Bismarck's mortgage to vanity*—he was sweating a lot. He was
bathed in it. Everything nettled him. His shirt clung to him.
He felt hemmed in and oppressed. He put his hand inside his
shirt, laid it on his skin, felt the hot stubbly hair, *Keetenheuve
no stripling, Keetenheuve a male of the species, a buck, aromat-
ic, hairy chest, covered by his clothes, covered by civilization,
domesticated animal, no evidence of buck*—and underneath
there was the pounding heart, the little pump that was struggling to cope. He had wanted to oppose them: his heart had
beat joyfully. He had met them (and himself): his heart beat
irregularly, timidly, he panted for breath like a hunted animal.
Was he afraid? He wasn't afraid. But he was like a swimmer,
swimming against a strong current and knowing he won't
make it, he will be carried away on the current, he makes no
headway, the effort is pointless, and it would be easier to let
himself drift, be lulled into death.

He passed construction sites. They were working overtime.
The government was building, the ministries were building,
the building inspection authorities were building, the federa-
tion and the various *Länder* were erecting centers, foreign
embassies were immuring themselves here, cartels, industrial
conglomerates, banking groups, oil companies, steel plants,
coal mining associations, electricity producers sited their
administrative centers here, as though they mightn't be

required to pay taxes in the shadow of the central government, insurance companies put by and built up, and reinsurance companies where insurers insured themselves against
insurance losses couldn't even find enough space to store
their policies, to house their lawyers, to put up their actuar-
ies, invest their profits, flaunt their wealth. They wanted, all
of them, to find a roof as near the heart of government as possible; it was as though they were afraid the government might
leave without them, as though one day it would no longer be
there, and their new headquarters would have become dread-
quarters. Was Keetenheuve living through a new age of
Founding Fathers? It was an unfounded, unbounded, well-
groundedly groundless age *you have built on shifting sand.*
Keetenheuve Verdi singer in Bonn, on the front of the stage he
mastered bel canto on fleeting sand oh how treacherously ye
have built. Poor little member of parliament between security
bunkers. The worm in the wood. Nail to their coffin. Sick worm.
Twisted. Rusty nail. Just as well the insurers will outlast him. He
was not insured. Would die like that. A burdensome corpse. No
memorial to Keetenheuve. Freed humankind from nothing. Felt
his way through earthworks. Traps. Blind. A mole. —He
reached the playground, and, just like this morning, there
were two girls sitting on the seesaw. Two thirteen-year-olds.
As Keetenheuve looked at them, they stopped bouncing up
and down, one of them squatted down on the ground, the
other hung suspended in midair. They giggled. They whispered something to each other. One of them gave a tug to her
little skirt, pulled the material down over her thigh. Corrupt.
Corrupt. What about you? Weren't you tempted by youth, by
smooth cool skin? Hair that didn't yet smell of death? A
mouth that didn't breathe out putrefaction? It smelled of

vanilla. In the ruins there was someone roasting almonds and sugar in a copper pan. *Try my burnt giant almonds* called a rain-soaked sheet. Keetenheuve bought fifty pfennigs' worth of the giant almonds and tried them. They tasted bitter. The sugary coat cracked between his teeth. A brittle and sticky mass lay on his tongue. The burnt almonds tasted of puberty, of boyish lusts in dark matinee cinemas: on the screen swelled the dirty freckled white breasts of Lya de Mara, you had a mouthful of sweets, and a new ache stirred in your blood. Keetenheuve stood chewing in front of a shop window full of fraternity accoutrements. The owner of the shop windows was living off the same pubescent feelings. Everything was there again, time ran backwards, there hadn't been any wars. Keetenheuve saw white and colored fraternity caps, dueling-society ribbons, drinking jackets, he surveyed fencing gear, sabers, tankards with the fraternity symbol on the lids, ceremonial books with golden nails in the binding, and metal clasps. Those things were being manufactured and sold, they paid the lease for the window and the shop, and provided the owner of the business with a living. The founding years were really back, the same taste, the same complexes, the same taboos. The sons of the master builders drove to university in their own runabouts, but in the evening they put on their silly hats, they aped their grandfathers, and they did something very strange, they rubbed a salamander; Keetenheuve had an unattractive vision of young men full of beer, stupidity, and ill-defined, sometimes nationalistic feeling, bawling songs, and grinding up some kind of lizards between their beer steins and the table. Keetenheuve chucked the rest of the almonds in the gutter. The paper bag burst and the sugar almonds bounced across the paving stones like marbles.

The infant Keetenheuve plays with agate stones on the pavement. Bonn insurance company director runs up to Keetenheuve with white cap, fraternity ribbon and saber. Director runs Keetenheuve through. Keetenheuve takes a burnt almond and pops it in the director's mouth. He tugs at the director's jacket, and little ten-pfennig pieces come tumbling out of his sleeve onto the pavement. Little girls come by, and start collecting the ten-pfennig pieces: they cry out: more and more and more coins come tumbling, skipping, and rolling onto the pavement. Keetenheuve laughs. The director is cross and says: Seriousness of the situation—

Keetenheuve crossed the market square. The market women were cleaning their stalls. *Joke for Mergentheim: A blind man crosses the fish market, sniffs, says: "Ah, girls." Bedroom at the Mergentheims'. Sophie getting dressed for the party, Corps Diplomatique in Godesberg, she pulls a diaphanous corset over her sagging body. Mergentheim is unexcited. He is tired. He says: "Keetenheuve came to see me." The corset pinches Sophie. She'd like to slit the seam. She's hot. Mergentheim says: "I don't think I should be on first-name terms with him any more." Sophie thinks: What's he babbling on about now, this corset is killing me, nylon silk, taut and diaphanous, I could rip open the seam, I'm not getting changed again. Mergentheim says: "I'm his enemy. I ought to tell him. I ought to tell him: 'Herr Keetenheuve, I am your enemy.'" Sophie thinks: What am I putting on this diaphanous corset for? If François-Poncet* saw me like this, you can see everything anyway, all the folds, the rolls of fat. Mergentheim says: "I*

---

*André François-Poncet, the French member of the tripartite Allied High Commission in West Germany, and therefore halfway between an ambassador and a provincial governor.

feel mean like this." Keetenheuve walked through the market rubbish, rotten, stinking, decomposing, rancid, and spoilt things lay at his feet, he slipped on something, *an orange, a banana, a good fruit ripened to no purpose, picked to be wasted, born in Africa, perished in the market in Bonn, not even consumed, not even metabolized on the journey through the greedy human. Sausage, meat, cheese, fish, and everywhere flies. Heavy bluebottles. Maggots in their bellies. Their weapon. Sliced sausage destroyed on the plate. That's what we eat. That's what they'll tuck into in the Hotel Stern. I could go along there. Middlemen in the lobby, field shovels for the border patrols, patent water cannon, artificial diamonds, waiting for a call from the minister. He'll send a car over. Let's have the diamonds, let's have the patent for the water cannon, the shovel, pretty collapsible shovel you can tuck in your waistcoat pocket, wear it under your suit, no one will notice, goes down well everywhere, spectacular efficiency, six hundred cubic meters of German soil in an hour, comrade burying comrade. This is England. This is England. You are tuned to the Voice of America.* This time Keetenheuve wouldn't speak. He wouldn't fight them on the airwaves. *Keetenheuve unknown soldier on an unknown front. Pointing forward? Pointing back? Anyone with nerves will fire in the air. Attention! We're not fighting birds here! Keetenheuve a good man, no hunter. White hands. Writer man.* On the balcony of the Stern Hotel stood a delegate from the Bavarian sister party. He was looking down the Mangfall valley. Cows coming in off the pastures. Jingle of cowbells. The year was advancing. The pensions were all full of Prussians: Ave Maria. The Bavarian party, like any of the other little parties, might be the one to tip the scales one way or the other. Much courted. When push came to shove, it voted with the government, in spite of its reservations about the Federal Republic.

There were people lining up in front of a cinema box office. What were they hoping to see? The great German comedy. Keetenheuve joined the line. Ariadne guided him, Theseus, who was willing to risk the dark, Ariadne said: "Please move into the middle!" She had a snotty squeaky voice. As an usherette, she had been put in charge of a naughty humanity that didn't move into the middle in time. Keetenheuve sat, and he sat in the appropriate attitude for his time, he was part of a passive audience. Just now he was a passive audience for advertising. On the screen, razors, driving licenses, neckties, fabrics, lipstick, hair dye, and a trip to Athens were offered to him. *Keetenheuve market potential, Keetenheuve consumer. Useful.* Keetenheuve bought six shirts a year. Fifty million West Germans bought three hundred million shirts. From one vast bale, the material was fed into the sewing machines. Coils of material snaked around the citizen. *Captive market.* Maths lesson: If a man smokes ten cigarettes per day, how many will he smoke in a year, therefore fifty million smokers will get through a volume of tobacco six times the size of Cologne Cathedral. Only, Keetenheuve didn't smoke. *Darn it!* He was pleased. Here was the newsreel. A minister was opening a bridge. He cut a ribbon. He swaggered over the bridge. Swaggered after him other swaggerers. The President visited the exhibition. A child welcomed him. *Our Führer loves children.* A minister was departing. He was taken to the railway station. A minister was arriving. He was picked up. The Miss Loisach contest. Bikinis on the Alps. Nice ass. Big atomic mushroom over the Nevada desert. Skiing on artificial snow on the beaches of Florida. More bikinis. Big crowds. Even

nicer asses. Cut to Korea: Meeting of two grim-faced enemies; they go into a tent; they come out again; one of them
climbs grimly onto a helicopter; the other, still more grimly
into his limousine. Gunfire. Bombs falling on some city.
Gunfire. Bombs falling on some jungle. Miss Macao contest.
Bikini. Stunning Sino-Portuguese ass. Sport brings people
together. Crowd of twenty thousand watching a ball. So boring. But then the camera's tele-lens pulls out a few individual
faces from the crowd: terrifying faces, chins thrust out,
mouths twisted with hatred, murderous eyes. *Do you want
total war? Yeah yeah yeah* From his seat in the dark cinema,
Keetenheuve watched the faces that the treacherous tele-lens
had violently pulled out of the shelter and anonymity of the
crowd, completely beside themselves, cast up on the screen
as on a dissecting table by the power of light (which according to Newton was an uncertain substance, floating chilly and
aloof over earthbound matter), and he was afraid. Were these
human faces? What had happened, and to what chance did
he owe it *Keetenheuve pharisee*, that he too wasn't scrambled
in this twenty-thousand-strong mass (there were ministers
seated on the benches too, and they were caught by the camera's eye, ministers had the common touch, either they really
had it, or else they pretended to: gifted mimics) following the
ball with outthrust chin? His heart didn't race here, his blood
didn't throb, he felt no rage: get the ref by the throat, lynch
the bastard, he's bent, penalty ref, never a penalty, whistles!
Keetenheuve was offside. He was outside the force field of
this assembly of twenty thousand. They were united, they
were an accumulation, a dangerous aggregation of zeros, an
explosive mixture, twenty thousand excited hearts and twenty thousand empty heads. Of course they were waiting for

their Führer, their number One, who would face them down, and turn them into a colossal number, a people, the new bastardized golem that was called a people, one Reich, one Führer, total hate, total explosion, total destruction. He was all alone. He was in the same position as the Führer. *Keetenheuve Führer.* But Keetenheuve couldn't charm the multitude. He couldn't animate the people. He couldn't fire them. He couldn't even cheat the people. As a politician, he was like a bigamist, who couldn't get it up when it was time to bed Frau Germania. But in his imagination and often enough in fact, and always in his strivings, he was on the side of the people's rights! On the screen, the cinema was now selling itself; short clips from forthcoming dreams were being shown. Two old men were playing tennis together. But these old lads were the romantic leads in the next film, pertly clad in little shorts, and they could easily be Keetenheuve's older brothers, because when Keetenheuve had been a stripling, he could remember seeing these gents in films. But they weren't just tennis players, they were also property owners, because it was a historical film that was being trailed here *moving and dramatic*, and the property owners had lost everything, all their worldly goods had been lost, all that was left to them were their respective properties, the big house, the fields and woods and tennis courts and their natty shorts and of course a couple of thoroughbred horses, which they would one day again ride for Germany. A voice-over declared: "A ravishing woman comes between two lifelong friends. Which of them will win her?" A chunky matron hurtled up to the net in a girly dress, and it was all taking place in the very best society, in a world that no longer existed in that form. And Keetenheuve wondered whether such a world ever had existed. What was this? What were they trying to pretend? A popular German writer called one of her many books *Highlife;* she or her publishers had given the German book the English title, and millions who were unfamiliar with the word "highlife" gobbled up the book. Highlife—tiptop society, magic talisman, what was it, who belonged to it? Korodin? No. Korodin wasn't highlife. The Chancellor? Nor him. The Chancellor's banker? He wouldn't have had people like that in his house. So who was highlife? Ghosts, shadows. The actors on the screen, the ones who were playing at highlife, they were the only ones who were it, they and a few celebrities from the world of magazines and advertisements, the man with the spruce mustache who pours champagne with such inimitable style, the man who smokes everyone's tram cigarette in his polo kit, and the blue smoke twines around the beautiful horse's neck. No one on earth would ever pour champagne or sit on horseback like that, and why should they—but these types were the real shadow kings for the people. A second trailer gave notice of a color film. This time the voice-over cried: "America in the Civil War! The Deep South, land of burning passions! A ravishing woman comes between two lifelong friends!" Two lifelong friends and a ravishing woman—on both sides of the water that seemed to be the only concept the screenwriters knew. On this occasion, the ravishing woman sat on a bareback mustang, and rode in three colors, till it hurt Keetenheuve's eyes to watch. Her two friends—also in three colors—snuck through shrubbery and shot at each other. The voice-over commented: "Such derring-do!" Keetenheuve didn't have a friend he could shoot at. Was he supposed to fire at Mergentheim, and have Mergentheim fire at him? Not such a bad idea really. Sophie could play the ravishing woman.

She'd be up for it. She wasn't a spoilsport. And now it was
time for the German comedy. Keetenheuve was shattered.
The comedy flickered. It was a ghost comedy. The romantic
lead put on a disguise. He dressed as a lady. Okay, there were
such people as transvestites. But Keetenheuve didn't think it
was funny. The transvestite got into a bath. Well, even transvestites have to wash. What was so funny about that? A
woman walked in on him in the bath, rightly naked and no
longer wrongly in disguise. Laughter in front of Keetenheuve
and laughter behind him, laughter on either side of him. Why
were they laughing? He didn't understand. It frightened him.
He was excluded. He was excluded from their laughter. He
hadn't seen anything funny. A naked actor. A thrice-divorced
woman who walked in on him in the bath. Surely these events
were more sad than funny! But all around Keetenheuve they
were laughing. They howled with laughter. Was Keetenheuve
a foreigner? Was he among people who laughed and cried dif-
ferently than himself, who were different from himself?
Maybe in his feelings he was a foreigner, and the laughter
came out of the darkness and washed over him like a powerful wave that threatened to drown him. He groped his way out
of the labyrinth. He rushed out of the cinema. It was panic
flight. Ariadne squeaked after him: "Right for the exit! Right!"
Theseus flees Minotaur lives

The day was drawing to a close. There was still one last
shimmer of the dying sun in the sky. It was suppertime. They
sat in their dowdy rooms, they sat in front of their made beds,
they chewed and they listened apathetically to the wireless:
Take me with you, captain, on your journey to the stars. Only
a very few people were out on the streets. They were the ones
who didn't know where to go. They didn't know where to go,

even if they had a room, even if their bed was made, and beer
and sausages were waiting for them, they didn't know where
to go. They were people like Keetenheuve, but they were different from Keetenheuve too—they didn't know what to do
with themselves. There were youths standing outside the cinema. They went to the cinema twice a week, and on other
days they stood outside it. They were hanging around. What
were they hanging around for? They were hanging around
waiting for life to begin, and the life they were waiting for did-
n't begin. Life didn't turn up for them outside the cinema, or
if it did come and was standing next to them, they didn't see
it, and the people they could see, that they later ended up
sharing their lives with, they weren't the ones they were hoping to see. If they'd known it was only going to be them, they
wouldn't have bothered standing around waiting. The boys
were waiting in a group on their own. Boredom was in them
like a disease, and you could already see in their faces that it
would be the death of them. The girls were off on their own.
They were less afflicted with boredom than the boys. They
were fidgety, and they hid it by putting their heads together
and gossiping and teasing each other. The young men were
looking at the film stills for the hundredth time. They saw the
actor sitting in the bathtub, and they saw him wearing
woman's clothing. What was he playing at? A queer? They
yawned. Their mouths became a round hole, the entrance to
a tunnel where emptiness came and went. They stuck cigarettes in the hole, to tamp the emptiness, they pressed their
lips around the tobacco, and they looked mean and self-
important. They might become MPs one day; but probably
the army would get them first. Keetenheuve didn't have a
vision: he didn't see them lying in shallow graves, he didn't

see them without their legs, begging on pram wheels. Just then he wouldn't even have felt sorry for them. He had lost the gift of second sight, and his empathy had run out. A baker's boy was eyeing the box office. The cashier sat in the box office like a waxwork figure in a hairdresser's window. The cashier smiled a stiff, sweet, waxwork smile and wore her permed wig thinly and stiffly. The baker's boy was wondering whether he could rob the cashier. His shirt was open to the navel, and his very short baker's pants barely covered his rump. His chest and his bare legs were dusted with flour. He didn't smoke. He didn't yawn. His eyes were alert. Keetenheuve thought: If I was one of the girls, I'd want to go down to the riverbank with you. Keetenheuve thought: If I was the cashier, I'd worry.

He met lonely people undertaking desperate strolls through town. What was on their minds? What were they going through? Were they frustrated? Were they looking for partners for the lusts that were fermenting inside them? They wouldn't find any partners. The partners were everywhere. They walked past one another, men and women, they soaked up images, and in their rented rooms and in their rented beds they would remember the street and they would pleasure themselves. A few wanted to get drunk. They wanted to talk. They looked longingly at the windows of pubs. But they didn't have any money. Their wages were portioned out; so much for rent, for laundry, a bit for food, some to support their families; they should be pleased to hang on to the job that supplied the money that needed to be portioned out. They stopped in front of the shop windows and they studied expensive cameras. They speculated over the merits of a Leica as against a Contax, and they couldn't even afford a kiddies' box

Keetenheuve went into the wine bar with wood-paneled walls. It was quiet and pleasant; only it was still hot in the bar, and he was sweating. An elderly man was sitting over his wine, and reading the paper. He was reading the editorial. The headline ran *Will the Chancellor Get His Way?* Keetenheuve had read the article; he knew that his name appeared in the editorial as a possible obstacle in the Chancellor's way. *Keetenheuve roadblock.* He ordered a wine from the Ahr, which was always good here. The old man, while informing himself of the prospects for the Chancellor, stroked an old dachshund that was sitting quietly beside him on the bench. The dachshund had a clever expression; it looked like a statesman. Keetenheuve thought: One day I'll be sitting like that, old and alone, looking to a dog for companionship. But there was still the question whether he would have even that: a dog, a glass of wine, and a bed somewhere in town.

A priest entered the wine bar. A girl accompanied the priest. The girl must have been twelve or so, and she was wearing red ankle socks. The priest was big and strong. He looked as though he was from the country, but his face was that of a scholar. It was a good face. The priest gave the wine list to the girl, and the girl shyly read out the names of the wines. The girl was afraid she would have to have lemonade; but the priest asked her if she wanted wine. He ordered an eighth for the girl, and a quarter for himself. The girl grasped the wineglass with both hands, and drank with careful little sips. The priest asked: "How is it?" The girl replied: "Goood!" Keetenheuve thought: You don't have to be shy, he's glad of your company. The priest took a newspaper out of his cassock. It was an Italian newspaper, a newspaper from the Vatican, it was the *Osservatore Romano*. The priest put on a pair of spectacles and read the editorial in the *Osservatore*. Keetenheuve thought: That newspaper's no worse than any other, it's probably even better. Keetenheuve thought: The article will be well written, they are humanists, they know how to think, they will be supporting a good cause with good arguments, but they will suppress the view that there are equally good arguments for supporting the opposite cause. Keetenheuve thought: There is no such thing as truth. He thought: There is belief. He wondered: Does the editor of the *Osservatore* believe what he prints in his paper? Is he a cleric? Has he taken orders? Does he live in the Vatican? Keetenheuve thought: That would be a nice life; evenings in the gardens, evenings strolling down by the Tiber. He saw himself as a priest in a cassock and a black hat with a red ribbon *Keetenheuve Monsignore. Little girls curtseying to him, and kissing his hand.* The priest asked the little girl: "Do you want some mineral water to go with your wine?" The little girl shook her head. She drank her wine undiluted, with appreciative little sips. The priest folded up his *Osservatore*. He took off his glasses. His eyes were clear. His face was calm. It wasn't an empty face. He enjoyed his wine, the way a wine grower might. The little girl's socks under the table were red. The old man stroked his clever dachshund. It was quiet and peaceful. The waitress was sitting quietly and peacefully at one of the tables. She was reading a magazine serialization of *I Was Stalin's Girlfriend*. Keetenheuve thought: Eternity. He thought: Fixity. He thought: Belief. He thought: This peace is deceptive. And he thought: The heat in here, the silence in here, it's a moment in eternity, and contained in this moment are we, the priest and his *Osservatore Romano,* the little girl with her red socks, the man and his dog, the waitress who's resting, Stalin and his unfaithful girlfriend, and me, the parliamentarian, the protean, weak and ailing, but at least still turbulent.

All of a sudden, everyone paid. The priest paid. The old man paid. Keetenheuve paid. The wine bar was suddenly empty. Where to? Where to? The old man and his dog were headed home. The priest walked the little girl back. Did the priest not have a home? Keetenheuve didn't know. Maybe the priest would go and see Korodin. Maybe he would go to a church, and spend the night in prayer. Maybe he had a beautiful home, a broad baroque bed with carved swans, old mirrors, an important collection of the seventeenth-century French, maybe he would go and browse in it a while, maybe he fell asleep on cool linen, and maybe little red socks twinkled through his dreams. Keetenheuve felt no craving to return home; his parliamentarian's apartment was a functional pied-à-terre, a doll's chamber of fear, where he felt one thing—that if he died there, no one would mourn. All day long, he'd been running scared of the dismal place.

The streets of the neighborhood were empty. The lights in the windows of the clothes shops burned to no purpose. Keetenheuve studied the lives of the shop window families. A radio station had been questing for the ideal family. Here they were. The clothes shop owner had had them for ages. A grinning father, a grinning mother, a grinning child stared delightedly at their price tags. They were happy because they were cheaply clothed. Keetenheuve thought: If the designer thought of putting the man in a uniform, how he would grin, how they would grin and admire him; they would admire him until the windows burst with the pressure of the explosions, until the wax melted down in the heat of the firestorm. And the lady in the next-door window, with a fashionable hairstyle, a lustful mouth, and a nice provocative thrusting belly, was pleased with her inexpensive dress. It was an ideal population standing there, ideal fathers, ideal housewives, ideal children, ideal mistresses, *Serial reportage* I Was Keetenheuve's Shop Window Dummy *Keetenheuve contemporary personality, Keetenheuve moral exemplum for magazine readers*, they grinned at Keetenheuve. They grinned encouragingly. They grinned: Go for it! They led a clean, cheap, ideal life. Even the provocatively thrusting belly of the fashionable doll, the little slut, was clean and cheap, it was synthetic: in her womb was the future. Keetenheuve could buy himself a doll family. An ideal wife. An ideal child. They could share his parliamentarian's doll's apartment with him. He could love them. He could put them in the cupboard when he didn't love them any more. He could buy them coffins, lay them out, and bury them.

The town had plenty to offer the lonely wanderer. It offered him cars, it offered him stoves, refrigerators, pots and pans, furniture, clocks, radios, all these objects were lying there in windows lit up as if for the personal benefit of Keetenheuve in a striking isolation, they were a devilish temptation, they were at present unreal cars, unreal stoves, pots and pans, or cupboards, they were magic charms or curses cast in the guise of utilitarian objects. A powerful magician had cast a spell, they were solidified air pressed into chance shapes, and the magician had enjoyed making ugly things as well, and now he was pleased that mankind desired these things and was prepared to work for them, to murder and steal and cheat for them; yes, mankind was prepared to kill itself if it couldn't meet the payments, honor the signature it had given the devil to acquire the magic goods. A shop with red light was pure black magic. A man stood in the window, cut open. Keetenheuve saw the heart, the lungs, the kidneys, the stomach; they were large as life, and clearly visible to him. The organs were connected to one another by glass tubes, by transparent laboratory snakes, and through these tubes flowed a pinky juice that the magic drink Sieglinde was supposed to keep flowing. The open man carried a skull with brushed teeth, and his right arm, which had been stripped of skin, exposing the strands of muscle and nerve, his right arm was raised in the fascist greeting, and Keetenheuve thought he could hear the "Heil Hitler" that this ghost had yelped out at him. The creature was without sex organs, it stood impotently among a store of hygiene goods, as they called themselves, and Keetenheuve took in rubber douches, contraceptive pills, all kinds of slimy pastes and sugared pills, there was a stork of artificial resin, and a luminous sign that read: *The best for your children.*

Keetenheuve thought: Don't take part, don't participate, don't sign on the dotted line, don't be a consumer or a subject. For a while in the quiet nocturnal streets of the capital, which was now reverting to small town, Keetenheuve dreamed his ancient dream of ataraxy. The dream gave him strength, as it gave everyone strength. His strides echoed. *Ascetic Keetenheuve. Keetenheuve disciple of Zen. Keetenheuve Buddhist. Keetenheuve the great freer from the shackles of self.* But the stimulation he felt stimulated his gastric juices, the spiritual swing to his step woke his appetite, the great freer from the shackles of self felt hunger, felt thirst, he wasn't in the mood for liberation, which would have to begin now, right away, immediately, if it was to succeed. His strides echoed. They made hollow sounds in the quiet street.

Keetenheuve went into the town's second wine bar. This wine bar wasn't so quiet, it wasn't so formal as the first one, there was no priest here, no little girl in red socks to gladden the eye, but the establishment was still open, they were still serving. The regulars at a couple of tables were engaged in debate. They were fat men and fat women; they had businesses here, they had a comfortable living, they had lit up their shop windows, they were in league with the devil. Keetenheuve ordered wine and cheese. He was pleased he had ordered cheese. The Buddhist didn't want any animal to be slaughtered for his sake. The slightly smelly cheese salved his conscience. It tasted good. On the wall were the dying words of the vintner to his sons: You know, you can make wine from grapes also. The wine Keetenheuve drank was good. And then the Salvation Army girls walked into the bar.

Only one of the girls was wearing the red-and-blue uniform and the bonnet of the soldiers of the Lord, and with the other, you couldn't tell if she belonged to the Salvation Army at all, or if she was a novice who didn't yet have a uniform, or if she had just come along by chance, freely from friendship, or against her will, forced by circumstances, under protest, or just out of mere curiosity. She was perhaps sixteen. She was wearing a crumpled dress made of a cheap synthetic, her young bosom pushed out the sleek fabric, and Keetenheuve was struck by the expression of astonishment in her face, a look of constant surprise, mixed with disappointment, regret, and rage. The girl wasn't strictly speaking beautiful, and she was small as well, but her freshness and her truculence made her pretty. She was like a young colt that had been yoked up, and was frightened and bucky.

Hesitantly, holding copies of the *War Cry* in her hand, she
followed in the wake of the uniformed girl, who might be
twenty-five, a pale and suffering face in whose taut pallid
expanse was an almost lipless mouth. Her hair, what
Keetenheuve could see of it under the bonnet, was cut short,
and if she took off the unflattering headgear, she would look
like a boy. Keetenheuve felt himself drawn to the pair.
Sensitive and open-minded Keetenheuve. The uniformed girl
held the collection tin out to the regulars' table, and the fat
business people pulled faces and pushed five-pfennig pieces
into the rusty slit. Their fat wives looked stupidly and arro-
gantly off into the middle distance; they pretended not to be
aware of the Salvation Army girl and the collection tin. The
girl took her can back, and her face expressed apathy and
contempt. The business people didn't look up at her face. It
never occurred to them that they might be despised; and the
Salvation Army creature didn't have to trouble to hide her
contempt. Then the guitar adorned with pious slogans jan-
gled against Keetenheuve's table, and the girl, contempt on
her face, held out the can to him—a grim and arrogant angel
of salvation. Keetenheuve wanted to talk to her, but shyness
prevented him, and he spoke to her only in his thoughts. He
said: Why don't you sing! Sing your hymn! And the girl replied
in Keetenheuve's imagination: This isn't the place! And
Keetenheuve in his imagination replied: Every place is the right
place to sing the Lord's praises. And he thought: You're a little
dyke, I've seen your like before, and you're terrified lest something you've stolen might be taken away from you. He put
five marks in the collecting can, and he felt ashamed
because he was putting five marks in the slit. It was too
much and too little. The little sixteen-year-old in mufti

watched Keetenheuve and watched him in astonishment. And then she pushed out the chapped lower lip of her curved and sensual mouth, and her face showed honest rage and indignation. Keetenheuve laughed, and the girl felt embarrassed and she blushed. Keetenheuve would have liked to ask the girls to sit down with him. He knew the other table would make a stir if he did; but he didn't care, yes, he would have welcomed it. But he was shy of the girls, and by the time he had got up his courage to ask them, the uniformed one was standing by the door, shouting to the little one, who hadn't taken her eyes off Keetenheuve, to get a move on. The girl trembled like a horse that hears the hated cry of the coachman and feels the tug on the reins; she turned away from Keetenheuve and cried back: "I'm coming, Gerda."

The girls left. The bell over the door rang. The door fell shut. The instant the door shut, Keetenheuve was back in London again. On the wall of an underground station, he saw a great map of the great city of London, with the sprawl of its suburbs into the countryside, and on the map there was a speck of fly dirt in London's docklands. That was where he was, Keetenheuve, at a tube station in the docks. The train that had ejected him had gone on its way; there was a roar and an icy blast in the tunnel. Keetenheuve stood on the platform and froze. It was Sunday afternoon. It was a Sunday afternoon in November. Keetenheuve was poor and alone and a stranger. Up on the street it was raining. It was a slant, lashing rain, coming out of low clouds, out of broody masses of fog that sat like heavy woolly hats on the roofs of the scabby, dirty houses and the tarred warehouses, sucking up the slothful, acrid smoke from the ancient crusty chimneys. The

smoke smelled of bogland, it smelled of peat fires in wet bogland. It was a familiar smell, it was the smell of Macbeth's
witches, and in the air was their cry, fair is foul, and foul is
fair! The witches had traveled into the city on the backs of the
fogs, they squatted down on roofs and gutters, they had a
rendezvous with the sea wind, they were touring London,
they pissed in the ancient precincts, and then they howled
lecherously as the storm buffeted them, as it hurled them
onto the bed of the clouds, shook them, and clasped
them wildly and lustfully. There was whistling and sighing in
every quarter. The beams of the warehouses creaked round
about, and the wind-skewed roofs groaned. Keetenheuve
stood in the street. He heard the witches cackle. The pubs
were shut. Men stood around idly. They listened to the witches. The warm pubs were shut. Women stood shivering in
alleyways. They listened to the witches' racket. The gin was
behind lock and key in the pubs. The randy witches laughed
and howled and pissed and copulated. The sky was full of
them. And then, out of the fog and the wet, out of the peat
smoke, and the gale and the witches' sabbath, came music,
came the Salvation Army people with their banners, with
their *War Cry*, with fifes and drums, with peaked caps and
bonnets, with speeches and hymns, trying to banish the
demons and to deny the insignificance of men. The Salvation
Army ranks formed into a spiral snail, formed a ring, and
there they stood and shouted, and tootled and drummed their
Praise the Lord, and the witches went on laughing, they split
their cloudy sides, they pissed, and they lay down on their
backs before the wind. The yellow gray black skies over the
dirty square in London's docklands looked like the swollen
lust-chafing thighs and bellies of pregnant witches. The cosy

little pubs were shut, and the gloomy homely dives. And even
if the pubs had been open, who would have had a shilling to
spend on the black, frothy, gluey beer? And so of a Sunday,
the men and women and the poor and also *Keetenheuve poor
immigrant* had nothing better to do than form up around the
Salvation Army people, and they listened to their music, and
they listened in silence to their singing, but they didn't listen
to the speeches, they heard the witches, they felt bony fingers
reaching for them, they felt the chill and the damp. And then
they went away, a hunched, freezing, sorry-looking procession, their arms folded, their hands in their pockets. Men and
women, *Keetenheuve immigrant SA marching along,* behind
the Salvation Army flag, to the beat of the Salvation Army
drum, and the witches laughed and ranted and the wind
rammed them hard, repeatedly, lovely sea wind from the
Arctic wastes, won't you warm up, won't you get a little excited, we are the witches from the heath, we've come to be at
the ball in good old London town . . . They came to a shelter
and there they were made to wait, because the Salvation
Army also wanted to remind them what poor people they
were, and poor people had to wait. And why shouldn't they
wait? There was nothing waiting for them. The shelter was
warm. Gas fires were burning. They hummed, their flames
glowed yellow and red and blue like flickering will-o'-the-
wisps and there was a sweetish smell in the room, like a dull
opiate. They sat down on wooden benches without arms or
backs, because for the poor such benches are good enough.
The poor are not allowed to be tired. The rich are permitted
to lean. Here there were only the poor. They propped their
elbows on their thighs and their chins on their hands, and
they leaned forward, because they were exhausted from

standing, from waiting, from feeling lost. The band played "O Come, All Ye Faithful," and a man they called the Colonel, and who looked like a colonel from the *"Daily Sketch" Colonel Keetenheuve at a game of cricket at Banquo Castle*, held the sermon. The Colonel had a wife (who didn't look anywhere near as posh as he did, with his picture in the *"Sketch,"* she looked just about fit to be his washerwoman, and scrub his underpants), and after the Colonel had spoken (What had he said? Keetenheuve had no idea, no one had any idea), the Colonel's wife called upon the people in the hall to proclaim how bad they all were. Now, there is a confessional side to many people, and also an inclination to masochism, and so a few stepped forward and owned up to thinking wicked thoughts they had never thought, all the while they anxiously tried not to tell about the serpents they carried in their bosom, the venomous creatures. Their evil deeds remained unconfessed. Perhaps it was advisable not to mention them here. There might be plainclothesmen in the hall. And what was an evil deed if you had to confess it here in public, and before God? To torture a dog is a wicked deed. To beat a child is a wicked deed. But was it wicked to want to rob a bank? Or was it wicked to plan to murder a powerful wicked and universally respected man? Who could tell? You needed a very alert conscience to discriminate. Did the Colonel of the Salvation Army have such a conscience? He didn't look the sort. His clipped mustache looked martial, more Army than Salvation. And if the Colonel had happened to have such a sensitive conscience, what good would it do him, because a sharp, fine, and well-developed conscience would be precisely the one that could never decide whether a bank robbery was an ethical or an unethical undertaking. Confession was

followed by tea. It was ladled out of a large steaming cauldron
into aluminum mugs. It was black and very sweet. You burnt
your lips on the hot rim of the aluminum, but the tea felt good
sliding across your tongue, and trickling warmly into your
belly. The gas flames buzzed, and their soft and lethal fumes
mingled with the sweet smell of the tea and the harsh whiff
of unwashed bodies, the pong of rain-soaked steaming
clothes, to make another kind of fog that reddened before
Keetenheuve's eyes and made him giddy. All longed to be outside, they longed for the tempest, they longed for the
witches—but the tempting pubs weren't yet open. In Bonn,
they wanted to close as well. The regulars got up to go from
their tables. The business people put on fake smiles, and
reached out their plump hands, they squeezed fat gold-
ringed fingers, each knew what the other was worth, they
knew one another's bank balances. Then they went to turn
out the lights in their shop windows. They took their clothes
off. They emptied their bladders. They crept into bed, the
fat businessman, the fat businessman's wife, the son will go
to college, the daughter will make a good marriage, the
woman yawns, the man farts. Good night! Good night!
Who's freezing out in the open?

Keetenheuve saw the lights going out in the windows.
Where would he go? He walked aimlessly. And in front of the
department store, he ran into the Salvation Army girls, and
this time he greeted them like old friends. Gerda gnawed her
thin bloodless lips. She was livid. How she hated men, the
unmerited gift of the penis had turned their heads. Gerda
would have run away, but she doubted whether Lena, the little sixteen-year-old, would have followed her, and so she had
to stay and suffer the proximity of the predatory man.

Keetenheuve walked up and down with Lena in front of the
shop windows, up and down in front of the darkened dolls'
rooms, and while Gerda looked on with pinched mouth and
burning eyes, he heard the refugee's story. Lena told it in a
gentle dialect that softly swallowed some of the syllables. She
came from Thuringia, and she was training to become a
mechanic. She claimed she had certificates as a mechanic,
and had already worked as a toolmaker. Her family had flown
to Berlin with Lena, and from there they had been flown into
the Federal Republic, and had lived in camps for a long time.
Lena the little mechanic wanted to end her apprenticeship,
and then she wanted to earn a lot of money as a toolmaker,
and then she wanted to study and become an engineer, as she
had been promised back East, but in the West everybody just
laughed at her, and said a workbench wasn't a place for girls,
and if you were poor you couldn't study. So some labor
exchange put Lena in a kitchen, put her in the kitchen of a
hotel, and Lena, the refugee from Thuringia, was set to rinse
plates, the fatty leftovers, the fatty sauces, the fatty skins of
sausages, the fatty trimmings of roast meat, and all that fat
nauseated her, she vomited into the vat of pale blubbery fat.
She ran out of the fatty kitchen. She ran onto the street. She
stood by the side of the road, and waved to cars, because she
wanted to reach her paradise, which was a shiny factory with
oiled workbenches and a well-paid eight-hour day. Lena was
picked up by traveling salesmen. Fatty hands groped her breasts.
Fatty hands reached up her skirts, and yanked at her knicker
elastic. Lena resisted. The traveling salesmen swore at her.
Lena tried truck drivers. The truck drivers laughed at the little mechanic. They reached up her skirts. When she yelled,
they shifted down into first, and threw her out of the cab. She

reached the Ruhr. She saw the chimneys. The blast furnaces were burning. The steel rolling mills were working. The forges were forging. But outside the factory gates sat the fat porters, and the fat porters laughed when Lena asked if they had a job for a trainee mechanic with lots of experience. At least the fat porters were much too fat to reach up the trainee mechanic's skirt. And so Lena had ended up in the capital. What do you do if you're homeless, where do you go if you're hungry? You go to the railway station, as if the trains would bring you a change of luck. Plenty of people approached Lena. One of them was Gerda. Lena followed Gerda, the Salvation Army girl, and she toured the town with the *War Cry* in her hand, and she was surprised by everything she saw. Keetenheuve thought: Gerda will touch your breasts as well. He thought: And so will I. He thought: It's your destiny. He thought: We're like that, it's our destiny. But he told her he would try to find a job for her at the end of her apprenticeship. Gerda's mouth opened angrily. She said plenty of people had offered that to Lena, and their promises hadn't been worth much. Keetenheuve thought: You're right, I want to see Lena again, I want to touch her, she's tempting, and particularly tempting to me; that's what it is. *Vicious Keetenheuve.* But he still resolved to take up Lena's case with Korodin, who had contacts with factories, and maybe with Knurrewahn or one of his party colleagues who was up on the labor exchange situation. He wanted to help her. The mechanic should be given her lathe. *Virtuous Keetenheuve.* He asked Lena to meet him at the wine bar the next evening. Gerda took Lena's hand. The girls disappeared into the night. Keetenheuve remained behind in the night.

Night. Night. Night. A bad moon. Summer lightning. Night.

Night. Nightlife. There were efforts to get something going in the station area. Lemurs. Lemurs in the bar staring at a scrawny ghost, trying to set a record for nonstop piano playing. The ghost was sitting at an old grand in sweaty socks, and, surrounded by brimming ashtrays and empty Coca-Cola bottles, hammered out tunes that you could hear from any loudspeaker. From time to time a waiter went up to the ghost and, with an apathetic expression, stuck a cigarette in his mouth, or poured Coca-Cola down his gullet. Then the ghost would nod like Death in the puppet theater—an expression of gratitude and solidarity. Night. Night. Lemurs. The Rhine valley express flashed past. Flashed on its way to Cologne. At the station in the Café Kranzler, fat men were sitting, singing: "I've got another suitcase in Berlin." They looked across at the fat women and sang: "I miss the old Kurfürstendamm," and the fat women thought: ministerial councillors, government councillors, embassy councillors, and they wiggled fattily in a Berlinerish fashion, pig's liver with apple and onions, and blew their noses Berlinerishly: "Come on, then, little fella, your hands on my flowerpots," and the agents, the travelers, the assistants, thought: Woman like a cloud, just like my old lady at home, phwoarh, thirty smackers, only my old lady will do it next Sunday for free, better get myself a magazine, else I'll forget what a woman looks like. "I'll pass." They played games of skat, and drank their wheat beer with shots out of long straight glasses. Night. Night. Lemurs. Frost-Forestier was going to bed. The Frost-Forestier industry was being put to bed. He exercised on the bars. He stood under the shower. He rubbed his fit, well-muscled body dry. He drank two gulps of cognac out of a brandy balloon. The great wireless was speaking news. All quiet in Moscow. Appeals to the Soviet people. The little wireless screamed: "Dora has diapers. Dora has diapers." On the table lay a photocopy of the interviews with the generals on the Conseil Supérieur des Forces Armées. Mergentheim's telephone number scribbled on the sheet. Also: Ask about Guatemala?? The black paper with the white writing looks like a corpus delicti. Frost-Forestier winds his alarm clock. It's set for half past five. Frost-Forestier's bed is narrow. It is hard. A thin blanket covers Frost-Forestier. Frost-Forestier opens a volume of the works of Frederick the Great. He reads Frederick's dodgy French. He examines an engraving, a picture of the King with the face of a greyhound. Frost-Forestier turns out the light. He falls asleep as on command. The other side of the curtains of generalissimo red, there's a screech owl in the park. Night. An owl screeching. It signifies death. *A dog has barked. Jewish joke. Signifies death. Keetenheuve superstitious.* Night. Night. Lemurs. On the first floor they were choosing the beauty queen of the night. Evening dresses like flapping washroom curtains. A professional Rhinelander, cheery chappie, stood by the mike and asked the ladies to step forward. Giggles. Embarrassed looks at the oiled floor. The professional Rhinelander, cheery chappie, cheeky chappie, gets his way. *Keetenheuve whip in the lower house.* The professional Rhinelander, cheery chappie, cheeky chappie, wending his way among the tables, champagne tables, more-wine-tables, champagne and wine salesmen, took the ladies by the hand, led them on to the smooth parquet of judgment, presented them, exposed them, offered them up, derailed housewives, aborted mothers, robes out of the Domestic Advice Bulletin *classical and plain*, what do I do about semen stains, can you tell me some slimming recipes, Frau Christine always offers the most asinine advice, stiff, awkward, limitlessly conceited movements. Keetenheuve stood in the doorway, *Keetenheuve had customer, bottle baby, won't buy his round, sucks on his pacifier*, he thought of parliament, the second reading of the bill, no bill for beauty contests, Mr. Speaker, Ladies and Gentlemen, a decision of immeasurable consequence, we vote in division, I jump through the wrong door, annoy the party, this here is a mutton jump, little sheep to the right, little sheep to the left, the professional Rhinelander, cheery chappie, cheeky chappie, hup two three, hup two three!, waits for the bill to pass into law. Keetenheuve thought: What are you playing at, you'll offend them all mightily, not one of these geese is worth plucking, but every one of them imagines she's beautiful, thinks she's irresistible, even her stupidity is no match for her vanity, they'll be offended. But the professional Rhinelander, hup two three!, cheeky and cheery, wasn't one to be troubled by such concerns. He chirpily persevered with the work now begun. He gave numbers to his golden gaggle, asked the honored guests, asked the wine buyers, asked the bucks wanting fucks to write down the number of their preference, of their queen, on one of the ballot papers distributed throughout the room. But there wasn't a beauty in the room. They were all charmless. All ugly. They were the ugly daughters of the Rhine. Wagalaweia, dimwits, rejects. Take another look! There was one animally attractive specimen. Meat market. A pink raven. Keetenheuve chose her. *Keetenheuve discharges democratic duty. Good citizen Keetenheuve.* She had curved sensuous lips, cow's eyes, unfortunately, Europa *Keetenheuve Jupiter*, a round bust, trim hips, slim legs, and the notion of taking her to bed was not disagreeable. The night is warm. Van de Velde's complete marriage. Darling, what position would you like me to adopt for you? *Keetenheuve Van-de-Velde-husband.* He was curious. What were the odds? Was his favorite in the running? Only one vote for the animally attractive one! She was the last of the bunch. A beanpole with pompadour hair and goose features was chosen; selling point "decent girl with good dowry." Attractiveness not in demand. Bedroom lights dimmed. All cats gray. Fanfare, drumroll, from the band. The professional Rhinelander, cheery chappie, cheeky chappie, presents boxes of sticky candy. Gracious smile from the winner. *Sweet lady, hear my song. Keetenheuve chanteur on the skids.* The wine buyers applauded and ordered up another bottle; excited bucks wanting fucks. Enterprising reps sought. Diligent workers. Did Keetenheuve work diligently? *Will Keetenheuve learn? No, he will not learn. Is he condemned? Yes, he is condemned. All those in favor? All those not in favor?* Night night. Lemurs. A better sort of place, a more distinguished location. François-Poncet hadn't turned up. Was in Paris, in his academician's tails. Palm-embroidered. Was working on a dictionary. Sat in Pétain's chair. She couldn't remember whose arm was embracing her, but it was a socially respectable arm, and the head that went with the arm belonged to a whiskey advertisement, King Simpson Old Kentucky Home American Blend, that inspired trust, and she danced under the summer lightning on a terrace by the Rhine, Sophie Mergentheim from the circulation department of the old *Volksblatt* in Berlin. Rooms in Berlin, rooms over the courtyard at the back, lightless rooms, expropriated, imprisoned, burned, destroyed, she was part of the whipped froth on the pudding, the crème de la crème, reddish sponge base, golden froth, caramelized, egg yolks rubbed in her blond hair. Mergentheim was telephoning. The host discreetly left

the room. Diplomat. What's he doing? Eavesdropping discreetly. Tapping into the line. Mergentheim was calling the
editor. He was making sure. They were running the article.
Copies had reached the station in time. Mergentheim was
sweating in his tails. He thought: He's my enemy, a man with
those views is bound to be my enemy. Night. Night. Lemurs.
Keetenheuve descended into the basement. "Bei mir biste
scheen"*—that's what they were playing in the basement.
"Bei mir biste de scheenste auf der Welt"—this was catacomb
air, but not the catacombs under the cathedral, not Korodin's
burial site going back to Frankish-Roman times, this was
Keetenheuve's nightspot from the period of the Western
alliance, there wasn't any smell of mold or incense for that
matter, there was a powerful smell of cigarette smoke, of
schnapps, of girls and men, people were dancing a mixture of
boogie-woogie and Rhinelanders, and energetically in both
cases, this was a place for young people who didn't wear caps
and didn't need sabers to get in touch with themselves, this
was an *echt* catacomb, a place of concealment underground,
a gathering place for youthful opposition to the old beds of
the town, but the young opposition was gurgling away like
ground water, it made a splash for one night in the fountain,
and then it dribbled away in lecture halls, in seminars for
grinds, on office chairs and at the lab assistant's workplace.
"We're All Going up to Heaven," played the student band.
Keetenheuve stood by the bar. He drank three shots of
schnapps. He drank them one after the other, knocking them
back. He felt old. He wouldn't get to heaven. The young people were spinning and whirling around him. A steaming bub-

*"Bei mir bist du scheen," the number by the Andrews Sisters, from 1937.

bling yeasty ferment. Bare arms, bare legs. Open shirts. Bare
faces. They mingled. They blurred. They sang: "Because we're
so good, because we're so good." Keetenheuve thought: You're so
good, you'll lie down in the despised beds of your parents, you
won't make yourselves any new beds of your own, but maybe
by that time the old beds will be burning, maybe you'll be burning as well, maybe you'll be in the ground. There was a throng
around the bar, but it didn't concern him. They didn't touch
him. He stood off on his own. Elke would have been a link con-
necting Keetenheuve to the young world. So he didn't venture
to ask them to have a drink with him. Neither boy nor girl did
he venture to ask to have a drink with him. *Keetenheuve the
stone guest.* He took himself off. *Little Keetenheuve doesn't play
nicely with others.* Night. Night. Lemurs. Korodin was praying.
He was praying in an attic. The room was unfurnished, but
for a hassock in front of a crucifix, which was hanging sober-
ly on a whitewashed wall. Korodin was kneeling on the hassock. A candle was burning. Flickering. The attic window was
open. The summer lightning had moved nearer, and its flash-
es lit up the room. Korodin feared the heavenly fire, and in
not closing the window, he was mortifying himself. He
prayed: I know I am evil; I know my life is not righteous; I
know I ought to give everything to the poor; but I know too
that to do so would be pointless; no poor man would become
rich, no man would be made better by it. Lord, punish me if
I'm mistaken! The crucifix, carved by a master out of rose-
wood, looked in the light of the storm to be doubled over in
pain, sick, suffering, rotting. It was an image of torment. The
torment remained silent. It gave Korodin no reply. Korodin
thought: I ought to go. I ought to give everything away. It's all
wrong. It's just a distraction. It's just in the way. I should just

go. Go and keep going. Don't know where. I have nowhere to
go—and he guessed that it was important not to have anywhere to go. The lack of destination was the real destination.
But he feared the lightning. He feared the onset of the rain.
He continued to pray. Christ remained mute. Night. Night.
Lemurs. Drunks shouting around the station. They shouted:
"Infantry!" And they were gone. They shouted: "Give us back
our Kaiser Bill!" And they were gone. Boys lurked in doorways, selling themselves. Gone. At the station, haggard pleasure mares ready for the knackers were waiting for a rider.
Gone. Thunder and lightning. The rain came down.
Keetenheuve stopped a taxi. He had no option. Time to go
home. Home to his doll's apartment. Home to the ghetto.
Home to the government ghetto, the parliamentarians' ghetto, the ghetto of journos, of officials and secretaries. Thunder
and lightning. He opened the French window that went—not
very far—from the floor to the low ceiling. The narrow foldaway bed was down, as he'd left it. Unmade. Open books lay
around. Papers. The desk was covered with papers, drafts,
sketches, half-written speeches, abandoned letters. Keetenheuve's life was a draft. It was a draft for a real life; but
Keetenheuve could no longer imagine real life. He couldn't
remember what it looked like; and he was certain he would
no longer live it. Among the papers was a letter from Elke.
Her last letter. Elke had been his chance, his one chance
at another life. Maybe. He had lost that chance. Gone.
Lightning. Lightning over a grave. He saw the weepy immor-
telles of the graveyard in the pale flicker of the lightning. He
breathed in the smell of moldy, damp yew hedges, the sweet
corruption of rotting roses in funereal wreaths. The graveyard
wall seemed to flinch in the lightning. Fear and trembling.

Kierkegaard. Nursemaid consolation for intellectuals. Silence. Night. *Keetenheuve timid night bird Keetenheuve night owl at the end of its tether Keetenheuve pathetic wanderer down cemetery avenues, ambassador to Guatemala lemurs accompany him*

5

HE AWOKE. HE WOKE EARLY. HE WOKE FROM UNQUIET sleep. He woke from unquiet sleep in the ghetto.

Every ghetto was surrounded by invisible walls and was at the same time open and exposed to view from outside. Keetenheuve thought: The ghettos of Hitler and Himmler, the ghettos of the transports and the victims, the walls and perimeters, the incinerator ovens of Treblinka, the uprising of the Jews in Warsaw, all the camps after the war, all the barracks that housed us, all the Nissen huts, the bunkers, the DPs and the refugees—the government, the parliament, officialdom and underlings, and now we are a foreign body in the sluggish flesh of our capital city.

What he could see were the four walls, the ceiling, door, and window of the tiny room, what he could see—curtains open, blinds up—were the façades of the other houses in the ghetto, jerry-built, flat-roofed, big-windowed, steel-framed tenements. They were a version of the tent towns of traveling circuses and freak shows; run up to be taken down. A secretary was taking a bath. He could hear the water flowing through pipes in the walls. The secretary washed thoroughly, soaped herself, rinsed herself, office dirt was dissolved, flowed down her breasts, sagging, unfortunately, flowed down her belly and thighs, spilled down the drain, tumbled into the underworld, entered the sewage system, the Rhine, the sea. The flushes of the toilets jerked and gushed. The parting of the ways for human and human waste. A loudspeaker wheezed: "One, two, three, and left, one, two, three, and right." A moron was exercising. He was skipping, you could hear it, a heavy body, naked, slap of bare soles on the boards. That was Sedesaum, the human frog. From a second loudspeaker shrilled a choir of children: "Let us sing and jump and shout." The voices of the children sounded drilled, they were bored, the singing was stupid. Frau Pierhelm the MP was listening to the children. Frau Pierhelm lived out of cans. She fixed herself a coffee out of the Nescan, poured a dribble of condensed milk into it, and waited for the radio program *We housewives and the Security Pact*. Frau Pierhelm had recorded the program in Cologne some two weeks previously.

Keetenheuve lay on his narrow foldaway bed. He stared up at the bed frame, a shelf covered with books, and he stared past it at the low ceiling, where cracks in barely dry plaster had run together into curving lines, a tangled web of roads, the general staff map of some unknown country. Now Frau Pierhelm was to be heard on the wireless: "We housewives must not, we housewives must, we housewives put our trust." What must Frau Pierhelm not, what must she, where did she put her trust? A fine dusting from the general staff map. The opening of a new front. Frau Pierhelm from Cologne exclaimed: "I believe! I believe!" Frau Pierhelm on the airwaves believed. Frau Pierhelm, the other side of the wall from Keetenheuve in the ghetto building, Frau Pierhelm, her cup full of the mix of Nescafe and condensed milk, in front of her an ashtray with her morning cigarette, Frau Pierhelm the honorable member, an ostrich, head buried in her chest of drawers, hunting for clean linen, who washed your clothes while you were securing the future of your country, Frau Pierhelm the politician was listening with satisfaction to Frau Pierhelm the orator, as she reached the conclusion that the pact gave security to German women, a ringing conclusion, if a little reminiscent of a recent advertisement for tampons.

It was still early. Keetenheuve was an early riser, as almost everyone in Bonn was a morning person. The Chancellor was preparing himself for the plenary session, rose-scented and fortified by the Rhine air, which sapped his opponents, and Frost-Forestier would long since have started up his powerful juddering machine. Keetenheuve thought: Will he venture something else, will he have a fresh offer for me today, Cape Town or Tokyo? But he knew Frost-Forestier wouldn't offer him another embassy, and, come evening, the knives would be out for him.

Keetenheuve was calm. His heart was beating calmly. He felt a little sorry to be missing out on Guatemala. He thought regretfully of passing up his death on the Spanish colonial veranda. Guatemala had been tempting. He hadn't fallen for it. He had made a decision. He was going to fight. The wirelesses were silent. All that could be heard was the morning song of the capital in summer: the clatter of lawn mowers, like ancient sewing machines, that were being dragged over the grass.

Sedesaum the human frog hopped downstairs. With every smacking step, the flimsy building shook. Sedesaum was a professional Christian, God help him, and since there wasn't a chapel anywhere nearabouts, he took his morning hop to the little dairy, to do a work of humility and publicity, and the Sunday color supplements had already featured the populist representative of the people *your concerns are my concerns* with milk bottle and bag of rolls in his arms, and besides, what he was doing there was an act of tolerance, the Samaritan was supporting his fallen brother, and they would give him extra credit for that in heaven. Sedesaum bought his breakfast at Dörflich's. Far and wide, Dörflich's was the only shop, which gave him a monopoly, you had no option but to take him your custom, but unfortunately Dörflich was a pain, he was the equivalent of a lapsed priest, he was a member of parliament who had been expelled from the orders of his party, but remained a consecrated parliamentarian. He had gotten tangled up in a disreputable and initially remunerative affair, which unfortunately the press had gotten wind of, and which then, stirred by denials and statements of support, had become impossible to hush up, and had ceased to be profitable; Dörflich was made a scapegoat and banished from his party into the wilderness, where, to the horror of all his colleagues in the parliamentary ghetto, he opened his little dairy business. Whether Dörflich hoped to wash himself whiter than white with his milk, speculating that his customers would give him their votes, or whether he was merely laundering the profits from his disreputable affair; whichever, "non olet," the only thing that perceptibly stank at Dörflich's was the cheese, though Keetenheuve thought he sometimes caught a whiff of carrion in Dörflich's vicinity, which wasn't from the cheese cloche. Actually, Keetenheuve thought it was sensible on the part of Dörflich to diversify away from the uncertain prospects of reelection, and into the milk trade. He didn't share the outrage of their parliamentary colleagues, and he went so far as to think: Each of us should have his own milk shop, so we're not left clinging to the raft of our perished ideas. And so it amused Keetenheuve to watch from the window of the ghetto block, as Dörflich brought in his wares out of the back of his parliamentarian's car, and Keetenheuve didn't mind that the Catholic and now whipless representative of the people was probably using the federal purse to pay for his transport overheads. But, his possibly immoral amusement aside, Keetenheuve did not like Dörflich, and Dörflich for his part loathed *Keetenheuve the intellectual scumbag.* And so Keetenheuve, when he went to Dörflich's once to try the milk, was duly served some that was off, and Keetenheuve thought: Well, who knows, who knows, maybe we'll see each other in the Fourth Reich, Dörflich's ministerial chair will already be parked in among his milk churns, and my death sentence will have been written.

Keetenheuve looked out of the window, and he saw the scene like a snapshot, like an interesting setup in a film, a piece of lawn was in shot, and on the fresh green carpet a girl in a starched white apron, and a white maid's bonnet (a maid of the kind that no longer existed, and that had suddenly reappeared in Bonn like a rash of ghosts), was pushing against a clattering lawn mower, then pan down the cool steel, glass, and concrete façade of the ghetto block facing Keetenheuve, to Dörflich's milk shop, and there was Sedesaum, bottle of milk and bag of rolls clasped in his little round arms, hopping out of the shadow of the blue- and white-striped awning,

small, vain, and humble, small, devout, and cunning, and just
like that, with the milk and the rolls transferred to his little
round belly, small, humble, and vain, small, cunning, and
devout, he would hop into the plenary session, a yea-sayer, a
singer unto the Lord, and the Lord didn't in fact have to live
over the tented starry sky as the Lord God of Sabaoth,
Sedesaum always found a way of squaring his earthly and his
heavenly duties, so that they harmonized in his conscience
and to the world, and there, as he hopped across the yard, his
right foot smacking down with vanity, his left foot smacking
down with humility, there came after him Dörflich, emerging
from the shadow of his awning, having left his milk business
in the hands of his lawfully wedded wife, and, in his blue suit
and the laundered shirt of old-fashioned respectability, he
seated himself at the wheel of his official parliamentarian's
car—now cleared of milk churns and bread baskets—to drive
to parliament and exercise the people's mandate. The sight
made Keetenheuve a little uneasy. He could not predict
which way Dörflich would vote. He liked to side with the
majority, but since he'd had the whip withdrawn, he had
taken to grandstanding, he sought support among the country's malcontents, he cast his line in murky waters, and so it
was to be feared that this time, albeit for selfish and dodgy
motives, he would vote with the opposition. Keetenheuve was
ashamed to have such an ally, stinking of old Nazism and
aspiring toward a new Nazism (that wind was yet to rise), as
he was irked and troubled and made to doubt by the chance
coalitions that arose, by siding with the obstinate, the offended, the dictatorial, the at best mediocre, whom some schis-
matic whim had managed to antagonize. Not until he saw
Frau Pierhelm and Sedesaum leaving the building together—

he hopping, she head aloft, determination in her stride—poor knights of the old union of the firm hand, camp followers of conservatism and the Montan-Union (not that they were on the board, but it hadn't escaped them where profits were made, where the little spring sprang, where it dribbled into the electoral potty, not that they had sold themselves, heavens no, the policy was their policy, it was what they had been taught at school, and they had never seen the need to rethink it since, children in the political kindergarten, avid for the teacher's Good morning, Class), did Keetenheuve once more feel justified in opposing them, and setting them, bellwethers in the slaughterhouse, gadflies in their fleeces. But the lead sheep, it's why he is a bellwether, goes unwaveringly on its way, and the herd, as is in its nature, follows, warning cries only serve to accelerate its progress into catastrophe, as each follows the animal in front. The shepherd, meanwhile, has his own ideas about the destination of the sheep. He leaves the slaughterhouse alive, and dictates from that bloody site his *Memoirs of a Shepherd,* for the enlightenment and edification of his fellow shepherds.

That day, the parliament was sealed off by police, and the unit showed the hysterical zeal of any trained organization that has been drilled to see ghosts on the exercise ground, and they held the house of the people occupied and surrounded with weapons and water cannons and Spanish cavalry, as if the capital and the country were mounting an uprising against the Bundestag (and that would have been the end of it), whereas Keetenheuve, who kept having to identify himself to the officials, had the impression that, apart from sightseers and onlookers, only a few inexpensively procured individuals, a few people bussed in on the cheap, a few pathetic claqueurs were demonstrating with their cries, and only gained any significance by the massive presence of the police that had been ranged against them. They shouted that they wanted to talk to their representatives, and Keetenheuve thought: They have every right to do so, why shouldn't they be allowed to talk to their representatives? He would have been prepared to talk to them; but it was questionable whether they had him in mind, whether they wanted to talk to him. *Keetenheuve man of the people no man of the people.* The rather scanty demonstration was finally rather sad, because it demonstrated the dull submissiveness of the people, which came out of a feeling that everything will come to pass anyway, we can't make any difference, because it couldn't hinder laws and decisions that it probably opposed, didn't even try to, but was prepared to bear the consequences of them;—the die had been cast once more. So the scene in front of the parliament was not unlike the scene at a film premiere, a crowd, not too large, of stupid and curious people, who had nothing better to do than collect outside the cinema, to wait for the familiar faces of stars. There's a whisper, here comes Albers, and a critic who's seen the film is tempted to agree with the urchins who are whistling; but the scalliwags aren't tooting because they think it's a rotten film, they're whistling because they like to make a noise, and the negative opinion of the critic would only mystify and perhaps even enrage them. Keetenheuve knew, as he approached the parliament, how tangled and doubtful his mission was. But where was the system that was preferable to parliamentary democracy? Keetenheuve saw no other way; and the shouters who wanted to abolish the parliament were his enemies too. *Shut the talking shop. A lieutenant and ten men are enough. And the*

Captain of Köpenick. That was why Keetenheuve felt ashamed of the spectacle in front of him. The President of the Bundestag had policemen protect his building, whereas any parliament worth its salt should be at pains to keep the armed organs of the executive as far away from itself as possible, and in the good old days of the parliamentary idea, the delegates would have refused to meet under police protection, because back then, whatever its composition, the parliament was opposed to the police, because what it represented was opposition, opposition to the power of the crown, opposition to the tyranny of the nobility, opposition to the government, opposition to the executive and its saber, and so it was a perversion and an enfeeblement of the representation of the people when from out of its midst a majority constitutes itself as a government, and claims full executive powers. What does this amount to, given a worst case, but an elective dictatorship?* The majority won't actually chop the heads off their opponents; but it remains a petty tyrant, and for as long as it's in power, the minority is routed, and condemned to pointless sterile opposition. The fronts were rigid, and unfortunately it was inconceivable that someone could get up from the benches of the minority in opposition and convince the ruling majority that he was right and they were wrong. Not even a Demosthenes could succeed in changing the policy of the government in Bonn from the opposition benches; even if one spoke with angels' tongues, one would be preaching to deaf ears, and Keetenheuve knew, as he passed the last barrier, that it was

---

*These very words were used in admonishment in England in the 1980s, by John Biffen, a former cabinet minister of Margaret Thatcher's.

actually futile to come here and talk in the debate. It would affect nothing. He could as well have stayed in bed and dreamed. And so the delegate approached the headquarters of his party in a frame of mind not of exaltation but of dejection: *Napoleon on the morning of the battle knowing how Waterloo will end*

In the party rooms, they were waiting for him; Heineweg and Bierbohm and the other committee room veterans, the procedural lynxes, the order paper demons, were once again casting reproachful looks in Keetenheuve's direction. Knurrewahn was inspecting the troops, and lo, not one sage head was missing. They had traveled up from the provinces to be there for the debate, the frowsty air of the provinces clung to their garments, they brought it with them into the chamber, a dull air from tiny rooms, where they seemed to lead isolated lives, because they too did not directly represent the people, no longer thought like the people, they too were— albeit small, very small—preceptors of the people, not exactly professors perhaps, but at least monitors, persons of respect or disrespect, in front of whom the people stayed mum. And they in their turn, the troops, they stayed mum in front of Knurrewahn, who occasionally felt that something was not quite right. He surveyed his taciturn lifeguard, roundheads and longheads, stout fellows on whom he could depend. They had remained loyal from the time they were persecuted, but to a man they were used to orders, a team that stood to attention in front of their sergeant, and Knurrewahn, in command, man of the people, of course, but now promoted to the circle of the gods, close to government and influential, Knurrewahn listened in vain for a yearning word from below, a cry of freedom, a heartbeat that came from the depths; no unused strength, barely able to be reined in, now stirred, no primordial desire for change, no courage to destroy the old order could be perceived, his messengers brought no echo from the streets and squares, the factories and workshops; on the contrary, it was they who were taking instruction, who were waiting for a word from on high, a nod, a command from Knurrewahn, they supported the centralized party bureaucracy, were, in fact, nothing other than the outer limits of that bureaucracy, and that was the root of the evil, they would travel back to their places in the provinces and make it known there that Knurrewahn wants us to behave in such and such a way, Knurrewahn and the party desire, Knurrewahn and the party instruct, instead of the other way around, instead of the provincial messengers coming to Knurrewahn and saying the people want, the people oppose, the people command you, Knurrewahn, the people expect you, Knurrewahn—nothing. Maybe the people knew what they wanted. But their representatives did not know, and so they pretended that at least there was a strong and clear party line. But where did that come from? From headquarters. It was impotent. The party's will was cut off from the seminal threads of popular feeling, the strands of power got lost in the invisible, and the result was stray emissions and fertilizations in the bed of the people. The party leadership knew its membership only as those who paid the annual subscription and, more rarely, as the ones to whom it issued its commands. That way, the machine worked without a hitch. And if Knurrewahn had decreed the dissolution of the party, the local groups would put it into effect, if Knurrewahn ordered the party to commit euthanasia in the national interest—well, the party had had a national heart complaint since 1914. Not many ever broke ranks (and thereby incurred suspicion). There was Maurice, the lawyer, and there was Pius König, the journalist, Knurrewahn needed them, but actually they made difficulties for him, and he found Keetenheuve a real handful. He took Keetenheuve by the arm, led him over to a window, and begged him not to become too vehement in the forthcoming debate, not to offend nationalist instincts (Did such exist? Were they anything more than complexes, neuroses, idiosyncrasies?), and he reminded him that the party was not principally and unconditionally opposed to rearmament in any shape or form, and that all it was opposed to was the form of rearmament being mooted just now. Keetenheuve had heard it all before. It made him sad. He was on his own. He was fighting death on his own. He was all alone in the fight against the oldest sin, the oldest shortcoming of mankind, the original folly, the original dementia, that a just cause could be advanced by the sword, that violence could improve anything. Pandora's box is a standard metaphor for the evil of female curiosity, but Keetenheuve would have liked to tell old Knurrewahn about a box belonging to Mars, which, once opened, disgorged all the conceivable ills of the world, far and wide, all-destroying and irresistible. Knurrewahn knew it too, he was aware of the dangers, but he was of the opinion (with the bullet lodged in his heart, he suffered particularly badly from the heart defect of his party) that he could keep the army in the control of a democratically accountable government, even though Noske* had once already lost his democratic grip on the army.

*Gustave Noske (1868–1946), SPD politician and minister of war in the first years of the Weimar Republic.

Keetenheuve was called to the telephone, he went into a cabin, and he heard the twittering of the busy deputies of Frost-Forestier, and then it was Frost-Forestier in person who murmured out of the earpiece to assure Keetenheuve that Guatemala would be okayed, that had been cleared, whatever happened; and Keetenheuve, admittedly slightly puzzled, had the distinct sense that it was Mephisto at the end of the line, even if he was now unmasked as a member of the conspiracy. He wanted a moment to get his thoughts together, to reconsider everything once more, and he had a long way to think, he had to think as far as the Saar and the Oder, he had to remember Paris, and Grünberg in Silesia and Ortelsburg in Masuria, he had to bear in mind America and Russia, the two identical/unidentical twins, Korea, China, and Japan, Persia and Israel and the Moslem states had to be included in his thoughts, and maybe India would be the Orient land from which salvation would arrive, the third force, balancing and conciliatory, and how tiny was the Fatherland in which he lived, and the tiny rostrum at which he would speak, while supersonic jets raced from one continent to another, atomic shells flew over the deserts to practice for the *panthanatos,* the universal dying, and death mushrooms, ripened in the most delicate brains, now flowered over tropical atolls. But then Maurice, the lawyer, went up to Keetenheuve and handed him a copy of Mergentheim's newspaper, saying, faithfully and lawyerishly, that surely there was some material there for Keetenheuve's speech. Keetenheuve held Mergentheim's newspaper in his hand, and indeed, he saw he had to remake his speech. He saw that his weapon had been twisted from his grasp, his explosive was damp. In a long article, Mergentheim presented a report on the interview with the generals on the

Conseil Supérieur des Forces Armées, to which, plucky scribe, plucky Goal Attack, he added a commentary to the effect that with generals tainted to that degree with triumphalism, it wouldn't be possible to set up a German-Allied army. Yes, Keetenheuve's powder was damp! They had got their hands on the press release that Dana had given him, and seeing as there'd only been one single copy of that rather obscure agency report here in Bonn, they must have helped themselves to his, the shadow of course, they had photographed it, and so beaten him to the punch, and so Frost-Forestier's call about the Spanish colonial death veranda in Guatemala was nothing more than the friendly scrap that was tossed to the toothless mutt. What had happened was clear to Keetenheuve, what would happen next almost as much. The Chancellor, probably not even party to the intrigue and briefly angry with Mergentheim, would react furiously to the article, he would have in his hands the assurances of the French and British governments that the generals' remarks were regrettable and unauthorized and taken out of context, and that the proposed military pact remained on course as a firm long-term policy objective.

The bell rang for the session. They streamed into the plenary, sheep on the left and sheep on the right, and the black sheep sat on the far left and the far right, but they felt no shame, they bleated noisily. Keetenheuve couldn't see the Rhine from his place. But he pictured its flow to himself, he knew it was just the other side of the large schoolroom window, and he thought of it as conjoining not sundering, he saw the water curling around the countries like a friendly arm, and the Wagalaweia sounded soothing, a lullaby, a peaceful berceuse.

The President was a heavyweight, and seeing as he belonged to the party of the just cause, he threw his weight on the scales. His little bell rang. The session was declared open.

There's tension over the stadium in Cologne. The 1st FC Kaiserslautern is playing the 1st FC Cologne. It's not important who wins, but twenty thousand spectators are on the edge of their seats. There's tension over the stadium in Dortmund. Borussia Dortmund is playing Hamburg SV. The result is a matter of sublime indifference; no one will starve if Hamburg come out on top, no one will die in agony if Borussia happen to score more goals; but twenty thousand spectators are trembling. The showdown in the plenary session affects everyone's lives, can mean everyone's death, it can bring this unfreedom and that slavery with it, it could mean your house falling down, your son losing his legs, your father being sent to Siberia, your daughter giving herself to three men for a tin of corned beef, that she'll share with you, you wolf it down, you pick up the stubs that someone else has spat into the gutter, or you make a fortune on rearmament, you grow fat from equipping death (How many pairs of underpants does an army require? If you set the profit at forty percent, you're being modest), and the bombs, the bullets, crippledom, death, exile will only catch up with you in Madrid, you've driven there in your new motor, had one last meal at Horcher's, joined the line in front of the American consulate, maybe you'll get to Lisbon, where the ships are at anchor, but the ships won't take you, the planes will lift over the Atlantic without you, is it worth it? No, that's not being too lurid; but there's no trembling expectation in the chamber, no thousands of rapt onlookers. Justifiedly, boredom spreads. The few handpicked spectators are disappointed by the game. The journalists doodle on their pads; they'll be fed excerpts from the speeches, and the result of the vote is a foregone conclusion anyway. The form of the two teams is well known, and no one is putting anything on the underdog. Keetenheuve thought: Why go to so much trouble, we could get the miserable final score in five minutes and no need for any speeches, the Chancellor wouldn't have to get to his feet, we could spare ourselves our arguments, and they could spare themselves their defense. Our heavyweight President would only have to say he thought the game would end eight to six, and if anyone disagreed, they could always count the sheep for themselves. There was the door for the jump. There were the girls with their trays of votes. Oh, and there was one representative of the people stifling a yawn. Oh, and there was another nodding off. Oh, and there was a third writing a letter home: Don't forget to call Unhold to come and look at the flush on the toilet, it's been dripping of late.

Heineweg raised a point of order. There was a vicious, hairsplitting debate on it, before, as might have been predicted, it was voted down.

On the platform, the newsreel lights went up, the camera tele-lenses pointed at the big star of the house, now climbing onto the rostrum in casual, practiced fashion. The Chancellor set out his policy. He was in a rather listless mood, and there were no fireworks. He wasn't a dictator, but he was the boss who had set everything in motion, taken all the steps, and he despised the rhetorical drama in which he was obliged to participate. He sounded tired and confident, like an actor having to do a run-through of an often performed play in the repertoire, because of changes to the cast. The actor/Chancellor was also the director of the piece. He told the other actors where to stand. He was a commanding figure. Keetenheuve thought of him as a cold and gifted arithmetician, who, unexpectedly, after years of irritable retirement, had been given the chance to enter the history books as a great man, the savior of his Fatherland, but Keetenheuve also admired the performance, the implacable and euphoric tenacity with which an old man stuck to his guns. Didn't he see that his entire plan would come to grief, not through his opponents, but through his supporters? Keetenheuve accepted that the Chancellor was acting in good faith. It truly was his view of the world that he was unfolding, it was a world that was burning, and he was calling for fire brigades, and establishing fire brigades to control and fight the blaze. But the Chancellor, thought Keetenheuve, was losing track of the situation, he suffered, thought Keetenheuve, from a characteristically German rigidity of outlook, and thereby he failed to notice, thought Keetenheuve, that other statesmen in other parts of the world also thought the world was ablaze, and that they too had called in their fire brigades and had equipped teams of men to go out and fight the fire. So that there was now the prospect of the variously instructed firemen getting in each other's way as they went about their tasks and, ultimately, of coming to blows. Keetenheuve thought: Let's not set up any more global fire brigades, let's all just say "the world isn't burning," and let's come together and tell each other about our nightmares, let's admit that we're given to seeing conflagrations, and we will learn from the fears of the others that our own fears are delusory, and we will have better dreams in the future. He wanted to dream of a paradise of earthly contentment, a world of abundance, a planet where toil was no longer necessary, a utopia without war and without want, and for a time, he forgot that this world too had been cast out of heaven, condemned to whirl ignorantly and mutely through black space, where behind the twinkling familiar stars there might be great monsters.

No one but Korodin seemed to be paying any attention to the Chancellor, and Korodin was listening for signs that God was using the statesman as his mouthpiece; but Korodin couldn't hear the voice of the Almighty, instead he had the somewhat irritating sensation of listening to his banker. Heineweg and Bierbohm risked the occasional heckle. Now they were calling out: "You put him up to it!" Keetenheuve was startled, because that didn't seem to make any sense to him. Only then did he notice that the Chancellor was quoting from Mergentheim's piece about the generals on the Conseil Supérieur, calling it treacherous. Poor Mergentheim! Still, he could take it. The statements of support were probably safely on the dispatch box, and there they were being read out, the denials from Paris and London, the assurances of loyalty, the words of friendship, the pledges of brotherhood, soon to become brotherhood-in-arms. The appointment was as good as in the bag, one could proceed to arm, and put on the helmet, the helmet adored by the burgher, the helmet that shows who's in charge, the helmet that gives a face to the faceless state, and only in the bosoms of the far right was there still the lurking and envious thought of the old enemy, and they thought of Landsberg, of the fortresses of Werl and Spandau, they cried out "give us our generals back" (and the great flounder came up out of the water and replied: Go home, they're already there); and the bullet burned in Knurrewahn's breast, and Knurrewahn was full of suspicion and worry.

Keetenheuve spoke. He too stood in the lights of the camera teams, he too would appear on the newsreels. *Keetenheuve matinee idol.* He began worried and pensive, as Knurrewahn would have him. He referred to the doubts and fears of his party, he warned of inherently unpredictable obligations, he turned the gaze of the world on the divided Germany, on the two diseased zones, to reassemble which was the first duty of any German, and even as he spoke, he felt: This is pointless, who is listening to me, who can be expected to listen to me, they know I have to say this and will go on to say that, they know my arguments, and they know I don't have a miracle cure that will have the patient up and about tomorrow, and so they continue to put their faith in the therapy that promises to save the one-half that they think is healthy and capable of life, where the Rhine happens to flow, and the Ruhr happens to flow, and where the chimneys of the Ruhrgebiet happen to rise.

The Chancellor held his head propped in his hands. He was impassive. Was he listening to Keetenheuve? It was impossible to tell. Was anyone listening to him? Hard to tell. Frau Pierhelm was hurling her advertising slogan, *Security for all women,* at the dispatch box; but Frau Pierhelm hadn't been paying attention either. Knurrewahn was leaning his head back, with his brush cut he looked like Hindenburg, or an actor playing some aging general; the century was reduced to imitating its own movie actors, even a miner looked like a film star playing a miner, and Keetenheuve couldn't see whether Knurrewahn was asleep, or lost in thought, or whether he was flattered at hearing his own thoughts coming from Keetenheuve's mouth. Only one person was truly listening to Keetenheuve, and that was Korodin; but Keetenheuve didn't see Korodin, who, in spite of himself, was enthralled and once more of the opinion that the delegate Keetenheuve was at a crossroads that must bring him to God.

Keetenheuve wanted to stop. He wanted to stand down. There was no point in continuing to speak if no one was listening to him; it was senseless to give out words without the belief that they could point the way. Keetenheuve wanted to leave the way of the beast of prey and go the way of the lamb. He wanted to lead the meek. But who was meek, and prepared to follow him? And beyond that, even if they all meekly grouped themselves around Keetenheuve, they might not wind up on a battlefield, but it was doubtful whether they would manage to avoid Gomorrah, the skull hill. Unquestionably, it was morally better to be murdered than to fall in battle, and the determination not to die in battle was the only possibility of changing the face of the earth. But was anyone prepared to climb onto the dizzying, perilous, ethical highwire? They preferred to keep their feet on the ground, allowed a damned weapon to be pressed into their hands, and died cursing with their guts ripped open, just as stupidly as the enemy. And if, so thought Keetenheuve, such an appalling death in battle was the will of God, then a cruel God shouldn't be afforded the support and the disguise of warfare, instead man should walk out onto the field, unarmed, and cry: Show us your terrible face, show it to us naked, kill and slaughter as you please, and don't give mankind the blame for it. And, as Keetenheuve looked around the inattentive, unmoved, bored faces all around, his eye lit on the Chancellor again, rigid, bored, his head in his hands, and he called out to him: "You want to have an army, Chancellor, you want to be included in the alliance, but what alliances will your general want to enter into? What treaties will your general break? Which way will your general march? Under which flag will your general fight? Can you tell us the colors, Chancellor, can you tell us the direction? You want an army. Your ministers want parades. Your ministers want to walk tall, want to *look their men in the eye again.* Fine. Forget about those fools, whom you secretly despise anyway, but, Chancellor, what about your dream of being buried on a gun carriage? Fine, be buried on a gun carriage, but your cortege will consist of millions of corpses, who won't even be buried in the cheapest pine coffin, who will burn wherever they happen to stand, who will be buried wherever the earth happens to fall on their bodies. May you grow old, Chancellor, may you live to a ripe old age, become honorary professor and honorary senator and honorary doctor at all kinds of universities. May you be transported on a rose-covered hearse, with all possible honors, to your final resting place, but forget the gun carriage—that's no distinction for a man as wise and important and inspired as yourself!" Had Keetenheuve really called out the words, or had he once again merely thought them? The Chancellor continued to prop his head in his hands. He looked drained. He looked not unpensive. The chamber was whispering. The President stared dully down at his paunch. The stenographers, looking bored, twiddled their pens. Keetenheuve got down. He was bathed in sweat. His party applauded perfunctorily. From the left there issued a shrill whistle.

Frau Pierhelm mounted the rostrum: security, security, security. Sedesaum hopped up to the stand, he could hardly be seen: God and Fatherland, God and Fatherland, God and Fatherland. God and world? Dörflich took possession of the

parliament and the microphone: Fundamental opposition,
loyalty to German principles, the enemy remains the enemy,
honor remains honor, war crimes committed only by the
enemy, declaration of honor urgently required. Was Dörflich
really called Dörflich? One might have thought his name was
Bormann; no wonder his milk soured on him. For a time
Keetenheuve even felt sorry for the Chancellor. He was still
sitting in the same attitude, with his head propped on his
hands. Maurice stepped forward with doubts founded on
international law. Korodin was still due to speak. He would
lead Christianity and Western civilization into battle, stand by
long-established cultural values, and rave about Europe. And
Knurrewahn would speak shortly before the vote.
Keetenheuve went out into the restaurant. The chamber
must have emptied a lot. There were many more deputies in
the restaurant than in the chamber. Keetenheuve spotted
Frost-Forestier, but he avoided him. He avoided Guatemala.
He didn't want a bone. Keetenheuve saw Mergentheim.
Mergentheim was drinking a coffee, recovering from a radio
appearance. He was holding court. People congratulated him
for having attracted the notice of the Chancellor.
Keetenheuve avoided him. He didn't want any memories. He
desired no explanations. He went out onto the terrace. He sat
down under one of the colorful parasols. He sat as though
under a mushroom. *Ein Männlein steht im Walde ganz still
und stumm.* He ordered a glass of wine. The wine was thin
and sugary. Keetenheuve ordered a bottle instead. He ordered
it on ice. People would notice. People would say: The big
cheese is drinking wine. Okay, he was drinking openly. He
didn't care. Heineweg and Bierbohm would be horrified by
the sight. Keetenheuve didn't care. The ice bucket would

offend Knurrewahn. That Keetenheuve did care about, but he poured himself a glass anyway. He drank the cold dry wine in greedy gulps. In front of him there were flower beds. In front of him there were gravel paths. In front of him was a fire hose attached to a hydrant. On the corner were policemen with dogs. The dogs looked like nervous policemen. A police van was parked in the stench next to the cesspit. Keetenheuve drank. He thought: I'm well guarded. He thought: I've come a long way.

He thought about Musaeus. Musaeus, the butler of the President, who thought he was the President, stood on the rose-grown terrace of the presidential palace, and he too saw the policemen, who had thrown their barriers around him too, he saw the police cars driving, he saw the dog handlers walking about under his nose, and he saw police boats fizzing across the river. Then Musaeus thought that he, the President, had been captured, and that the police were planting impenetrably thick rose hedges around the palace, to grow up around the palace, spiked with thorns, with suicide machines, trip wires and police dogs, the President couldn't get away, he couldn't take refuge with the people, and the people couldn't come to the President. The people asked themselves, What is our President doing? The people inquired, What is the President saying? And they informed the people: The President is old, the President is asleep, the President is signing the treaties that the Chancellor has put before him. And they told the people that the President was very pleased, and they showed the people pictures of the President, in which a pleased-looking President sat in a presidential chair, with a thick black cigar turning luxuriously to ash between his fingers. But Musaeus knew that he, the

President, was uneasy, that his heart beat uneasily, that he was sad, that something was wrong, maybe the treaties were wrong, or maybe the rose hedges, or the police with their cars and their dogs, and then Musaeus, the President, became ill-humored, all at once he took against the landscape, which lay in front of him like a beautiful old painting, no, Musaeus, the good President, he was too sad to enjoy the scenery any more, he went down to the kitchen, he ate a little chop, he drank a little claret, he had to do it—out of melancholy, out of gloom, out of sadness and heaviness of heart.

Keetenheuve went back into the plenary session. The chamber was filling up again. They were about to do again what they had come here to do, to give their votes and earn their democratic corn. Knurrewahn was speaking. He was speaking out of genuine concern, a patriot, someone whom Dörflich would string up if he could. But Knurrewahn wanted his army too, and he too wanted to join alliances, only not yet. Knurrewahn was a man from the East, and it was dear to his heart to have East and West joined together again, in his dreams he was the great Unifier, he hoped to achieve a majority at the next election, to enter government, and then he wanted to do the work of Unification, and after that he aspired to an army and membership of the alliances. It was striking how ready the old were at all times of history to sacrifice the young to Moloch. Parliament hadn't come up with anything new. They were voting by roll call. The votes were collected in. Keetenheuve voted against the government, and he wondered if that had been right, and if it had been politic of him. But he didn't want to be politic any more. Who would succeed the present government? A better government? Knurrewahn? Keetenheuve didn't believe

Knurrewahn's party would achieve an overall majority. Maybe one day there would be a great coalition of malcontents, with Dörflich at the head of it, and then the devil would be let loose. There they all were, at their wits' ends, the apologists of universal suffrage, the disciples of Montesquieu, and they didn't even realize they were arranging games for simpletons, that the separation of powers that Montesquieu had prescribed did not apply any more. The majority ruled. The majority ruled absolutely. What they had was a dictatorship of the majority. All the citizens had to do was choose under whose dictatorship they preferred to live. The politics of the lesser evil, that was the be-all and end-all of politics, the alpha and the omega of all voting and decision making. *The dangers of politics, the dangers of love*, you bought leaflets and you bought prophylactics, and suddenly you were saddled with children and responsibilities, or with syphilis. Keetenheuve looked about him. They all looked stunned. No one congratulated the Chancellor. The Chancellor stood there all alone. The Greeks deported their great men. Crosses marked on potsherds condemned Themistocles and Thucydides. Thucydides became a great man only in exile. Knurrewahn stood there all alone as well. He was folding up pieces of paper. His hands were shaking. Heineweg and Bierbohm looked reproachfully at Keetenheuve. They looked reproachfully, as if it were his fault that Knurrewahn's hands were shaking. Keetenheuve stood there in utter isolation. Everyone avoided him, and he kept out of their way. He thought: If we have a sprinkler system in the chamber, someone should switch it on, we need a downpour, we need a storm of gray rain to come and drench us all. *Keetenheuve the great parliamentary downpour*

It was all over. That was it. It had just been a bit of theater; now they could all go and take off their makeup. Keetenheuve left the chamber. He didn't flee. He walked slowly. No Furies were chasing him. Step by step, he detached himself from a bewitched existence. Once more he wandered along the corridors of the Bundeshaus, up the steps of the Pedagogic Academy, back through the labyrinth, *Theseus having failed to kill the Minotaur*, he encountered apathetic guards, apathetic cleaning ladies with buckets and mops set about the dirt, apathetic officials set off for home, their greaseproof sandwich paper carefully folded up in their briefcases, to be used again on the morrow, they had a tomorrow, they were durable characters, and Keetenheuve was not one of their ilk. He seemed to himself like a ghost. He got to his office. He switched the neon light on again. Twilit, two-faced, and pallid the delegate stood in the disorder of his life as a representative of the people. He knew it was all over. He had lost the battle. It was circumstances that had got the better of him, not the other side. The other side had barely listened to him. It was the circumstances that were unchanging. They were the trend. They were doom. What was left for Keetenheuve? He could knuckle under, go back to his party, run with the pack. Everyone ran with some kind of pack, bowed to necessity, conceded that it was necessary, perhaps even accepted it as the ananke of the Greeks, but it was nothing more than the daily trot of the herd, the push of fear, and a dusty way to the grave. Take up your cross, called the Christians. Serve the state, shouted the Prussians. *Divide et impera,* taught the poorly paid schoolmasters at boys' schools. A new batch of correspondence lay on Keetenheuve's desk. He swept it away. It had become completely pointless to write to him. He didn't want to play any more. He couldn't play any more. He was spent. He swatted his political life aside along with his letters. The letters fell to the floor, and Keetenheuve thought he could hear them groaning and wailing there, they cursed and abused him, there were petitions, there was bitterness, threats of suicide and threats of assassination, there was friction, bruising, and inflammation, a desire to live, a desire for pensions, for support, a roof, claims for jobs, exemptions, benefices, assistance, remission of penalties, a different age and a different spouse, the urge to work off their rage, to confess their disappointment, admit to being at a loss, or press their advice. Finished. Keetenheuve had no advice. He needed no advice. He picked up Elke's picture and the beginning of his translation of *"Le beau navire."* The folder with files, with new poetry, with the works of E. E. Cummings he left behind in his office *(kiss me) you will go.*

The neon light in Keetenheuve's office shone all night. It gleamed eerily out across the Rhine. It was the eye of the dragon of legend.

But the legend was old. The dragon was old. It wasn't watching over any princess. It wasn't guarding any treasure. There was no treasure, there were no princesses. There were depressing files, uncovered bills of promise, uncovered beauty queens, and sordid affairs. Who was going to watch over all that? The dragon was a customer of the regional electricity board. Its eye gleamed at two hundred and twenty volts, and it used five hundred watts per hour. Its magic resided in the eye of the beholder. The world was a soulless place. Even the peaceful Rhine was a figment of the onlooker's imagination.

Keetenheuve followed the riverbank into town. He encountered the stenographers from the Bundestag. They carried their raincoats draped over their arms. They strolled home. They dawdled by the river. They were in no particular hurry. They looked for their reflections in its murky water. Their forms wavered on the sluggish wash. They drifted on a tired warm wind. It was the tired warm wind of their existence. Joyless bedrooms awaited them. Perhaps one or other of them was expected by an unarousing partner. A few looked at Keetenheuve. They looked without interest. They had bored empty faces. Their hands had recorded Keetenheuve's words. Their memories had not stored his speech.

A pleasure steamer was nearing the shore. Little lanterns were burning on deck. A tour company was sitting over their wine. The men had colored party hats on their bald heads. They had long noses fixed on their own lumpy noses. The men with the colored hats and the long noses were manufacturers. They had their arms around their wives, who wore sweet scents, ugly clothes, and ugly hairstyles. They sang. The manufacturers and the manufacturers' wives sang "The North Sea beach where the seagull flies." In front of the paddle, almost under its dirty froth, stood an exhausted cook on a little platform. He looked across to the shore, with a dull and drained expression. There was blood on his bare arms. He had killed fish—sad mute carp. Keetenheuve thought: Would that be a life for me, with the North Sea beach and the Lorelei every day? *Keetenheuve sad cook on a Rhine pleasure steamer, kills no carp*

The lights were on in the presidential palace. All the windows were open. The tired warm wind, the wind of the stenographers, flowed through the rooms. Musaeus, the butler of the President, who thought he was the President, walked from room to room, while the actual President was committing one of his cultured addresses to memory. Musaeus went to see if the beds had been properly made. Who would sleep in them tonight? The federal ship with the President on board drifted along on the sluggish wash, in the tired warm wind, but there were dangerous rocks under the gentle current, and then the river would suddenly become a raging torrent, they would be threatened with shipwreck, with smashing apart in the thunderous roar of a waterfall. The beds were made. Who would sleep? The President?

A poster gleamed, lit up by spotlights, an illuminated tent had been set up on the banks of the Rhine, it stank of silt and rot and the artificial preservation of a corpse. *Don't miss Jonah the whale!* Children laid siege to the tent. They waved paper banners, and on the banners it was written: *Eat Busse's whale oil margarine with plenty of natural vitamins.* Keetenheuve paid sixty pfennigs and saw himself facing the great marine mammal, the biblical Leviathan, a mammoth of the Polar Sea, a kingly beast, primordial, contemptuous of man and yet a prey to his harpoon, a miserably abused and exhibited titan, a corpse pickled in formaldehyde. The prophet Jonah was thrown into the sea, the whale consumed him (the kindly whale, Jonah's savior, Jonah's destiny), for three days and three nights Jonah sat in the belly of the enormous fish, the sea calmed itself, the companions who had thrown him in the water rowed on into emptiness, they rowed calmly toward the empty, shoreless horizon, and Jonah prayed to God from the belly of hell, from the darkness that was the salvation of him, and God made his intention clear to the whale, and he ordered the good, the maltreated, the monkish animal used to fasting, to spit the prophet out again. Or perhaps, in view of the prophet's subsequent conduct, the beast merely had an acid stomach. And Jonah went to the great city of Nineveh, and he preached *Nineveh will fall in forty days*, and word got to the King of Nineveh, who dismounted from his throne, took off his royal purple, pulled on a sack, and rolled himself in the ashes. Nineveh did penance before the Lord, but Jonah was annoyed with the Lord for taking pity on Nineveh and saving it. Jonah was great and gifted, but he was also a small and peevish prophet. He was right: Nineveh was to have been destroyed in forty days. God, however, thought in leaps and bounds, he didn't follow the official guidelines for thinking that Jonah, Heineweg, and Bierbohm followed, and God was pleased with the King of Nineveh for discarding his purple robes, and he was pleased with the rueful people of Nineveh, and God let his bomb perish in the Nevada desert because they danced nice little boogies in His honor in Nineveh. Keetenheuve felt he'd been swallowed up by the whale. He too was sitting in hell, he too was far below the sea, he too was in the belly of the great fish. *Keetenheuve wrathful Old Testament prophet.* But if it had been he who was saved by God, and spat out of the belly of the fish, Keetenheuve similarly would have announced the destruction of Nineveh, but he would have felt great joy if the King had discarded his purple, discarded his royal robes borrowed from some theatrical costumers, and Nineveh had been saved. The children stood outside the tent. They waved their banners *Eat Busse's whale oil margarine with plenty of natural vitamins.* The children had pale, pinched faces, and they waved their paper banners terribly seriously, just as the advertising people expected them to.

A few steps farther, and Keetenheuve ran into a painter. The painter had driven to the Rhine in his caravan. He was sitting in the beam of its headlights at the edge of the river, he was looking pensively into the sunset, and he was painting a German mountain scene with an Alpine hut, a peasant woman, dangerous-looking cliffs, plenty of edelweiss and looming clouds, a nature that Heidegger might have invented, and Ernst Jünger might have bestrode, and people were clustered around the painter, admiring the master, and asking what he would charge for the piece.

Keetenheuve climbed a fortification, the old customs house, he saw ancient, weathered cannon that might have loosed off the odd shot in the direction of Paris as a friendly greeting from monarch to monarch, he saw frail, phthitic, waving poplars that hadn't taken properly, and behind him on a worthy plinth, he saw Ernst Moritz Arndt* in garrulous lecturer's mode. Two little girls were clambering about on Ernst Moritz Arndt's feet. They were wearing coarse, outsize cotton pants. Keetenheuve thought: I'd like to give you some better clothes. But in front of him now was the river, rising majestically out of the scene. From the narrow of its central course it broadened into the plains of the Lower Rhine, lent itself to trade, to mobility, to profit. The Siebengebirge sank into night. The Chancellor and his roses sank into the shadows of night. To the left were the arches of the bridge to Beuel. Lamps on the bridge shone like torches against the gloaming. The three carriages of a tram seemed to have stopped on the central span of the bridge. The tram looked completely decontextualized, for a moment it was a hyperrealistic image of a means of transport, a spectral abstract. It was a death

*Arndt (1769–1860), writer, poet, professor, and private secretary of Baron von und zum Stein.

tram, and it was impossible to imagine it actually going anywhere. One couldn't even think it would go to destruction.
The tram on the bridge was frozen or petrified, a fossil or a
work of art, a tram per se, without past and without future. A
palm was bored on the riverside gardens. There was no reason to suppose it was a palm from Guatemala; but
Keetenheuve thought of the palms in the Guatemalan plaza.
A hedge like a cemetery hedge surrounded the palm in Bonn.
There were scouts on the shore. They were talking some foreign language. They leaned over the railing and looked down
into the river. They were boys. They were wearing shorts. In
their midst there was a girl. The girl was in very tight black
trousers that showed the shapes of her thighs and calves. The
boys had their arms laid on the girl's shoulders. In the union
of the scouts there was love. It clutched at Keetenheuve's
heart. The scouts existed. Love existed. The scouts and love
both existed on that evening. They existed in this air. They
existed on the shore of the Rhine. But they were completely
unreal! Everything here was as unreal as flowers in a hothouse. Even the hot tired wind felt unreal.

Keetenheuve turned into the town. He got to the part of
town that had been destroyed. From a field of rubble, from
stumps of masonry, from a cellar landscape, there arose,
intact, a yellow air-raid sign marked *Rhein*. The inhabitants of
the town had once fled down to the river, to save their lives.
A large black car was parked among the ruins. A car with foreign plates was prowling along a rubble road. The word
School appeared on a warning sign. The foreign automobile
braked on a crater field. From out of the furrows, shapes crept
toward it. Keetenheuve glimpsed the shop windows again, the
window dummies, the swanky bedrooms, the swanky coffins,

the various pieces of sexual and contraceptive gadgetry; he saw all the modern conveniences that the business people were laying before the people in peacetime.

He went back to the less fancy wine bar. The corner tables all had regulars at them. The corner tables were discussing the vote in the Bundestag. The corner tables were grumpy, and they were displeased at the vote. But their displeasure and their grumpiness were sterile; they were displeasure and grumpiness in a vacuum. The corner tables took exception. Any other outcome of the parliamentary session would have provoked them to equal displeasure and grumpiness. They referred to the Bundestag with a preexistent irritation; they referred to the most recent debate as to an event that was irritating and presumptuous, but that didn't concern them or make them feel anything. What made these people feel anything? Were they longing for a taste of the whip to make them shout "Hurrah"?

Keetenheuve had no truck with glasses *Keetenheuve big drinker*, he ordered a bottle, a sexy, paunchy container of the good wine of the Ahr. Purple, mild, smooth the wine flowed out of the bottle into the glass, and from the glass down his throat. The Ahr was near. Keetenheuve had heard that its valley was beautiful; but Keetenheuve had worked, he had spoken and written, he had not visited the river and its valley and vineyards. He should have gone there. Why had he not gone walking with Elke beside the Ahr? They would have stayed the night somewhere. They would have left their windows open. It was a warm night. They would have listened to the murmuring waters. Or were they palms, clashing their blades, rustling drily? He sat alone *Ambassador Excellency Keetenheuve*, he sat on the veranda in Guatemala. Was he dying? He drank his wine quickly. E. E. Cummings' "hand-some man" drank greedily; U.S. poet Cummings' "blueeyed boy" drank greedily in great gulps; Mr. Death's "blueeyed boy" *member of parliament* drank greedily in great gulps the red Burgundy from the German river Ahr. Who kept him company from his schooldays on, spread his wings protectively over him, showed his curved beak, his raptor's claws? The German Aar.* He groomed himself, he fluffed himself up according to the markings of the old fighting birds. Keetenheuve loved every creature, but he didn't care for heraldic beasts. Was an emblem of nobility looming? Was some humiliation at hand? Keetenheuve needed no emblem of nobility. He didn't want to humiliate anyone. He was carrying Elke's picture in his breast pocket *on the left where the heart is.* As a boy he had read *Man is good. And now the grisly damp dark depths of the grave. Bei mir biste scheen. Schön schön schön.* The wireless loudspeaker over the corner table was whispering. "People in the Tirol give each other roses." *Roses in popular song, roses on the Rhine, blooming hothouse roses, rich wise rose growers going about with their clippers and cutting back the young growths, hedge cutters on gravel paths, wicked old rose magicians, assiduous wizards toiling sweating working miracles in the Rhenish hothouse heated by coal from the Ruhr. Bei mir biste scheen, bei mir biste cheil. Geil geil geil. Too much randy politics, too many randy generals, too much randy understanding, too many randy meals, too many stuffed shop windows in the world. Bei mir biste die Scheenste auf der Welt.* Yes, the best-looking shop front. "Don't leave the optics of the thing out of account." "They need to view it with the correct set of optics." "Yes,

---

*An old term for eagle, punning on *Ahr*.

Ministerial Councillor, the optics are everything! *Most beautiful beauty queen. Bikini. Atom test atoll. Beautiful boozer. Elke lost child of the ruins. Kaputt. Lost child of the War/ National Socialism/ Gauleiter parents. Kaputt. The most beautiful of the tribades "be-o by-o be-o boo would-ja ba-ba-botch-a-me."* The corner table speaker sings: "Because Texas is my home." *Busse's vitamin-enhanced lard.* The corner table businessmen nod. They are lads. They feel at home in Texas. Tom Mix and Hans Albers, heroes of businessmen's boyhood fantasies, ride across the corner table on bareback ashtrays. *Holder for an association flag. Flaps. Waves. Everything goes crazy.* Keetenheuve drank. Why did he drink? He drank because he was waiting. Who was he waiting for in the capital city? Did he have any friends in the capital city? What were the names of his friends in the capital city? Their names were Lena and Gerda. Who were they? They were Salvation Army girls.

There they were, Gerda, the strict one, with the guitar, Lena the trainee engineer, carrying the *War Cry,* and Lena made no secret of the fact that she wanted to go to Keetenheuve, and Gerda stood there pallidly, twisting her mouth. The girls had had a quarrel. It was evident. You will be robbed, thought Keetenheuve, and he was alarmed at his own cruelty, because he took pleasure in hurting the little dyke, he was ungentlemanly (though not unmoved), he would have her take down her guitar and sing and play—the song of the heavenly bridegroom. He thought it would be nice to take Lena the trainee engineer by the waist, and to have Gerda singing the song of the heavenly bridegroom. He looked into Gerda's pale face, he saw the rage in her face, he saw the twisted mouth, he observed the trembling pinched lips, the nervous, tormented flicker of the eyelids, and he thought: You're my sister, we're both part of the same miserable family. But he hated his reflection, the stupid mirror image of his isolation. A drinker will destroy a mirror; along with the splintering glass, he destroys the hated knight of the tottering form, his image as it keels down to the gutter. Lena, when motioned to, sat down, and Gerda, likewise motioned to, squatted down contrarily, because she didn't want to yield. The men at the corner tables looked up. They had a box seat to watch the beasts of prey fighting over their spoils. Keetenheuve took the collecting tin for the Salvation Army, got up, rattled it around, *Keetenheuve belated collector for the WHW,** held it out to the business people. They turned up their noses. Pretended not to know the little tin can any more, *no contributions for the Führer and his army.* They turned away, disturbed in their boyhood dreams. Keetenheuve just now was dreaming more powerful dreams, just as puerile as theirs. *Keetenheuve pedagogue and pedophile. Man with pronounced pedagogical eros. A friend of youth.* The corner table wireless speaker chanted: "And don't forget your swimming trunks!" A child sang, went screeching over hill and dale, a tape hissed. *A dog barked. Where? In Insterburg. Jewish joke. Mergentheim joke. Old* Volksblatt *joke. Who's alive? Who's dead? We're still alive. Mergentheim and Keetenheuve, arm in arm, old* Volksblatt *memorial, recommended to the protection of the citizen!* Lena wanted a brandy and Coke; she was blending in. Gerda wouldn't accept anything; Sapphic principles. Keetenheuve said: "A brandy would do you good." Gerda ordered a coffee; she ordered a coffee in order to guarantee herself the right to

---

*Stands for *Winterhelfswerk,* another bit of Nazi nomenclature, in this instance for a Christmas charitable collection.

remain in the place, whatever befell. Keetenheuve hadn't done anything for Lena the trainee engineer yet. He was sorry, genuinely. He had misspent his day. The waitress brought him some letter paper. It had the name of the bar on the top of it. *What is wine but preserved sunshine* it said. The letter couldn't fail to make a terrible impression on respectable addressees. *Keetenheuve man without decency.* He wrote a letter to Knurrewahn and he wrote a letter to Korodin. He begged Knurrewahn and Korodin to find a lathe for Lena, the trainee mechanic. He gave the letters to Lena. He said to her: "Korodin isn't sure whether he believes in God, and Knurrewahn isn't sure whether he doesn't. If I were you, I would try them both. One of them is sure to help." He thought: You won't take no for an answer, my little Stakhanova. He wanted to help her. But at the same time he knew that he didn't want to help her, that it was he who wanted to cling to her; he would have liked to take her away, she could live with him, she would eat with him, she had to sleep with him, he had appetite for human flesh again, *Keetenheuve old ogre*; maybe he could send Lena to the technical institute, she would take her exams, *Lena Dr. ing.*—and then what? Should he try it? Should he try and establish contact? But what did you do with an academically qualified bridge builder? Sleep with her? What did you feel when you held her in your arms? *Love is a formula*

He took Lena, and led her into the ruins. Gerda followed them. With every step, her guitar banged against her man-hating body and buzzed. It was a monotonous rhythm. The beat was like that of Negro drums, a complaint against the lash, against feeling abandoned, against yearning for dark forests. The black car was still waiting in front of the ruined setting. The foreign automobile was still parked on the rubble road. The moon was just breaking through the clouds. Frost-Forestier was sitting on some broken stones. In front of him, casual and bold, in the liquid moonlight, in his shirt open to the waist and his tight shorts, with floury bare calves and bare thighs, stood the beautiful baker's boy who had wanted to rob the cashier at the box office. Keetenheuve waved hello to Frost-Forestier; but the shadowy forms of the man sitting upright on the ruins, and the swaggering youth in front of him, did not move. They were like visions in stone, and everything was unreal and hyperreal at once. From the foreign car parked on the rubble road came a groan, and Keetenheuve almost felt the blood well out from under the door, and drip into the dust. Keetenheuve led Lena into a cleared area surrounded by low walls that had once been a room, and even some of the wallpaper was still visible, it might have been the room of a Bonn scholar, because Keetenheuve recognized a Pompeiian pattern, and the washed-out lusty body of a female Eros with ripped parts that resembled overripe fruits. Gerda followed Lena and Keetenheuve into the enclosure lit by the moon, and from the surrounding caverns, from buried cellars, from the hidey-holes of hunger and depravity, people whispered and crept and slithered closer as for some performance. Gerda set down her guitar on a stone, and the instrument gave back a full chord. "Play for us!" cried Keetenheuve. He seized Lena, the girl from Thuringia, he leaned down over her inquisitive expectant face, he groped for her slightly too curly, her soft, her Middle German lips, drank sweet saliva, strong breath, and warm life from her young mouth, he pulled up Lena the trainee engineer's flimsy dress, he touched her, and Gerda, even paler in the pale moonlight, took up her guitar, struck the chords, and in a high clear voice sang the song of the heavenly bridegroom. And from out of holes in the ground rolled the murdered, from craters crept the buried alive, from quicklime tombs crawled the strangled, from their cellars tottered the homeless, from their beds in the rubble came the whores, and an alarmed Musaeus came from his palace and saw misery, and the delegates were convoked in extraordinary nocturnal session on the burial ground from the Nazi years, aptly enough. The great statesman was chauffeured there, and was granted a vision into the workshop of the future. He saw devils and vermin and he saw them creating the homunculus. A train of Piefkes* climbed the Obersalzberg and met the coach tour company of the daughters of the Rhine, and the Piefkes copulated with the Wagalaweia girls, and bred the super-Piefke. The super-Piefke did the hundred-meter butterfly in under a minute. He won the Atlanta thousand-mile race in a German-built car. He invented the moon rocket, and feeling threatened, he armed himself against the planets. Chimneys popped up like erect penises, a poisonous smog wrapped itself around the earth, and in the sulfurous fumes, the super-Piefke called the World Nation into being, and introduced lifelong conscription. The great statesman tossed a rose into the smoke of the future, and where the rose fell, a spring burst forth, and the spring flowed with black blood. Keetenheuve lay in the eternal flow, he lay with the girl from Thuringia, with the Thuringian trainee mechanic, in the arena of the representatives of the people, in the arena of statesmen, he lay in the course of blood, surrounded by day

*Austrian slang for Prussian soldiers or, more generally, nasty German tourists, after one Piefke, a Prussian music master who composed a march to celebrate the Prussian victory over the Danes in 1864.

flakes and night rabble, and screech owls hooted in the air, and the cranes of Ibycus screamed, and vultures sharpened their beaks on the scarified walls. A scaffold was set up, and the prophet Jonah came riding up on Jonah, the good-humored dead whale, and sternly he supervised the erecting of the gallows. The delegate Korodin dragged along a great golden cross, under whose weight he was bent double. With a huge effort he set up the cross next to the gallows, and he was very afraid. He broke some pieces of gold off the cross, and he tossed them into the group of statesmen and dele-gates, into the circles of night rabble and day flakes. The statesmen paid the gold into their bank accounts. The dele-gate Dörflich hid the gold in a milk churn. The delegate Sedesaum took the gold to bed with him, and called on the Lord. The night rabble and the day flakes called Korodin obscene names. Everywhere on stumps of masonry, in blown-out windows, on the broken pillar of the singer's curse, sat greedy heraldic animals, squatted stupid puffed-up murder-ous eagles with reddened beaks, fat complacent lions from coats of arms, with bloodied mouths, snake-tongued griffins with dark sticky claws, a bear growled menacingly, the ox of Mecklenburg mooed, and the SA marched, death's head units paraded, Vehmic killer battalions moved up with blare of brass, swastika banners unfurled from moor-slimed sheaths, and Frost-Forestier, a shot-through steel helmet on his head, called out: "The dead to the front!" There was a huge troop inspection. The youth of two world wars marched past Musaeus, and the pale Musaeus took the parade. The moth-ers of two world wars walked mutely past Musaeus, and Musaeus whitely saluted their mourning procession. The tail-coated statesmen of two world wars strode past Musaeus, and

Musaeus signed the treaties they laid before him. The generals of two world wars, heavily decorated, goose-stepped up; they stopped in front of Musaeus, drew their sabers, saluted, and demanded their pensions. Musaeus granted them their pensions immediately, and the generals seized him, took him up to the scaffold and gave him to the hangman. Then along came the Marxists with their red flags. They lugged a plaster bust of Hegel, and Hegel stretched and cried: "The great individuals in their particular duties are the realization of the substantial, which is the will of the world spirit." The emaciated nonstop pianist from the bar played the "Internationale." The inadequate beauties of the other bar danced the carmagnole. The police minister came driving along in water tanks, inviting people to a drag hunt. He dispatched trained dogs into the field, and shouted after them: Chase him, grab him, catch him! The minister was trying to catch the dog-loving Keetenheuve with his dogs. But Frost-Forestier spread a map of the world protectively in front of Keetenheuve, pointed to the Rhine, and said: "There's Guatemala!" The guitar crashed; its strings yowled. The singing of the Salvation Army girl resounded far beyond the ruins, rose over the rubble pile and its misery and fear. Keetenheuve felt Lena's sacrifice, and he felt all the sacrifice of all the years since his return, all the desperate determination to enter the flow of the mainstream, which remained infertile and ineffectual. It was an act of complete irrelation that he was performing, and he was a stranger, staring into a strange face, distorted by the deceptions of sexual pleasure. There was only sadness. There was no uprising here, there was guilt, no love, just a grave. It was the grave in him. He let go the girl and stood up. Before him he saw the air-raid warning arrow pointing people to the

Rhine. The air-raid warning arrow loomed unignorably in the pale moonlight, and pointed imperiously toward the river. Keetenheuve broke out of the circle of the rabble, that really had assembled here, drawn by the sad singing and the pretty strumming of the Salvation Army girl. Keetenheuve ran to the bank of the Rhine. Abuse and laughter followed him. A stone was thrown. Keetenheuve ran toward the bridge. In the illuminated windows of the department store on the approach the dummies were beckoning. They stretched out their arms appealingly to the delegate, who ran away from their blandishments for ever. Over. *It was over. Eternity had already begun.*

Keetenheuve reached the bridge. The bridge trembled under the force of the unearthly tram, and Keetenheuve felt the arch of the bridge was trembling under the weight of his body, under the force of his hurrying steps. The bells of the ghostly tramcars rang; it sounded like a malign giggle. In Beuel on the opposite side, a pattern of electrical bulbs made up the word *Rheinlust.* From a rural garden a rocket went up, exploded, fell, a dying star. Keetenheuve gripped the bridge rail, and once again he felt the supports trembling. There was a vibration in the steel, it was as though the steel was alive and wanted to betray a secret to Keetenheuve, the lesson of Prometheus, the puzzle of mechanics, the wisdom of the blacksmith—but the news came too late. The delegate was utterly useless, he was a burden to himself, and a leap from the bridge made him free.

About the Author

WOLFGANG KOEPPEN WAS BORN IN 1906 IN GREIFSWALD on the Baltic coast, the illegitimate son of a doctor who took no interest in his welfare. He was a student for a time, unemployed, and held an array of odd jobs, including those of ship's cook, factory worker, and cinema usher. At the same time, he began to write for left-wing papers and, by 1931, was in Berlin, writing for the *Berliner Börsen-Courier*. He published two novels with the Jewish publisher Bruno Cassirer, *Eine unglückliche Liebe* (*An Unhappy Love Affair*) (1934) and *Die Mauer schwankt* (*The Tottering Wall*) (1935), before emigrating to Holland for a short period in the mid-1930s. Prior to the war, he returned to Germany and spent the war years writing film scripts for UFA that were, as he put it, just good enough to keep him in work, and just bad enough not to be made. The end of the war saw him in Munich.

In 1948, he ghostwrote Jakob Littner's Holocaust memoir *Aufzeichnungen aus einem Erdloch* (*Notes from a Hole in the*

Ground), for which he was paid in food parcels. In 1992, the book was somewhat controversially republished under Koeppen's own name. The controversy was renewed when Littner's original manuscript, having been traced and translated into English by his relative, Kurt Grübler, appeared as *Journey through the Night*, published by Continuum in 2000.

In the 1950s, he completed the three novels that established him, alongside Günter Grass and Heinrich Böll, among the leading contemporary German writers: *Tauben im Gras* (*Pigeons on the Grass*) (1951), *Das Treibhaus* (*The Hothouse*) (1953), and *Der Tod in Rom* (*Death in Rome*) (1954). Though quite separate in terms of character, action, and setting, these three novels, taken together, comprise a kind of trilogy on the state of postwar Germany. German readers and reviewers were wholly unequal to them, and Koeppen, either discouraged by their reception, or too proud, or too lazy, wrote no more fiction thereafter.

For the remaining forty-odd years of his life, he was a sort of literary pensioner kept by Suhrkamp, his loyal publisher, and by a series of prizes and awards that, guiltily and belatedly, came his way, among them the Büchner Prize of 1962. He wrote three travel books, on Russia, America, and France, and a memoir, *Jugend* (*Youth*), that appeared in 1976, yet he never wrote the new novel that was touted and promised over several decades. In 1986, Suhrkamp published his collected works, somewhat surprisingly running to six volumes. He died in 1996, shortly before his ninetieth birthday. In the summer of 2000, a 700-page collection of *inédits* was brought out under the title *Auf dem Phantasieross* (*On the Wings of Imagination*).

About the Translator

MICHAEL HOFMANN, THE SON OF THE GERMAN NOVELIST Gert Hofmann, was born in 1957 in Freiburg. At the age of four, he moved to England, where he has lived off and on ever since. After studying English at Cambridge and comparative literature on his own, he moved to London in 1983. He has published poems and reviews widely in England and in the United States. In 1993, he was appointed Distinguished Lecturer in the English Department of the University of Florida at Gainesville.

To date, he has published four books of poems and a collection of criticism, *Behind the Lines,* all with Faber & Faber. He edited (with James Lasdun) a book of contemporary versions of the *Metamorphoses*, called *After Ovid*, and is currently editing *Rilke in English* for Penguin. He has translated works by Bertolt Brecht, Franz Kafka, Joseph Roth, and Gert Hofmann, among others. His translation of Wolfgang Koeppen's *Death in Rome* (now reissued in paperback by

W. W. Norton) shared the Schlegel-Tieck Translation Prize in 1993 when it first appeared in England. His translation of Joseph Roth's *Tale of the 1002nd Night* was awarded the PEN/Book-of-the-Month Club Prize for translation in 1998.